The Supernatural Tales
of Fitz-James O'Brien

The Supernatural Tales of Fitz-James O'Brien

Volume Two: Dream Stories and Fantasies

Edited, with Notes and an Introduction, by
Jessica Amanda Salmonson

Doubleday

NEW YORK

1988

Acknowledgments

Thanks to the University of Washington's Suzallo Library, the New York Public Library, and the Seattle Public Library. Thanks to Pat LoBrutto for help in obtaining scarce material. Thanks to Alfred Bendixen for his trip to the Columbia University Library in my behalf, though that particular trek was fruitless. Thanks to Jules Faye for miscellaneous help. Thanks to my agent Susan Lee Cohen for caring about my myriad odd projects.

U.S. CIP data applied for 87-36525

ISBN: 0-385-24649-8
Copyright © 1988 by Jessica Amanda Salmonson
All Rights Reserved
Printed in the United States of America
First Edition

To Francis Wolle,
who made this book possible.

Contents

Nights of Ambrosia

An Introduction by Jessica Amanda Salmonson

In a dark tavern below the streets, cigars, pipes, stale beer, and sweat scented the atmosphere.

A gray-bearded man leaned over his cup and sighed the agony of a vanished generation. A young man sauntered down the odorous steps, holding a handkerchief to his nose, and squinted through the smog. Then, emboldening himself, he put the handkerchief away and approached the drunk old man.

"Hullo," said he, but the oldster didn't hear. After a few moments of studying the hollow-cheeked profile, the youngster tried again. "Hullo, weren't you the Bohemian King?"

Rheumy eyes raised slowly. Livid, puffy lips opened slightly and Henry Clapp, Jr., once the city's most influential liberal wit, gazed into the bright young eyes of innocence as yet unbetrayed. "I'll be the King of Hell," said Henry, "if it will delight you to the price of a drink."

So he bought the old man a fresh cup, though it was unneeded, and looking at the famous, morbid, fallen man with unabashed curiosity, he asked of the "old times" of the Bohemian summer.

"Ah," said Henry, "those were indeed nights of Ambrosia," and he fell to weeping so that words failed him for a while.

"I'm working on a piece for the *Times*," said the cavalier young journalist, "about Pfaff's restaurant and your old crowd. Whitman's all the rage still, but not much came of the rest."

"Who knows what they might have become," said Henry, his voice softer. "Confounded mystery, death."

"You were chums with Fitz-James O'Brien, am I right? Those stories of his are still well-remembered. What sort of chap was he?"

Henry murmured sadly, "He glowed with fun and poetry. His like shall not be seen again."

"Wasn't he a rotter?"

Henry's tears were of a sudden dry and he began to rise unsteadily. His emaciated frame posed feeble threat, but his voice rang proudly. "Young man, if there were such rotters now, it would be a finer world. Off with you, lest I mistake you for a cockroach and do you in!"

The journalist was ready to stand his ground and insist on a gentleman's courtesy, but Henry's puffy lips were dribbling and the young man worried that his suit might be wetted. "I can see you're in no mood today, sir!" the journalist said reproachfully, already forming a rude commentary for the *Times* regarding the intemperate King of Bygone Glories. He withdrew rapidly from the cellar into the New York winter night.

Henry Clapp pressed a hand to his aching side and took back his chair, leaning more heavily above the cups, wondering how the world he had known had slipped away and why he was left alone to ponder the transience of joy and the lasting intensity of despair.

In the mid-1850s, Henry had lorded over a group of promising, radical young authors and poets, students and lawyers, playwrights and physicians who in economic terms were mostly failures but in terms of mad, heartfelt, libertine living—they were the city's finest.

They had worshipped Poe and like him, for the most part, died young —save for the most priggish members of the gang and a lucky one or two such as Whitman who'd wandered on to lesser wildness in the wake of the Civil War.

It had been predicted that Henry himself would end up in city government or otherwise part of the very establishment he and his ilk tweeked and maligned. What a subtle insult! But history would *not* remember him as another Edmund Clarence Stedman, Bohemian poet turned Wall Street banker (who, Henry never knew, would one day edit an important compendium of Victorian poets notable for its lack of Bohemians). Rather, he had chosen the slow death of alcoholism; being hauled off to the temperance hospital from time to time wasn't apt to change his mind. His rare moments of happiness, nowadays, were in understanding perfectly well that he had chosen his own method of doom and was pursuing it singlemindedly. Those who understood him patted his bowed back and bought him another, then left him to his broodings.

But at times, his drunken life became a darkened mirror of things past and he couldn't believe old chums weren't just about to join him. Drug abuse had taken his beloved George Arnold, already a forgotten poet, as well as Fitz-Hugh Ludlow, author of *The Hasheesh Eater*. Beautiful Ned

Wilkins, who Henry recalled "like a maiden out of a fairy tale," was abandoned by his important theatrical friends the instant he took ill, leaving only his Bohemian compatriots to read him Carlysle and the Bible as he lay gasping with pneumonia in his unheated garret. There were suicides as well, glorious romantic suicides; and there were young men who never returned from the Civil War, the most remarkable among them that Irish knight, Fitz-James O'Brien.

It would be long and long before the tragedy and romance of America's first Bohemians was forgotten.

Fitz-James O'Brien has been recognized as the most important short story writer in America between Poe and Bret Harte. Such was the opinion of the unrelated Edward J. O'Brien, founder of *Best Short Stories of the Year* and for three decades an acknowledged expert on short fiction.

The condition of literary arts in America of the 1850s was a very mixed thing, the peaks being in the area of novels and poetry. Without Fitz, the short story would appear moribund throughout the decade. Irving was retired. Poe had died in 1849. Hawthorne would begin the decade with his great novel *The House of Seven Gables* and never again equal himself, and in any case his best short works were long behind him.

That Irving, Poe, and Hawthorne were obsessed with the supernatural was one reason that "the feminine fifties" experienced a falling off in short story form and quality. Morbidness and weirdness were much out of fashion—except among the impoverished, eccentric Bohemians—and with the decade's casting off of the grand themes, authors had also cast off the important lessons of construction and effect. Magazine stories became once again nothing but compressed novels.

Among novelists Melville stands out to us today, but at the time he was castigated or ignored and sold poorly. Fitz was the first and for too long the only critic to recognize Melville's value. Harriet Beecher Stowe provided what has to be the decade's most significant work, for *Uncle Tom's Cabin* reshaped American political thinking and led ultimately to the Civil War. It certainly affected Fitz, who was to die in the frenzy of patriotic slaughter. Other than these and Hawthorne's longer works, the novels of the decade were singularly bad imitations of *Jane Eyre* and *Wuthering Heights*. Sentimentality was exaggerated (heroines burst into tears on every third page). Religious zeal was the other hallmark, so that the books are more important in the history of women in the ministry (novels being their only sanctioned outlet to preach) than as literature. Women completely dominated the literary scene—and had there been much of the Brontës in them, it might not have been such a sorry state of affairs.

As to poetry, Longfellow had written "Hiawatha," the second most popular poem of the century (arguably one of the worst as well, except for children) with Poe's "The Raven" still holding first place in American sentiment. Longfellow followed his success with "The Courtship of Miles Standish." The Bohemian Walt Whitman had published *Leaves of Grass* in its first incarnations. Poets were lionized and were often paid more than were artists in prose. Even Fitz mistakenly believed his lasting reputation would rest on his poetry, not his short stories, but this was partly because all around him he could see that poetry was more highly valued. His poems "Kane" and "The Sewing Bird" were notable successes for him, but to today's readers, it is his handful of macabre poems that retain their value, and Time has otherwise been a belittling critic of Fitz the poet.

When Fitz arrived in New York in 1852, a time when the great writers of our language were to be found chiefly in England (with Dickens at the head of their legion), he was a lion among sheep. However little it served him financially, he was instantly recognized for his genius.

"The Diamond Lens" didn't appear until 1858, in the premier issue of *The Atlantic Monthly*. By then he had published an impressive body of poems, stories, humor, and nonfiction; his plays and songs were known throughout the city; his widest audience had been in the prestigious *Harper's New Monthly Magazine*, for which he was a reliable contributor. His stories "What Was It? A Mystery" and "A Pot of Tulips" had been notable sensations, though it took "The Diamond Lens" to catapult him to the heights of fame. It remained by far the best-known story in the nation until Hale's "The Man Without a Country" and Stockton's "The Lady, or the Tiger?" Fitz reinforced his importance to *The Atlantic Monthly* with "The Wondersmith" less than a year later.

Thomas Bailey Aldrich, a young Bohemian in the 1850s but a staid Boston conservative later on, said it best in 1897: "Of course there were excellent stories before the *Atlantic* was born—Poe's and Hawthorne's— but the magazine gave the short story a place which it had never before reached. It began with 'The Diamond Lens.' "

The direction of short fiction might have been altogether different if not for *Harper's New Monthly Magazine* and *The Atlantic Monthly* and Fitz's contributions therein. That he learned from Poe's *methods* earned him the deserved title of Poe's successor. But he reinforced this impression by having, very often, Poe's obsession with the macabre. Fitz's revival of the fashion of strange tales meant that the finest magazines would feature similar stories right up until the 1920s as a matter of course; thereafter, pulp magazines would take up the torch, with a lessening of critical importance.

The importance of Fitz's macabre stories has overshadowed an additional body of supernatural works: the dream stories and lighter fantasies, many of which were never reprinted from magazines and newspapers. That Fitz's Bohemian circles were themselves in large percentage doomed fellows, and Fitz's own life ended in melancholy heroism, has made the macabre stories more attractive as adjuncts to the man. But his life was also filled with joy and comedy, not just sadnesses and pain. In their day, his other fantasies were nearly as influential ("The Diamond Lens" not withstanding) as his macabre tales. They were part and parcel with that portion of his creative endeavors that so well facilitated the nature of magazine fiction in decades to follow. "The King of Nodland and His Dwarf," "A Voyage in My Bed," "The Dragon-Fang Possessed by the Conjuror Piou-Lu," "From Hand to Mouth," and "Three of a Trade; Or, Red Little Kriss Kringle" were all widely circulated in the 1850s and/or 1860s. But only one of them ("The Dragon-Fang Possessed by the Conjuror Piou-Lu") was included in his 1881 collection, resulting in the others' obscurity to later generations.

These Dream Stories and Fantasies, added to the brilliant Macabre Tales gathered in Volume One of *The Supernatural Stories of Fitz-James O'Brien,* reveal the broader base of Fitz's lasting influence on the short story of Victorian America.

Had Fitz survived the Civil War, he might well have written novels as important as Hawthorne's *The Scarlet Letter* and *The House of Seven Gables.* It was his plan to attempt it. Whatever he might have written, we can say with some assurance that he would not have had to suffer another decade of impoverishment. *Harper's New Monthly Magazine* and *The Atlantic Monthly* changed the economic ground rules and magazinists could expect to be well-paid for their labors. The day had passed that authors of national renown could starve in their garrets or live "From Hand to Mouth." Fitz's dream of a kinder life might easily have been achieved, and he would have been with Tom Aldrich and Walt Whitman on the list of Bohemian survivors. Then again, though it is less likely, his fondness for the bottle might have ended him shoulder to shoulder with Henry Clapp, Jr.

As for Henry, if his ghost has been able to find anyplace in today's New York worthy of his haunting, perhaps he's still about and will notice (if only in the basement of the Strand) that his old friend's supernatural stories have at long last been collected into two handsome volumes. If so, I trust this brings a moment of joy to his anguished spirit—and to the gentle reader as well.

—Jessica Amanda Salmonson
Seattle, 1987

Envoi

The Enchanted Titan

I

Curse you! O, a hundred thousand curses
  Weigh upon your soul, you black enchanter!
Could I pour them like the coins from purses,
  I would utter such a pile instanter
As would crush you to a bloody pulp.
But my rage I fain am forced to gulp;
Anathemas are vain against cold iron,
  Nor can I swear this magic box asunder,
Where I've been stifling since the days of Chiron,
  Fretting on tempered bolts, and hurling muffled thunder.

II

Through the chinks I see the dim green waters
  Filled with sunshine, or with moonlight hazy;
Through them swim the oceanic daughters,
  Beautiful enough to drive me crazy.
The fishes gaze at me with sphery eyes,
And seem to say, with cold-blooded surprise,
What Titan is it, that's so barred and bolted,
  Caged like a rat in some infernal cellar?
Why even Enceladus, when the dog revolted,
  Was not so hardly treated by the Cloud-Compeller!

III

And all, forsooth, because I loved his daughter!
  Loved that child of spells and incantation;
Love her now, beneath this dreary water,

Love her through eternal tribulation!
I wonder if her lips lament me still,
In her enchanted castle on the hill?
Or has she yielded to the damned magician,
   And with my pygmy rival weakly wedded?
O Jove! the torment of this bare suspicion
   Preying forever on my heart, and like the Hydra headed!

IV

O bitter day, when spells, like snakes uprearing,
   Enwrapped my limbs, and, muscular as pliant,
Pinioned my struggling arms, until despairing
   I lay upon the earth, a captured giant!
Then came the horror of this iron box—
The closing of its huge enchanted locks;
Then the cursed wizard to the windy summit
   Of the tall cape a coffered prisoner bore me,
And flung me off, until, like seaman's plummet,
   I sank, and the drear ocean closed forever o'er me!

—F.-J. O'B.
Harper's, December 1859

Dream Stories

A Voyage in My Bed

I could not sleep. Hour after hour of intolerable weariness wore away, and found me still watchful and restless. My hands grew hot, and fever seemed to fill my veins as I tossed upon my bed. The very silence of the street seemed to assume a certain vacant monotony, and struck upon my senses with the apparent regularity of a tune. I grew maddened at this void of sound, and wished fervently for even the slightest noise to break the stillness. Then my brain began seeking for occupation. I endeavored, with an earnestness and depth of thought worthy of a better aim, to define amid the surrounding darkness the limits of my room, and by that to regulate my own position. Curiously enough, I had lost all perception, or rather remembrance of the exact position of my bed. I could not tell which was the head or which was the foot; and though I recollected distinctly all the features of the room, and knew in what direction the bed usually lay, I felt now as if I had suddenly been thrust into the chamber amid utter darkness, without the slightest clue to its shape or limits. If I had had no recollection of the features of my room, I should not have been so puzzled. I should simply have considered myself as inhabiting for the moment a dark space of which I knew neither the shape nor boundaries. But the perfect and distinct image which was painted on my brain of each article of furniture which the room contained, and its precise locality as regarded every other article in that room, thrust itself so pertinaciously upon me that I could not avoid attempting to realize it. Here, thought I, is the dressing-table, with two scent-bottles, one on either side —a silver shaving pot in the centre, and the razors and brushes lying on the end next to the window; there is the little book-shelf hanging at the further end of the room by red cords against the—— But stay; where *is* the wall? How far off is it from me at this moment? Does it lie at a right or obtuse angle with my body as I am now placed? Pshaw! the more I try to realize that confounded wall, the more bewildered I become. It seems to be continually shifting its position; and when I think I have it firmly fixed in a certain position—lo! it suddenly strikes me that I am quite wrong, and

that it lies in precisely an opposite direction. Well! let that pass. Suppose
we proceed with our inventory. Now I am quite positive as to the exact
spot which is covered by that small round table with the books on it.
When I arranged it this evening before getting into bed, I put it right
between my bed and the window, and I recollect remarking at the time
that it must be in the middle of the room, because its claw covered
precisely the red medallion which forms the very centre of my Turkey
carpet. Let me see—the carpet—carpet—hang it! where *is* the carpet?
Why, as I live I cannot tell for my very life which is the ceiling or which is
the floor; whether the carpet is above or below me! Where am I? How am
I? Have I been turned upside down, or has the world been suddenly
reversed? Where is the floor? where the walls? where the window? I feel
like Mahomet's coffin suspended in mid-air, and as if I was every moment
about to be let go. How am I lying? If I put my foot out of bed, what side
will it be on? I try by feeling the posts of my bedstead to discover which is
the head, but they are all four alike, and I can feel nothing but smooth
sticks of wood. What am I to do? I shall go mad—stark staring mad—if I
endeavor to solve these mysteries any longer. There is but one resource
left, and that is to make a grand effort, and—get up. Ay! but how? It is
easy to say get up, but if one does not know where the floor is, how is one
—— Besides, there is such a weight on my chest that drags me back when
I attempt to rise; and a most extraordinary fear has suddenly come over
me, so that I do not think worlds would tempt me to get out of bed into
the dark, fathomless void which encompasses me. It seems to me like
making up one's mind to step off the edge of the world into space. Ugh!
what an effort! one leg out of bed and dangling over the dark void in
which my couch is suspended. Shall I go on? Shall I trust myself any
further? Ha! what's this? A carpet—the floor—what joy! My brain is
suddenly revulsed with returning consciousness of locality, and I walk
firmly across the dark room, scramble hastily into my clothes, and cram-
ming my hat over my eyes, wander out through the door and down the
stairs, with a sort of indistinct idea pervading my mind that a walk will do
me good.

Do you know that I have lived in this house for four years, and it never
before struck me that the balusters that line the stairs are made of rope—
thick, twisted cables? but now for the first time I am conscious of the fact,
and they quiver in my grasp as I go fumbling down the staircase.

How very cold the hall-door feels as I open it. How smooth and polished
too. Why, it is marble—pure, white marble! I did not know that we were
so luxurious. Pooh! nonsense; how stupid of me! To be sure it is marble—

always was marble. Don't I recollect a year ago, when the pet monkey tried to scramble up the front, and failed because it was so smooth and slippery?

At last I am in the street. The cool fresh air blows over my temples, and fills me with a luxurious sense of languid pleasure. It must be near morning, for the stars are growing pale, and the eastern brim of the sky seems covered with the white leprosy of dawn. The city is as yet, however, still and silent as a desert, and my footsteps sound—no, by the by, it has just struck me that they do not sound. I feel as if I was walking upon some dull, elastic substance, and on looking down I discover for the first time that the streets are paved with India-rubber. What a great improvement this is! No more noise—no more rattling of carts, or trampling of horses; all living things will fleet by as swiftly and silently as a dream.

Three o'clock! tolled by the iron pulse of that old cathedral. How picturesque it looks half wrapped in shadow and jutting out its great stone elbows half-way across the narrow street. But the deuce! now that I think of it, I don't recollect ever seeing that cathedral before, though I suppose I have traversed this street five times a day for the last four years. How very strange! There is something very peculiar, too, about the aspect of all the other houses. I remember them well enough, but somehow they don't feel quite the same. Oh! I suppose it is the twilight that deceives me; I have never been out so early before, and the shadows that precede the dawn are mocking me with mysteries. I will defy them; I will leave them soon behind. Rapidly, rapidly do the streets fleet by as I run along; bridges, churches, houses are past, and the country comes near. On still I run with unfailing breath and firm step, and mile-stone after mile-stone passes me by, until at last I stop. I am out of breath, and this seems a sweet place to rest in.

I see a road. It is cool and shady; the autumn tints are hovering half timidly upon the green threshold of summer, and the glossy leaves of the beech trees that line the path are beginning to look brown about the edges. There is no dust: a cool rain has fallen over night, and the morning sun has not yet had time to swallow up the glittering drops that tremble on the leaves. The last primroses of the year blossom hardily amid the grassy banks that bound the highway, and seem as if they were determined to see the summer out. There is a fresh and delicate fragrance on the air; it is like the perfumed breath of some young virgin. The road is still and silent; not a foot-print is to be traced in the yielding soil which forms its surface. No one has passed this way yet; but there are indications that cannot be mistaken of some one's approach. The sparrows suddenly whirr out of the hedge just where the road makes an angle; that rabbit, who has been for the last half hour coolly devouring his breakfast of rib-leaf by the road-side, erects his long ears—sits up on his haunches—listens attentively for a second or two, and them scampers off to his hole as if a weasel was at his heels. A moment more, and the dull echo of footsteps sounds along the damp soil; the next two persons turn the angle of the road and walk forward beneath the shadow of the trees. One is a girl, the other a man. The man, who walks first, is a tall athletic fellow, with a thick neck and a bad scowling countenance. He is dressed in a loose fustian suit, and has a soiled red silk handkerchief knotted carelessly around his throat. He swings a short heavy stick in his hand, and lounges on with the heavy reluctant gait of the confirmed vagabond. The girl follows him, her slender, delicate form bending beneath the weight of a heavy bag which she carries on her back. She must be either daughter or sister of the big hulking fellow who walks before her, for though her face is beautiful and womanly, and it would be difficult to trace in those fair patient features and deep-blue eyes any of the coarse sensuality which breathes in the face of her companion, yet there is an indescribable tone of resemblance spread over her entire form—a likeness if you will, but newly incarnated, elevated, purified. Heavens! how one's blood boils to see that fair, delicate creature panting, struggling, sinking, under that cruel burden, while her huge gladiator of a father walks onward lazily, looking up at the sungleams that struggle through the trees, whistling indolently to himself snatches of old tunes, knocking off the heads of the road side flowers as he passes with his heavy stick! By Saint Denis, if that silk-worm playing amid the leaves had not wound his delicate cords around me and fettered my limbs, I would seize the fellow by the throat, and choke the sluggish life out of him!

Poor girl! thou art faint indeed. Thy supple back is bent and bruised beneath thy cruel load. Thy knees tremble, and the round proportions of thy face are contracted into harsh painful lines with muscular exertion. She stops an instant to recruit her shattered strength. She leans her burden, still on her shoulders, against the green bank that hems in the road, while her thin hand wanders mournfully amid the cool grass and the primroses that blossom by her side. The wretch who accompanies her detects this movement by the sudden cessation of her light footsteps on the road. He turns round with a savage scowl.

"Curse you," he says, "what ails you now? Why don't you come on?"

"I am very faint and tired, father; indeed I am. Let me rest for a moment, and I will be quite ready."

O voice of woman! whether thou art laden with accents of anger, supplication, or pity; whether thou fallest on man's ear garmented with that deep scorn that riots secretly in thy nature, and which only *one* wrong can ever thoroughly arouse; or whether thou art robed in those low, mild words of consolation that rob charity of all its sting, and makes pity light to be borne; or whether thou comest fire-winged with passion, and clad in sighs that burn, yet do not kill; thou art the only music in nature that can satisfy the cravings of the soul—the only harmony that can move the rocks of man's being and deify his dreams!

As the girl uttered her excuse, she looked wistfully at the man, and made a motion of entreaty with her hand; but he was soulless—a savage that no melody could charm—and the sweet plaintive tones of her voice fell unheeded on his ear. He moved a step or two towards her, and raised his stick threateningly.

"Come, no shamming now, my lady; I'm not going to stand any of your nonsense; you ought to know me well enough by this time, I think. Get up this moment and come after me, or by—— I'll——"

"What?"

The fellow started. The syllable was pronounced in a clear sonorous voice, that rang like the thrill of glass through the pure air, and for a moment it was a matter of doubt where it came from. The mystery, however, was solved the next instant, by the parting of the hedge that topped the bank behind, and the apparition of a young man in the gap. He was very young, not more than nineteen; but there was fire in his blue eye, and determination in his full muscular lip.

"What?"

The syllable still seemed to linger on the air, and the brutal pedestrian still stood irresolutely in the centre of the road, with one foot advanced towards his daughter, the short stick poised threateningly in his hand, and his face turned with an air of vulgar astonishment and stupid wonder to the spot from which this sudden interruption had proceeded. And the girl was a picture. Lying against the dark green bank, her heavy load tottering and half-supported by her fragile shoulder; one delicate hand grasping a tuft of damp grass tightly, while her face was upturned to the stranger with a mingled look of wonder, fear, and admiration. Youth gazing upon youth! it was a harmony of life; and there in the pathway, with frowning brow and clenched hand, stood the Discord that made it beautiful!

"What I like," said the man at last, in a rough brutal voice, and slamming his hat over his eyes with what was meant to be an independent bang. "She's my daughter, and I'd like to see the man that would step between me and her."

With a look of ineffable disdain, the youth turned to the girl, and said, in a low, sweet voice:

"You are very weary. Let me carry that load for you until you are rested."

Then did the pair stare indeed at the stranger; but with what different eyes. To hear a gentleman—for such his dress and air betrayed him to be —offering to carry a filthy sack for a common beggar-girl! Why, it was like the Arabian Nights acted in broad daylight, and on a country road!

The girl did not reply; but she looked at the stranger with one of those deep, wondering, grateful looks, which men seldom see more than once in a life-time, and then she turned to her father.

"Come! none of this nonsense; the girl's able to do for herself, and if she isn't, it's time for her to learn. Here, Nan, you slut, get up at once; I'm in a hurry."

The girl rose from the bank with a deep sigh and an air of patient grief, and tried to walk onwards; but she had not tottered three steps, when, with a single bound, the stranger cleared the hedge, and stood in the road between father and daughter.

"The girl is faint with fatigue!" he cried, earnestly. "You cannot be so cruel as to insist upon her proceeding."

"Come, come, my chicken, I ain't going to stand any of your nonsense. You just leave my girl alone, will you?"

"But you will kill her! Have you no pity for your daughter? Look! I will send a servant with you, wherever you are going, if you will only let him carry that load."

"She shall carry it, by G—d!" said the man, with a sudden outburst of fury. "Out of the way, you whelp!"

The young man planted his feet firmly on the ground, looked full in the speaker's face with a clear and unwavering glance, and said simply:

"She shan't."

Then did the savage nature of the vagabond break out in all its power. The muscles of his face contracted; his throat swelled, and his veins grew almost black with passion. He took a step forward, and said, in a tone somewhat between a hiss and a growl:

"You'd better leave this place."

The young man smiled slightly, but did not move. Then, without another syllable being uttered by either, the struggle commenced. The girl laid down her load by the road-side, and knelt in the long grass to watch.

Not a word was spoken; all was so silent that the birds in the boughs above scarce turned their heads to look at the deadly combat taking place beneath. It was a strange scene. So early in the morning, in that quiet country road, where one would expect to meet nothing but mild shepherdesses and their swains, to see two men battling silently for life; and in the long grass that lined the road-side, a fair girl kneeling, watching, fainting, praying, as the fight went on!

The youth was slender and lightly formed; but there was plenty of muscle in his round limbs, and his movements were as elastic and wary as those of a young panther. His antagonist was powerful, but heavy; and with greater strength, possessed less agility. The pair were well matched; and the struggle was intensely interesting, because it was equal.

With arms locked, and set teeth, through which the short gasping breath hissed as it went and came, the combatants struggled silently. Nothing was heard but the cranching of the gravelly soil as their feet dug into it in the effort, as it were, to grasp the earth. Several times the large man lifted the youth from off his feet, and swung him round with immense strength; but each time he preserved his balance with wonderful skill, and landed again on his legs, light and unshaken by the shock. He did not attempt for an instant to throw his antagonist, but evidently acted on the defensive, trusting to his own power of endurance to weary the other out. And the large man did soon begin to show symptoms of fatigue. His efforts became each moment more rapid and convulsive, and his throat seemed to swell and his mouth to open with incipient exhaustion. His large hands appeared to be slipping now and then from their hold, though the next instant they tightened with fresh energy. But he cannot last. His breathing is thick, and his limbs are failing him. Now, youth, that championest the young! athlete in the arena of mercy! now, put forth all the strength that nature and thy cause can lend thee, and hurl the scoundrel to the earth! A grinding of feet into the loose gravel, a moment of terrible, infernal contest, and—Bravo! well done, young hero; thy opponent lies stunned, motionless, and bleeding on the path; and thou, fresh from victory, art bending over the fainting girl, and whispering tenderly!

A few moments' interval, and the conquered man recovers his senses. He lifts his head slowly from the ground and looks round with an air of stupid bewilderment; he scarce knows where he is. Suddenly his eye lights upon the pair talking by the road-side—the youth and maiden. A scowl of intense hatred flits over his face, but it is mingled with fear. His coward nature, once subdued, dare not rise again against the victor. He strives to get up. Oh! if this cursed silk-worm had not wound his impalpable fetters so inextricably around me, I would rush upon him and complete what the youth has only begun; but I am powerless as a slave.

The man arose and stood erect, with a scowl upon his face. The blood streamed across his cheek from a broad jagged cut in his temple, and he had the look of a demon who had been wounded by a god. He made a sign to the girl, savage and imperative, to follow him. She turned pale, and looked up into her protector's face. He told her to stay where she was, and not obey her father. But it seemed as if the latter held some invisible chain by which he dragged her to his side; for as he signed to her, she lifted up the heavy sack and commenced tottering towards him, despite the entreaties of the youth. She evidently walked against her will, for her eyes continually turned towards her champion with a sad, regretful glance. Then as the young man saw her gradually, and step by step, drawn away from him, a change came over his whole bearing. His eye became preternaturally piercing and his form grew straighter, and seemed to expand. He held out his arm, and pointed with his gathered fingers straight at the man's eyes. Then, as if by magic, the progress of the girl suddenly ceased. At the same instant her father's form became rigid and motionless as a statue, while his eyes were gradually glazed over with a sort of lifeless film. After pausing for an instant to observe the effect of his spell, the youth seized the trembling girl in his arms, and parting the green screen of the hedge with one hand, bounded through the gap. The elastic branches, rustling, closed again; but between the fading blossoms of the laurels I could see two forms, with clasping arms, tread the green distance of a summer glade. The sunlight fell upon their hair, and trembled round them like a net of gold. Their eyes were turned on each other; their lips met. Oh! what would I not give to follow them beyond those dark shadows; but this silk-worm!

The man stood straight before me in the road—a horrible effigy. He was frozen into stone, and every line of his garments seemed as hard and sharp as if it had been but freshly chiselled from the block. He looked as solid as the great Pyramid; staring, staring right into my heart with his cold lifeless eyes. Oh, it was horrible to be obliged to bear it! If I could only have moved. If I could only have touched him with the very tip of my little finger. But the chains of the silk-worm were woven above, around, beneath me, and had twisted themselves into an iron lattice-work about my tongue. I could not endure it any longer. I strained every muscle of my body to bursting; the foam gathered on my lips, and my eyes stood out in their sockets, burning and blood-shot; and yet, not a motion. Again, again I tried, and—yes; O joy! I heard the yellow fetters crack. They stretched, they glistened in the sun. In another moment I should be able to dash that cursed stone man to the earth. One more effort; it was done. The wondrous filaments flew asunder with a sound like thunder, and I darted from my silken prison on the frozen effigy. I raised my hand to strike—

Oh-h h! bless my soul! what's this? how I've hurt my hand! But where am I? Why, this is my bed. And the Stone Man? There's the broad sunlight, too, gushing in at my windows. I suppose I was dreaming; yes, I must have dreamed something or other, but I don't know exactly what. But it's very late. I must make haste, or I shall be late for business. Betty-y-y!

A Terrible Night

"By Jove! Dick, I'm nearly done up."

"So am I. Did any one ever see such a confounded forest, Charley?"

"I am not alone weak, but hungry. Oh for a steak of moose, with a bottle of old red wine to wash it down!"

"Charley! beware. Take care how you conjure up such visions in my mind. I am already nearly starving, and if you increase my appetite much more it will go hard with me if I don't dine off of you. You are young, and Bertha says you're tender—"

"Hearted, she meant. Well, so I am, if loving Bertha be any proof of it. Do you know, Dick, I have often wondered that you, who love your sister so passionately, were not jealous of her attachment to me."

"So I was, my dear fellow, at first—furiously jealous. But then I reflected that Bertha must one day or the other marry, and I must lose my sister, so I thought it better that she should marry my old college chum and early friend, Charley Costarre, than any one else. So you see there was a little selfishness in my calculations, Charley."

"Dick, we were friends at school, and friends at college, and I thought at both those places that nothing could shorten the link that bound us together, but I was mistaken. Since my love for, and engagement to your sister, I feel as if you were fifty times the friend that you were before. Dick, we three will never part!"

"So he married the king's daughter, and they all lived together as happy as the days are long," shouted Dick with a laugh, quoting from nursery tale.

The foregoing is a slice out the conversation with which Dick Linton and myself endeavored to beguile the way, as we tramped through one of the forests of Northern New York. Dick was an artist, and I was a sportsman, so when one fine autumn day he announced his intention going into the woods for a week to study Nature, it seemed to me an excellent opportunity for me to exercise my legs and my trigger finger at the same time. Dick had some backwoods friend who lived in a log-hut on the shores of Eckford Lake, and there we determined to take up our quarters. Dick, who said he knew the forest thoroughly, was to be the guide, and we accordingly, with our guns on our shoulders, started on foot from Root's, a tavern known to tourists, and situated on the boundaries of Essex and Warren counties. It was a desperate walk; but as we started by daybreak, and had great faith in our pedestrian qualities, we expected to reach the nearest of the Eckford lakes by nightfall. The forest through which we traveled was of the densest description. Overhead the branches of spruce and pine shut out the day, while beneath our feet lay a frightful soil, composed principally of jagged shingle, cunningly concealed by an almost impenetrable brush. As the day wore on, our hopes of reaching our destination grew fainter and fainter, and I could almost fancy, from the anxious glances that Dick cast around him, that in spite of his boasted knowledge of the woods he had lost his way. It was not, however, until night actually fell, and that we were both sinking from hunger and exhaustion, that I could get him to acknowledge it.

"We're in a nice pickle, Master Dick," said I, rather crossly, for an empty stomach does much to destroy a man's natural amiability. "Confound your assurance that led you to set up as a guide. Of all men painters are the most conceited."

"Come, Charley," answered Dick, good-humoredly, "there's no use in growling so loudly. You'll bring the bears and panthers on us if you do. We must make the best of a bad job, and sleep in a tree."

"It's easy to talk, my good fellow. I'm not a partridge, and don't know how to roost on a bough."

"Well, you'll have to learn then; for if you sleep on the ground, the chances are ten to one but you will have the wolves nibbling at your toes before daylight."

"I'm hanged if I'll do either!" said I, desperately. "I'm going to walk all night, and I'll drop before I'll lie down."

"Come, come, Charley, don't be a fool!"

"I was a fool only when I consented to let you assume the *rôle* of guide."

"Well, Charley, if you are determined to go on, let it be so. We'll go together. After all, it's only an adventure."

"I say, Dick, don't you see a light?"

"By Jove, so there is! Come, you see Providence intervenes between us and wolves and hunger. That must be some squatter's hut."

The light to which I had so suddenly called Dick's attention was very faint, and seemed to be about half a mile distant. It glimmered through the dark branches of the hemlock and spruce trees, and weak as the light was, I hailed it as a mariner without a compass hails the star by which he steers. We instantly set out in the direction of our beacon. In a moment it seemed as if all fatigue had vanished, and we walked as if our muscles were as tense as iron, and our joints oily as a piston-shaft.

We soon arrived at what in the dusk seemed to be a clearing of about five acres, but it may have been larger, for the tall forest rising up around it must have diminished its apparent size, giving it the appearance of a square pit rather than a farm. Toward one corner of the clearing we discerned the dusky outline of a log-hut, through whose single end window a faint light was streaming. With a sigh of relief we hastened to the door and knocked. It was opened immediately, and a man appeared on the threshold. We explained our condition, and were instantly invited to walk in and make ourselves at home. All our host said he could offer us were some cold Indian corn cakes, and a slice of dried deer's-flesh, to all of which we were heartily welcome. These viands in our starving condition were luxuries to us, and we literally reveled in anticipation of a full meal.

The hut into which we had so unceremoniously entered was of the most poverty-stricken order. It consisted of but one room, with a rude brick fireplace at one end. Some deer-skins and old blankets stretched out by way of a bed at the other extremity of the apartment, and the only seats visible were two sections of a large pine trunk that stood close to the fire-place. There was no vestige of a table, and the rest of the furniture was embodied in a long Tennessee rifle that hung close to the rough wall.

If the hut was remarkable, its proprietor was still more so. He was, I think, the most villainous looking man I ever beheld. About six feet two inches in height, proportionately broad across the shoulders, and with a hand large enough to pick up a fifty-six pound shot, he seemed to be a combination of extraordinary strength and agility. His head was narrow, and oblong in shape. His straight Indian-like hair fell smoothly over his low forehead as if it had been plastered with soap. And his black, bead-like eyes were set obliquely, and slanted downward toward his nose, giving him a mingled expression of ferocity and cunning. As I examined his features attentively, in which I thought I could trace almost every bad passion, I confess I experienced a certain feeling of apprehension and distrust that I could not shake off.

While he was getting us the promised food, we tried, by questioning him, to draw him into conversation. He seemed very taciturn and reserved. He said he lived entirely alone, and had cleared the spot he occupied with his own hands. He said his name was Joel; but when we hinted that he must have some other name, he pretended not to hear us, though I saw his brows knit, and his small black eyes flash angrily. My suspicions of this man were further aroused by observing a pair of shoes lying in a corner of the hut. These shoes were at least three sizes smaller than those that our gigantic host wore, and yet he had distinctly replied that he lived entirely alone. If those shoes were not his, whose were they? The more I reflected on this circumstance the more uneasy I felt, and apprehensions were still further aroused, when Joel, as he called himself, took both our fowling-pieces, and, in order to have them out of the way, as he said, hung them on crooks from the wall, at a height that neither Dick or I could reach without getting on a stool. I smiled inwardly, however, as I felt the smooth barrel of my revolver that was slung in the hollow of my back, by its leathern belt, and thought to myself, if this fellow has any bad designs, the more unprotected he thinks us the more incautious he will be, so I made no effort to retain our guns. Dick also had a revolver, and was one of those men who I knew would use it well when the time came.

My suspicions of our host grew at last to such a pitch that I determined to communicate them to Dick. Nothing would be easier than for this villainous half-breed—for I felt convinced he had Indian blood in him— nothing would be easier than, with the aid of an accomplice, to cut our throats or shoot us while we were asleep, and so get our guns, watches, and whatever money we carried. Who, in those lonely woods, would hear the shot, or hear our cries for help? What emissary of the law, however sharp, could point out our graves in those wild woods, or bring the murder home to those who committed it? Linton at first laughed; then grew serious; and gradually became a convert to my apprehensions. We hurriedly agreed that, while one slept, the other should watch, and so take it in turns through the night.

Joel had surrendered to us his couch of deer-skin and his blanket; he himself said he could sleep quite as well on the floor, near the fire. As Dick and I were both very tired, we were anxious to get our rest as soon as possible. So after a hearty meal of deer-steak and tough cakes, washed down by a good draught from our brandy flask, I, being the youngest, got the first hour's sleep, and flung myself on the couch of skins. As my eyes gradually closed, I saw a dim picture of Dick seated sternly watching by the fire, and the long shape of the half-breed stretching out like a huge shadow upon the floor.

After what I could have sworn to be only a three-minute doze, Dick woke me, and informed me that my hour was out; and turning me out of my warm nest, lay down without any ceremony, and in a few seconds was heavily snoring. I rubbed my eyes, felt for my revolver, and seating myself on one of the pine-stumps, commenced my watch. The half-breed appeared to be buried in a profound slumber, and in the half-weird light cast by the wood embers, his enormous figure seemed almost Titanic in its proportions. I confess I felt that in a struggle for life he was more than a match for Dick and myself. I then looked at the fire, and began a favorite amusement of mine—shaping forms in the embers. All sorts of figures defined themselves before me. Battles, tempests at sea, familiar faces, and above all shone, ever returning, the dear features of Bertha Linton, my affianced bride. She seemed to me to smile at me through a burning haze, and I could almost fancy I heard her say, "While you are watching in the lonely forest I am thinking of you, and praying for your safety."

A slight movement on the part of the slumbering half-breed here recalled me from those sweet dreams. He turned on his side, lifted himself slowly on his elbow, and gazed attentively at me. I did not stir. Still retaining my stooping attitude, I half closed my eyes, and remained motionless. Doubtless he thought I was asleep, for in a moment or two he rose noiselessly, and creeping with a stealthy step across the floor, passed out of the hut. I listened—Oh, how eagerly! It seemed to me that, through the imperfectly-joined crevices of the log-walls, I could plainly hear voices whispering. I would have given worlds to have crept nearer to listen, but I was fearful of disturbing the fancied security of our host, who I now felt certain had sinister designs upon us. So I remained perfectly still. The whispering suddenly ceased. The half-breed re-entered the hut in the same stealthy way in which he had quitted it, and after giving a scrutinizing glance at me, once more stretched himself upon the floor and affected to sleep. In a few moments I pretended to awake—yawned, looked at my watch, and finding that my hour had more than expired, proceeded to wake Dick. As I turned him out of bed I whispered in his ear, "Don't take your eyes off that fellow, Dick. He has accomplices outside; be careful!" Dick gave a meaning glance, carelessly touched his revolver, as much as to say, "Here's something to interfere with his little arrangements," and took his seat on the pine-stump, in such a position as to command a view of the sleeping half-breed and the doorway at the same time.

This time, though horribly tired, I could not sleep. A horrible load seemed pressing on my chest, and every five minutes I would start up to see if Dick was keeping his watch faithfully. My nerves were strung to a frightful pitch of tensity; my heart beat at every sound, and my head seemed to throb until I thought my temples would burst. The more I reflected on the conduct of the half-breed, the more assured I was that he intended murder. Full of this idea, I took my revolver from its sling, and held it in my hand, ready to shoot him down at the first movement that appeared at all dangerous. A haze seemed now to pass across my eyes. Fatigued with long watching and excitement, I passed into that semiconscious state, in which I seemed perfectly aware of every thing that passed, although objects were dim and dull in outline, and did not appear so sharply defined as in one's waking moments. I was apparently roused from this state by a slight crackling sound. I started, and raised myself on my elbow. My heart almost ceased to beat at what I saw. The half-breed had lit some species of dried herb, which sent out a strong aromatic odor as it burned. This herb he was holding directly under Dick's nostrils, who I now perceived, to my horror, was wrapped in a profound slumber. The smoke of this mysterious herb appeared to deprive him of all consciousness, for he rolled gently off of the pine-log, and lay stretched upon the floor. The half-breed now stole to the door, and opened it gently. Three sinister heads peered in out of the gloom. I saw the long barrels of rifles, and the huge brawny hands that clasped them. The half-breed pointed significantly to where I lay with his long bony finger, then drawing a large, thirsty-looking knife from his breast, moved toward me. The time was come. My blood stopped—my heart ceased to beat. The half-breed was within a foot of my bed; the knife was raised; another instant and it would have been buried in my heart, when, with a hand as cold as ice, I lifted my revolver, took deadly aim, and fired!

A stunning report, a dull groan, a huge cloud of smoke curling around me, and I found myself standing upright, with a dark mass lying at my feet.

"Great God! what have you done, Sir?" cried the half-breed, rushing toward me. "You have killed him! He was just about to wake you."

I staggered against the wall. My senses, until then immersed in sleep, suddenly recovered their activity. The frightful truth burst upon me in a flash. I had shot Dick Linton while under the influence of a night-mare! Then every thing seemed to fade away, and I remember no more.

There was a trial, I believe. The lawyers were learned, and proved by physicians that it was a case of what is called *Somnolentia*, or sleep-drunkenness; but of the proceedings I took no heed. One form haunted me, lying black and heavy on the hut floor; and one pale face was ever present —a face I saw once after the terrible catastrophe, and never saw again— the wild, despairing face of Bertha Linton, my promised bride!

A Day Dream

Dimes came to me the other night and suggested to me in a mysterious kind of way, that we should visit the Five Points together. I am constitutionally prudent, and I demurred.

"There is a good deal of murder knocking about the streets nowadays, my dear Dimes," said I. "Society is unsafe. A respectable man can not even keep a quiet, orderly house, under the supervision of a middle-aged female of irreproachable morals, but he is found hacked to pieces in his room one fine morning. The corners of the streets are rounded off into gangs of ruffians ready to garrote any passenger who has a three-cent-piece on his person. The police are every where but where they ought to be; and, as a general thing, take more interest in elections than in assassinations. On the whole, my dear Dimes, I don't think I will go."

"But," said Dimes, "there's no danger. We will go with Captain Currycomb of the 150th ward, as efficient an officer, let me tell you, Sir, as any in the city of New York. He will show us every thing, and I'd like to see the man that would touch us while under his protection. Besides, look here."

Whereupon, Dimes pulled out an exquisite revolver, mounted in ivory and silver, and no larger than some night-keys that I have seen young men who live in cheap boarding-houses carry. It was a seducing weapon. Murderously enticing. I held it in my hand for a few moments, felt the silky lock, passed my fingers over the polished stock, and looked along the delicate barrel, on whose blue mirror-like surface the light played as on a lake. I found myself speculating suddenly on what would occur if I were to shoot Dimes. I saw the precise spot in his temple—a little above the left eyebrow—where the bullet would enter. I saw the sudden spasm—almost invisible, so slight was it—that convulsed his frame as the ball struck him. I saw the rapid flash of the eye on me—so rapid that we have no term to measure it with—one glance of terror, reproach, amazement, and then his legs bent, and, doubling up under him as if the bones had been suddenly withdrawn, he rolled on the floor.

I found myself remarking as I stood over him, that the murdered man had fallen in a strange attitude. He lay on the floor with his body bent forward, his forehead touching the earth, and his arms extended in front. I was reminded instantly of the pictures of a Moslem at prayer with his head toward the Holy City; and then my memory almost instantly recalled a large book bound in Russia leather, called the Oriental Annual, which I had read when a child, and which contained the picture of a Turk at his devotions.

I then busied myself again with Dimes. He lay still in the same position, dead. He had died almost instantly. That last fleeting look he gave me was the flash of his passing soul. The carpet on which he lay was a white ground with a pattern of ivy leaves trailing across it. Plainly discernible on this white carpet was a small red stream that slowly, slowly flowed from Dimes's temple, until it reached a bunch of ivy leaves, where it spread into a little round pool. I recollect very well the whimsical thought suggesting itself to me that this round patch of blood nestling among the ivy leaves bore a rude resemblance to a cluster of the scarlet berries of the plant itself.

I had hardly conceived this idea, when, as if by the sudden loosing of some cord, a huge blackness fell upon me, and I awoke to the awful responsibility of murder. Up to that time I had looked curiously at the incident, but now I became agitated. My heart beat. My temples were bedewed with a cold sweat. The dead man seemed no longer like the praying Moslem in the picture, but rather like some dark fiend about to lift himself from the earth and destroy me. I ran here and there, and hastily made preparations for flight. Somehow, whatever I did, I seemed to stumble against the corpse. I saw with horror that my boots left tracks of blood on the carpet. I tried to take them off, but they seemed glued to my feet. I raved and blasphemed, and ran to the fire-place, where I scraped the soles upon the ashes—but the blood would not dry; it still left wet prints on the floor wherever I moved. I felt my brain whirling. Then came a knocking at the door. Should I answer, or remain silent? What to do? The knocking grew louder—the door shook. They were bursting it open! I ran to the window—it was fifty feet from the ground! I rushed back to the yielding door, set my back firmly against it—but in vain; some unseen, irresistible force urged it inward. I strained every muscle—life and death were on it—I could not any longer—

"Here, Dimes," said I, "take your pistol. I should be afraid to carry such things about me. I'm afraid I have a dash of the assassin in my blood.

Nevertheless, I'll avail myself of Captain Currycomb, and go with you to the Five Points."

"Do you know, my dear fellow," said Dimes, "that just now when you were cocking that pistol, you looked quite wild about the eyes!"

I laughed and said nothing. Dimes would have distrusted me for evermore, if he knew that I had contemplated his murder even in a day-dream.

The Other Night

The other night we had a dream. We had been poring all day over Adam Eagle's volumes, laboriously deciphering a quaint essay on the moral principles of animals, in which the writer endeavored to prove that beasts possessed conscientiousness, and performed their various avocations as much from a sense of duty as from instinct. The writing was queer and cramped, and pained the eyes to read it. The pages were so soiled with mould and damp as to be entirely illegible in some places, and some idle urchin had been busy pricking architectural designs on the paper, some of which, though very ingenious in themselves, sadly interfered with the perusal of the manuscript. We grew very weary; yes, Adam! we absolutely grew drowsy over thy hallowed volumes! A sensation of cobwebs overspread our frame; a species of impalpable but tenacious threadwork seemed to encompass each limb, and weave itself around our long hair. It appeared as though a thousand busy little sprites were engaged in hanging a tiny leaden weight to each particular hair of our eyelashes. Little balls of sand were apparently stuffed into the corners of our eyes, making us blink terribly. We found our fingers constantly wandering over our eyelids, and poking themselves into all corners of our face. Our moustache suffered considerable persecution. We were fidgety, and twirled the ends into watch-springs over and over again. The room was certainly too hot! No; it is the dressing-gown! Off goes the offending garment, and we luxuriate in shirt-sleeves. What hideously tight shoes these are! Where are our slippers? Of course we never can find any thing when we want it. The slippers are not to be seen. A short search after them enlivens us a little. We then feel a sudden disposition to be reflective. Our head rests frequently on one hand, and we assume a pensive attitude. It is not that we are sleepy! oh, no; *that* has gone off long ago. We merely wish to—wish—to—in—to—to—Pshaw! this is really too absurd; dozing at this hour of night, with so much work before us. Nonsense! we will make an effort. A basin of cold water and a sponge will do it, and we shall be as brisk as a bee. We perform an ablution, and enter the study, endeavoring with faint success to look lively, as we pass the looking-glass. It is, however, a dreary effort. We notice that we look pale, and that our hair has a limp and tired aspect. There is work to be done, however, and we fasten our mental fangs into it furiously. It is very interesting, at least we try hard to persuade ourselves of the fact, and we devour it. Our eyebrows, however, annoy us a little, we do not very well know why; but we keep plucking at them, and passing our finger absently along our temples. But we still read on, read firmly and systematically. The words have sometimes an unaccountable inclination to fraternize, the tail of one intertwining itself with the head of another, and the effect is rather confusing, as thus: "Thenightwas-chillandcoldand-rain," &c. It does not matter much, though. A little patience, and they will settle themselves down again in their proper places. The lamp is very annoying. One moment it looks bright and clear, the next it is as dull as a New-York gas-lamp on a dark night, or the City-Hall clock on every night. Thinking it may be something in ourselves, we keep our eyes wide open, and stare at it; but the sprites are again busy hanging their little weights on our eyelashes, and we feel our lids gradually dropping. We catch ourselves nodding, with a convulsive jerk, and hem and blow our nose audibly, in order to drown conscience. The noise has the effect of terrifying a mouse, who, emboldened by the silence, had come out from his hole, and was amusing himself with eating a corner off of "The Pilgrim's Progress." We feel pleased at inspiring such terror. The reflective mood comes on again; the chin drops into the hollow of the hand, and we pretend to be speculating on the origin of fear. But nod—nod—nod. There seems to be a swaying of the universe. Room, book-shelves, lamp, furniture, all rock and nod, and we alone maintain a just equilibrium. All things get cloudy; but whether this arises from the atmosphere, or from our hair falling into our eyes, we cannot tell. Mist is every where; we seem to be sitting in mist; no, it is a sea; it looks like mist, it is so smooth and blue: we are sitting in an arm-chair, with brass nails, on a smooth blue sea. That is, it is very like a sea; but it can't be one exactly, for a sea has rocks, and all the rocks here are books—great, rugged folios, over which the waves of vapor burst and foam. Presently this ocean mist divides, and the book-rocks clang their huge covers with a noise like sea-shore thunder, and an aged figure emerges from the sea. It is the Solitary. It is Adam Eagle himself. Adam Anadoymene! He is clad in an old linsey-woolsey dressing-gown. There are papooshes on his feet, and his right hand, all thin and withered, is stained to the bone with ink. His countenance is noble and mild, with traces of suffering marked upon it. And the white hair falls back in rich masses from his forehead, like a cataract of snow. But his eyes are strange. They seem to behold nothing material. They do not even see me, the adorer, the worshipper of the seven volumes. Their gaze is illimitable. They seem to be striving even to pierce beyond the farthest beyond. They know no clouds or intervening mists. They spiritually tunnel mountains, and speed unheeding through the valleys far away. Were we standing on the outer edge of the disc of Neptune, straight in the focal line of those eyes, we would feel convinced that they saw not us, but were piercing through us into backward space. While we were watching the Solitary intently, a strange murmuring noise, like that which one makes when one springs a number of book-pages, keeping the thumb pressed against the edges, rustled around us, and again the smooth blue sea-mist divided, and straight in Adam Eagle's path an angelic form, of sculptured vapor, rose up and floated buoyantly. Never did mortal eyes behold a fairer thing, boy or woman, spirit or etherealized matter—we knew not which it was. Its beauty was not of sex or form, and lay not within lines. It was boundless and universal grace. It had scarce hovered an instant in the air, when the Solitary beheld it. That he did see it, could only be inferred from the sudden flaming of his eyes; for in all other respects, his gaze seemed to be as distant as before. But his eyeballs burned suddenly, and light seemed to scintillate from them, and make prismatic bows against the vapory outlines of the apparition. His lips moved as if in inward speech, and he extended his long, thin, transparent hand, as though he would magnetize and compel the spirit. Then the latter seemed to smile all over, and laugh even in the very folds of its impalpable drapery; and began with a slow even motion to describe a great circle. As if drawn by some viewless magnetic relation, the Solitary glided over the smooth, blue sea-mist, and followed its track. With extended hand, he glided after it in the great circle, burning with eagerness to increase his speed and overtake it, but restrained by some invisible law which regulated his motion. When the beautiful spirit had described the great circle, it commenced another of less diameter than the first, and moved with a slightly increased velocity, which communicated itself to Adam Eagle. The next circle was smaller still, and the velocity heightened. And still the disembodied Grace floated on before with its universal smile, and still the Solitary pursued it with imprisoned eagerness. Smaller and smaller grew the circles, swifter and swifter grew the pursuit, until at last both narrowed into a furious whirl. Adam's long white hair streamed back, as if some good spirit were trying to tear him from his vain pursuit, and his large reflective eyes were starting from their sockets, as though they would leap out and fasten themselves upon the vapor-shape. But always, even in the last swift eddies of the chase, when all features were confused into a dim outline, the Shape maintained the same unvarying and universal smile, that lightened its very drapery. Swift, swift; round and round. The circles must end in a centre, where all motion ceases. Adam gasps for breath, as his transparent fingers almost touch the object of his pursuit—another whirl, and they are spinning on one pivot. A sudden stoppage. The Solitary opens wide his arms to grasp the Shape. The universal smile in which it is clothed deepens into a sun-burst of laughter; all is brightly dim for an instant; and then, Adam Eagle is alone! A moan breaks from his lips, as down from the upper sky there fall upon his beating temples a few gentle snow-flakes; his head drops upon his breast; the smooth, blue sea-mist divides again, and he sinks slowly, leaving behind him painted on my heart a picture of unutterable anguish. Then the rustling sound breaks forth again, the book-rocks clang their covers like sea-shore thunder, and I commence sailing over the blue sea-mist in my brass-nailed arm-chair. The voyage is pleasant enough, but somehow or other, owing to my steering improperly with a paper-cutter, we run ashore upon a reef of book-rocks. We feel that our last moment is come; the vapor of the sea-mist foams up about us, and our arm-chair is gradually sinking. We fire guns of distress with a gold pencil-case, and prepare a raft. But to our horror we discover that the blue sea-mist will support nothing but brass-nailed arm-chairs. We are slowly settling down; the sea-mist is on a level with our chin; another moment, and we are lost; when, oh! joy, an albatross comes floating by. We seize one of his wide wings, and are suddenly upborne into the highest heaven, and then dashed as suddenly against the earth. On recovering from the shock, we find that we have upset the ink-bottle, and are lying on the floor, embracing a folio edition of Vertol's Knights of Malta.

The Crystal Bell

It was a country tavern, and I sat in the bar-room for lack of something
better to do. Heaven knows there was little enough to amuse one in that
dreary temple of Bacchus. There were five newspapers, the newest a
month old, lying on the table—I knew every advertisement in them.
There was a picture of the favorite Presidential candidate hanging over
the fire-place, which, if it at all resembled the gentleman in question,
entitled him to a glass-case in Barnum's Museum rather than to a chair in
the White House. A book for registering names lay on a sort of desk in the
corner, but since my arrival the pages, though dated, were destitute of a
single name. Apple-jack, bad gin, and blazing brandy in bottles of eccentric colors, filled a glass press behind a counter, which was called by courtesy a bar; and behind this stood a wooden image called by courtesy a
landlord.

When a man has no books, and no acquaintances at a country tavern,
he is apt to fall back on the landlord. I have met in my time very amusing
landlords—landlords who could talk about fishing, and shooting, and politics, and perhaps retail to you some of the gossip of the neighborhood; for
it is wonderful how a man in the strait in which I was, will find amusement in the doings of people he knows nothing about. But the landlord of
the Hominy House was not to be relied upon in such an emergency. You
were not to take any such liberties with him, Sir, let me tell you. He took
you into his house, as it were, under protest. He gave you a bed with an air
that seemed to say he regretted doing it, but still he did not like to refuse;
and you ate your dinner before him in fear and trembling, lest he should
reconsider his hospitality and order you out of the house.

Whether it was a natural inflexibility of joints, or whether it was a high
sense of personal dignity, I do not know; but certainly General Dubbley,
the landlord of the Hominy House, in the village of Hopskotch, New
Jersey, was the most dignified man I ever saw. The halo which he threw
round a glass of whisky and water was perfectly wonderful. You might
have imagined you were drinking "green seal" to judge by the lofty expres-

sion of his countenance as he handed you the bottle. At the dinner-table he fairly awed the appetite out of one; and I shall never, as long as I live, forget the thunder-cloud which gathered on his brow when, one day, I unluckily asked to be helped to soup twice. When Lafayette passed through Hopskotch, General Dubbley was one of the committee that received him. I did not know him at that period, not having been born, but I have formed a theory that from this epoch may be dated his tremendous dignity. Whether this interview with the French patriot had any thing to do with turning the General's hair green, I can not say; but it is, nevertheless, a fact that he was remarkable for possessing a lock of bright verdant olive on either side of his head. This eccentricity of color, I presume, must remain forever a mystery.

As I was saying, I sat in the bar-room. General Dubbley stood behind the bar counting the contents of the till with Olympian dignity. Quarter-dollars seemed to become thunder-bolts in his hands. I was very weary. Weary of Hopskotch, weary of Dubbley, weary of the Presidential candidate over the mantle-piece, who seemed to have been born with a patch of strawberries on each cheek; weary of the old newspapers; weary of every thing, in fact, except the memory of my dear Annie to whom I was engaged, and on whose account I had left New York and immured myself, in mid-winter, at the Hominy House, in order, before our marriage, to settle some matters connected with my property, which lay near Hopskotch. I yawned in the very teeth of General Dubbley.

The door opened ere my teeth closed again, and a man entered, and, shaking off the snow that lay in thick flakes on his coat, advanced to the wood fire that blazed and crackled on the broad hearth, and spread out his hands to the cheering warmth. He was a very seedy-looking man. He had but one coat on—an old, threadbare evening coat—which was tenderly buttoned across a chest which seemed afraid to breathe too lustily lest it should burst the frail buttons. His shoes were old and soaked, looking as if he had found them after they had been boiled for soup by Lieutenant Strain and his companions on the Isthmus. His trousers were also wet, and very scanty, and shrank from contact with his shoes as if they had been as sensitively constituted as the mimosa. Poor fellow! he looked as if he had not had a dinner in his stomach, or a cent in his pocket for a very long time.

As he entered, the General raised his head from the till and looked at him severely. I saw the poor man shrink a little, but presently he seemed to muster up sufficient courage to go up to the bar.

"Can I have a bed here to-night?" he asked, in a timid voice.

"Full, Sir, full!" said the General, frowning until his old eyebrows fairly creaked; "besides, we seldom have accommodation for strangers."

The poor man gave a glance at his threadbare coat, and smiled. But, oh! how sad the smile was! Patient, but very sorrowful!

"It is a very bad night," said the stranger, pleadingly; "and I am not particular as to where I sleep. Any where would do for me."

Unphilosophical stranger! A worse method than a confession of heedlessness of comfort could not have been adopted to win the General's favor. If he had blustered up to the bar and shouted for a bed of rose-leaves with every leaf ironed out, the majestic Dubbley might have overlooked the seedy coat; but not to care where he slept! that settled him.

"Sorry, Sir, but can't accommodate you;" and with this brief intimation the Jove of Hopskotch commenced once more to make quarter-dollars look like thunder-bolts.

The stranger sighed; looked wistfully at the bright fire; gave another hopeless glance at the wooden Dubbley, and then moved slowly to the door. It was more than I could stand. Olympus had no terrors for me at the moment.

"Stay!" I cried, advancing from the obscure corner in which I had been seated; "stay, Sir, for a moment. This weather is too inclement for any human being to wander in at night. I have not the pleasure of knowing who you are, but there are two beds in my room, and I esteem it my duty to offer you one of them. Pray accept it."

I almost lost the murmured thanks with which the seedy man accepted this impetuous offer, in the consideration of General Dubbley's countenance. I don't think I ever beheld such a picture of astounded dignity. My heart sank after my speech was fairly out; for really I expected nothing more than to be turned out myself; and, what is more, I believe that I would have gone. To my surprise, however, the General took another tone.

"If Mr. Massy was willing to proffer such indiscriminate hospitality," he said, "*he* was perfectly satisfied."

For the first time the truth burst upon me that the General was not so awful as he looked, and that by the aid of a little resolution he might even be reduced to the position of a landlord. I plucked up courage from this supposed discovery, and having opened the breach, pushed on.

"I want some supper, General Dubbley," said I, peremptorily.

"Sir, you have had your supper," answered the General, clutching madly at the last rag of his importance that was being torn so ruthlessly from him.

"No matter; I wish to sup again. I sometimes sup frequently during an evening."

I was reckless with victory, and began to talk wildly.

"You shall be served, Sir."

And the General abdicated his thunder-bolts and disappeared into the kitchen. I had conquered. A hand was laid very gently on me, and the stranger now spoke audibly to me for the first time.

"I am very, very much obliged to you," he said, "for all this kindness; but if in getting this supper you put yourself to inconvenience on my account, may I beg that you will countermand it?"

"Not at all," I replied, diplomatically; "but as you have reminded me of it, perhaps you will favor me by supping with me—that is, if you have not supped?"

"I have not dined," said the stranger, with a feeble smile. "I see through your kind *ruse*," he added; "and to a gentleman who can act so feelingly as you have done, I have little shame in confessing that if I have not dined, it was because I had no money."

"Come, come!" said I, trying to bluster away those confounded tears that always *will* get in my eyes when I hear such things, "Come, we will have a jolly good supper together, and then we will talk of business matters afterward. Let us sit by the fire until it is ready, and, meanwhile, drink this."

So saying, I invaded the General's Olympian domains, and pouring out a stiff horn of apple-jack, forced it upon my new friend. It did him good, I am certain, for I saw the dim eyes brighten and the thin cheek flush; and it was not the fire-light that did it, cheery as it was.

I never met a more delightful man than this seedy stranger. He had been every where, seen every thing, done every thing, knew every body. He was a finished scholar, an original critic, a delightful singer, an epitome of wit. He so fascinated me, that we sat up in my room until almost twelve —an unearthly hour in Hopskotch, where the people go to roost with the chickens—and it never once entered into my head to ask him who he was, what he was called, or how it was that he was wandering about in the snow without any money. I even went to bed without locking my door, or putting my watch under my pillow.

It was the gray dawn of the morning when some one sitting on my bedside awoke me suddenly. I started upright in an instant, and beheld my friend. He was completely dressed, and in the dim light seemed like a departing ghost. For a moment, in the incoherence of my ideas, I had a confused idea that he was about to rob me, and seized him instinctively by the arm.

"Don't be alarmed," he said, with a smile. "I intended to awake you, and before I went—for I am going immediately—I wished to thank you for your extreme kindness to me. God bless you for it! I have but little to offer you in the way of return, but what I have is yours. Here is a crystal bell," and he drew a tiny glass bell from his pocket, a thing like a child's toy. "It was forged in distant lands, where the sun makes the rocks vocal, and its maker sang over it in the furnace the spells known only to the children of the East. It is the touchstone of truth. Whoever utters a falsehood to him who bears it about, that moment the crystal bell will vibrate. Scoff at the story now, if you will, but try the talisman—it will never betray you. Farewell!"

And laying the little bell upon the counterpane, before I could sufficiently collect my scattered senses he glided to the door and went out, closing it softly after him.

I took up the bell mechanically, and examined it. It was entirely formed of what seemed to be the purest crystal. The tongue was also of crystal, but flexible as the finest watch-spring. I tried to ring it, but although the ball at the end of the pendant tongue visibly struck the clear sides of the bell, it did not emit the slightest sound. I tried it again and again, and always with the same result.

I got up and looked for my watch. It was safe. My pockets were untouched; my drawers intact. My seedy friend, therefore, was not an impostor. Again I returned to the mysterious bell, and agitated its crystal tongue in vain. Not even a muffled tinkling was to be drawn from it. Had the pendulum been a feather it could not have been more silent.

All day long I felt wretchedly uncomfortable with the crystal bell in my pocket. I scarcely answered the sneering inquiries after my seedy friend with which General Dubbley assailed me. I scarcely took the trouble to inform him that I had not been robbed. I was indifferent to the display which he made of his counting his spoons in my presence. The last words of my mysterious guest continually rang in my ears—"Whoever utters a falsehood to him who bears it, that moment the crystal bell will vibrate."

Annie Gray! sweet, truthful, pure-eyed Annie Gray! why was it that your face continually rose up before me whenever I touched the magic bell? Whenever I drew it forth, and looked through its crystal walls, why was it that your fair countenance seemed dimly visible within, but clouded with some horrible shadow? And when I thought of you, why did the name of that hateful Aubyn always flicker in big letters before my mind's eye?

I suffered positive torture. Here was I, engaged to be married to one of the sweetest girls in New York, beloved by her to my heart's content, and rich enough to satisfy her every wish, when in comes a stranger, who puts what he calls a talisman for testing truth into my hands, and straightway I begin to doubt the dear girl whom I had never doubted before. Did she really love me, or was it only for my wealth that she became mine? Did she not rather prefer that horrible Harry Aubyn, who danced so well, and who talked so charmingly about nothing? The more I tried to conquer this abominable fantasy of jealousy the more positive it became, until at last I had worked myself into such a fever of excitement that I could bear suspense no longer. Yes! I would instantly hurry to New York and test this wondrous gift! It was folly—madness; I knew that well enough, but still I would test it—test it all the more willingly, for I had such faith in Annie. But why did she encourage that empty dandy, Harry Aubyn?

In less than two hours I was in New York, ringing madly at Annie Gray's door.

As I entered the drawing-room hastily, out walked Mr. Aubyn. We saluted coldly, but I could have strangled him at the moment, if such things were permissible in this century. I must have been rather pale and disordered-looking, for I had scarce entered the room when Annie's first words were,

"Oh, Gerald! has any thing happened?"

Dear girl! how could any but a madman doubt that anxious, fond look —that quivering lip? I kissed her forehead, and reassured her.

"Annie, dear, why do you have that Mr. Aubyn here in my absence? You know I don't like him."

"Why, Gerald, I really can't help if he calls. I don't care about his visits, I assure you; but I can not be rude to him, I have known him so long."

Gracious heavens! was it fancy? or did I hear a faint, crystalline tinkling in my pocket? A cold shiver ran through my frame; but I endeavored to dissemble my agony, and, with a forced smile, went on.

"So you don't like him really, you little puss! Come now, confess that at one time you did care a little—a very little—for Aubyn, your old play-mate?"

"Why, what ails you, Gerald? You look so queer. I assure you, I never cared any thing for Harry Aubyn."

Tinkle! tinkle! tinkle! in my pocket. I felt the blood rush to my head; it was a Niagara of emotion, but I subdued it.

"And you love your poor Gerald, then, better than any body else; better even than the old school-fellow you have known so long?"

"What a fool you are, Gerald! Of course I do," and she kissed me gently on the forehead.

Tinkle! tinkle! tinkle! in my pocket. Plain, clear, distinct. Every vibration of the crystal bell thrilled through my frame. If the bells of every cathedral, headed by Tom of Lincoln, had pealed altogether at my ear they could not have moved me half so much as that sharp, shrill crystal tintinnabulation from that horrible bell.

I could bear it no longer.

"Traitress!" I shouted, flinging away the tender arms that wound around my neck. "Hypocrite! I despise you! Yes, madam, the eyes of your dupe were opened in time. You shall not laugh at the credulous Gerald Massy."

"Gerald! are you mad?"

"Not quite; though a week after our marriage I would have been, impostor that you are! But I know you. Know that you don't love me. Know that you have lied to me three times within this last half hour."

She tried to embrace me; but I flung her off. She wrung her hands, and the big tears rolled over her cheeks, and her gentle head was bent, as if stricken with some great blow. She acted her part excellently well.

"What can you mean, Gerald? I have never deceived you in thought or word. If you have proofs of my hypocrisy advance them, but do not storm me down with assertions."

"My proofs are here!" I cried, holding up the bell triumphantly—the triumph of despair. "Here! look on this talisman, falsest of women, and tremble!"

"But, Gerald, are you sane? I see nothing but this bell."

"And this bell, as you call it, has told me within the last half hour that you are a worthless woman."

One tigress-like leap, and she caught it from my hand. With flaming eyes she held it aloft, and then dashed it on the ground. A crash, like the bursting of a thousand hand-grenades—a thundering of cathedral bells, that seemed to shake the world; and, looking up, I saw General Dubbley standing over me in a dignified attitude.

"Mr. Massy," said he, "the dinner-bell has been ringing these ten minutes; but you appear to have been sleeping so soundly that you have not heard it. Dinner waits."

And so it was a dream. No seedy friend—no talisman—no falsehood in sweet Annie Gray. I rubbed my eyes and went into dinner; but as I ate my soup under the awful eye of the General, I confess I regretted the non-reality of that portion of my dream in which I had subdued the Thunderer of the tavern.

I never told Annie Gray that I had ever doubted her even in a dream, until we had been a month married.

How I Overcame My Gravity

I have all my life been dallying with science. I have coquetted with electricity, and had a serious flirtation with pneumatics. I have never discovered any thing, nevertheless I am continually experimentalizing. My chambers are like the Hall of Physics in a University. Air-pumps, pendulums, prisms, galvanic batteries, horse-shoe magnets with big weights continually suspended to them: in short, all the paraphernalia of a modern man of science are strewn here and there, or stowed away on shelves, much to the disgust of the maid-servant, who on cleaning-day longs to enter the sanctuary, yet dare not trust her broom amidst such brittle furniture. To survey my rooms, you would infallibly set me down as a cross between Faraday and Professor Morse. I dabble in all branches of Natural Philosophy. I am continually decomposing water with electricity, and combining gases until they emit the most horrible odors. I have had four serious explosions in my laboratory, and have received various warnings from the Fire Marshal. The last was occasioned by the obstinacy of an Irish maid-servant, who, happening to behold a large mass of phosphorus in the dark, would insist on "putting it out" with a pail of water. The consequence was, of course, a conflagration that was near destroying the entire establishment. My friends visit me with fear and trembling. They are never certain that the bell-pull may not be the pole of an electromagnetic battery, and when they seat themselves in a chair seem to expect some unwonted phenomenon to exhibit itself. You will at once perceive, therefore, that I am an enthusiast. People when they pass me in the street point me out to their friends, and whisper, "Very clever man, but *so* eccentric!" I have gotten an immense reputation for ability, yet I don't believe that my best friend would trust me with the management of the most trivial business matter. Nor am I so much surprised at this. I will confess that I am continually suffering losses on my own little property, and it would seem my fate to form relations with all the bankrupts and swindlers in the United States. These drains on my estate I always hoped to make good by an invention. I am a very worldly fellow at bottom, let me tell you, notwithstanding all my scientific pranks. I keep an eye out for the main chance; and I always held the hope that even when my affairs were going most to ruin I would eventually light upon some lucky discovery which would make every thing right again. There's Professor Morse. He lit upon an invention, and see what's the result. Why, he's asked over to Moscow by the Emperor of Russia to be present at his coronation, and is given a palace to live in, with a whole Ukraine of horses and Cossacks at his disposal!

For a long time I had turned my attention to solving the problem of aerial locomotion. I fancy even now that I hit the white when I enunciated my grand principle of progression by means of atmospheric inclined planes; and at the time I made a model of a machine which illustrated my theory very fairly, but I had not capital enough for experiments on a large scale; and so great was the prejudice against all kinds of ballooning among moneyed men that I could not find the means to exploit what is incontestably a great physical truth.

One day as I was walking down Mercer Street, in the neighborhood of Bleecker, I came opposite to the establishment of Chilton, the chemist, which stood on the corner. Revolving a thousand formless projects in my brain, my eyes, wandering like my mind, happened to light on the open door of the chemist's store. There, on a table placed a little way inside the entrance, I beheld a number of brass instruments lying, the shape and construction of which I was unfamiliar with. Idly and half-mechanically I crossed over and entered the store for the purpose of examining them. The young man in attendance advanced to meet me—for I am known as a sort of amateur *savant*—and asked how he could serve me.

"What is this?" I asked, taking one of the instruments that had attracted my attention from the table. "It seems to me to be some novelty."

"It is truly a novelty," said my friend, the budding chemist. "It is a trifle—an ingenious trifle, certainly—discovered by a Connecticut genius, and its operations have as yet been entirely unaccounted for."

"Ah!" I cried, becoming suddenly interested, "let us look."

The machine which I held in my hand may be thus briefly described. Imagine a brass globe, some three inches in diameter, having its axis playing in a narrow but tolerably thick rim of brass, just as a terrestrial globe revolves in its horizon. The only difference being that the globe was not central in the rim, or horizon; one of its poles being nearer to the end of its axis than the other. This peculiarity, I afterward discovered, was not essential to its working, being merely a matter of convenience. The remainder of the apparatus consisted of an upright steel rod, fixed in a heavy wooden platform, candlestick fashion, and pointed like an electrical conductor.

"How does it work," I asked, after examining it attentively, "and what principle does it illustrate?"

"It overthrows an established principle," answered my young friend, "and I am not clear as to what one it gives in place of it."

"Let us see it."

"Willingly."

So saying the young man took the globe, which revolved with little friction in its brass horizon, and winding a string round that portion of the axis which occupied the greatest space between the globe and ring, held the latter against his breast, and pulling the string violently, as boys pull the string of a humming-top, caused the globe to revolve with marvelous swiftness on its axis. The globe being thus in a rapid state of revolution in its horizon, he now showed me on the under surface of the last, and in a right line with the poles of the axis, a small cavity drilled, which admitted of the machine being placed on the upright pointed steel rod, without any chance of slipping. This cavity was *not a hole*, only an indentation in which the point of the upright rod fitted, just as the axle of a watch wheel is received into the jewel. When this pivot, so to speak, was placed by the young chemist on the steel-pointed rod, the globe and its horizon, to my utter astonishment, proceeded to revolve in a plane at right angles to the revolution of the globe! There was a weight of some six pounds supporting itself in the air, and revolving with a regular motion! If my reader will take a long wedge of iron, heavier at one end than the other, and place the light end on the point of a rod stuck into the earth, and at right angles with it, and then conceive that wedge of iron revolving around the point where it touches the upright rod, he will have a pretty clear idea of the marvel which I witnessed at Mr. Chilton's.

The attraction of gravitation then was overcome! In the same position in which I saw it maintaining itself, if the revolution of the brass globe was checked the whole apparatus would instantly tumble to the earth. Why, then, did the simple centrifugal force of the globe enable it to thus marvelously poise itself in air? I was bewildered, and though my brain, from habit of dealing with problems, instantly groped for a reason, it could find none satisfactory.

"Has no explanation been offered of this wonder?" I asked the chemist.

"None, Sir," was the reply; "at least none that were in the least logical or conclusive. Several people have sent us elaborate explanations, but when all have been divested of their scientific phraseology, they amount but to one arbitrary assertion of the fact that it revolves contradictorily to the laws of gravitation."

I bought one of the toys and went home. I was lost in wonder. What became of Newton's famous apple now? It was rotten to its core. Had the wind or some other subtle power impressed upon it such a force as to cause it to revolve with immense rapidity it would never have fallen, and Newton would never have discovered the so-called principle of the attraction of gravitation.

The more I pondered the more the marvel grew upon me. I spun the toy for hours, and was never weary of beholding it move in its appointed circle, self-sustaining and mysterious. After all, I considered it as only wonderful to me, because I have been so long in the habit of accepting the theory of gravitation as an established fact. This new force, whatever it is that supports this toy in air, is not a whit more mysterious than the assumed force which is said to draw all things toward the centre of the earth, and keep the planets in their places. Ask what it is, and people tell you "the attraction of gravitation." Ask them what "the attraction of gravitation" is, and they will tell you "the force which draws matter to the centre of the earth," and so the game of science runs. Arbitrary names are forced on you as facts. From battledore to battledore the shuttlecock is sent flying. The result becomes the definition and the explanation.

It was in one of those moods of mind in which a man sometimes finds himself, groping for day through a horrible and oppressive darkness, yet certain that the chink through which it will flow lies somewhere within reach, that I suddenly lit upon the conviction that in this new discovery I held the secret of aerial locomotion!

I argued in this way: If a violent rotary motion is sufficient to overcome the gravitating tendency of brass, it surely is that of human flesh. Neither is it at all necessary that the body of the person wishing to soar aloft should itself revolve. That would be fatal to life. But here, in this toy, I see the revolution of a brass globe supporting a heavy brass horizon, and if I were to put another weight, say a cent, on that brass horizon, it would still be supported; therefore if a machine on the same principle, and proportionately large, be constructed, it will support a man as this supports a cent. I had lit upon the truth that "a body revolving on its own axis with sufficient velocity becomes self-supporting, and can be impressed with a force that shall impel it in any given direction!"

With all the fever of a man of science and an enthusiast I set to work. My machine cost me long nights of labor and brain-work. I will endeavor to describe it.

It was a copper globe of vast dimensions, hollow inside, and traversed by a huge axis, which buried its poles into an enormous horizon of iron. In the interior of this globe, parallel with the axis and a little above it, ran a false axis, also of iron, but playing loosely in holes bored in the globe itself, so that when the globe revolved this axis did not turn. On this bar of iron was placed a seat, which was intended for my own accommodation. This arrangement, it will be perceived, insured to any person placed on the seat an equilibrium, no matter how quickly the globe by which he was surrounded revolved. It was, in fact, the same principle on which ships' lamps are suspended. There the lamp always remains horizontal, no matter how heavily the vessel rolls.

The machinery by which the globe was caused to revolve on its axis is much too complicated to admit of any description unaccompanied with diagrams; suffice it to say, that it was so powerful as to insure a revolution of this enormous copper sphere at the rate of sixty times in a second. A vast iron pillar, answering to the upright steel rod of the toy, I had also constructed. This was destined to receive and sustain the brass horizon. A machine constructed after the manner of the ancient catapult was also arranged for the purpose of launching the globe into air so soon as it had attained the necessary revolutionary velocity. The power of this catapult was cunningly graduated to certain distances. Assuming that the globe while revolving possessed no weight, it would with a slight push travel forever through space unless the resistance of the atmosphere lessened and conquered its motion. But the globe would only revolve for a certain time, and in proportion as the velocity of revolution decreased so would its tendencies to the earth return; thus knowing precisely how long this velocity would last, and in what ratio it would decrease, I was enabled to calculate to a pound what force to impress upon it by the aid of the catapult, in order to send it any given distance.

Every thing being complete, and having invited a few friends to witness the experiment, I took my seat on the false axis with a beating heart, and gave the signal by which the attendants were to set the globe in motion. In an instant the copper sphere was whirling around me with a velocity that I could not measure, but could only guess at from the humming noise that to me in the interior sounded like the thunder of a thousand skies. The interior of the globe was lit by pieces of massive flint glass set firmly in a belt form round the centre. These windows, from the rapidity of motion, blended together in a zone of light that flashed continually before my sight. My seat on the axis, poised in the midst of this terrible whirl, remained steady and unaltered. Suddenly I felt a jerk, a singular sensation quivered through my frame, and, rather by instinct than sensation, I knew that the catapult had launched me into space.

I had calculated my distance for St. Paul's, Minnesota, and had accordingly set the catapult to the scale of force necessary to cast the globe that distance, making the proper allowance for the decrease of velocity. Would I succeed? I confess at this moment I felt grave doubts. A thousand things might happen. The theory was perfect, but how many perfect theories had failed in practice! My elevation might be improperly calculated, and the machine be dashed to pieces against some intervening mountain. A few seconds would, however, decide all, as I had calculated that the journey would not consume more than four minutes and a half.

While occupied with these considerations I chanced to glance at the belt of light formed by the quickly-revolving windows. It seemed to me to have changed its shape strangely. Instead of its previous regularity of form, it had become, as it were, ragged and uneven. On looking closer, and examining it as narrowly as I could examine any thing passing in such rapid revolution, I fancied that I saw it widen gradually before my eyes. And, as if to confirm my suspicions, a blast of cold air fell on my cheek, and immediately after a hollow roaring filled the globe.

The horrid truth burst upon me. I had forgotten to make the solidity of the copper globe more than equal to the centrifugal force, and the machine was bursting to pieces when I was at my highest elevation.

My brain seemed to whirl with the globe on making this discovery, and with staring eyes I glared at the awful rent that was so rapidly increasing. A hurly-burly like that of the infernal regions filled my ears. It was the air rushing into the globe. Then came a crash and a horrid splitting sound. Instinctively I grasped the immovable axis on which I was seated. Another crash, and I saw dimly the huge mass of copper surrounding me fly into a thousand vast fragments, and I knew that I was falling. I gave one wild shriek, and—

"Mr. Wisp! Mr. Wisp! What are you doing? Let the tea-urn alone, Mr. Wisp!"

I looked up from the carpet on which I was lying, and saw my wife, Mrs. William Wisp, extricating the silver tea-urn—fortunately not filled —from my embraces. I was never able to explain to the good woman why I abstracted that article of plate from the side-table during my dream; and for the first time in the history of science an inventor was to be found congratulating himself that his invention had not succeeded.

Three of a Trade;

Or, Red Little Kriss Kringle

The city was muffled in snow, and looked as calm and pale and stately as a queen in her ermine robes. It was night, and the tinkling of innumerable sleigh-bells made the frosty air musical. The sleighs themselves sped silently through the streets, painted blackly against the white snow as they passed, like so many phantoms winging their way to a festival on the Brocken Mountains.

It was late, for the corner groceries were shut. The last draught of poison had been drained over the counter. The last victim had staggered home to his trembling wife. The red, unwholesome light that flared over the door had been extinguished, and the bar-keeper was snoring in his bed behind the flour-barrels.

In the bleak shelter afforded by the projecting wooden awning of one of the corner groceries in Greenwich Street, close to where that thoroughfare nears the river, and huddled up against the side of the large coal-bin that stood hasped and padlocked on one side of the entrance, two little figures were visible in the dim glimmer of the night. Two little children they were, sitting with their cold arms embracing each other, their chill cheeks pressed together, and their large, weary eyes looking out hungrily into the blank street.

Down by the wharves they saw the tall, slender masts of ships piercing the sky like the serried lances of some band of gigantic Cossacks. Among the black hulls, a few late lights still shone, and the air rang occasionally with the voice of a drunken sailor, who, from some friendly door-step, where he had involuntarily cast anchor, chanted his experiences of a young West Indian lady of color, who rejoiced in the horticultural name of Nancy Banana.

Presently a mystic music seemed to fall from the arched skies upon the city. It was the chimes from old Trinity ringing the Old Year out and the

New Year in. The thrilling notes of the changes following each other in measured flow, vibrated through the air like music made by the feet of marching angels. They jubilantly seemed to scale the slope of heaven. The wild melodious clangor floated over the great silent city. Myriads of aerial Moors, clashing their cymbals, seemed to march over the house-tops. The clock was trembling on the stroke of twelve, and Time had one foot already in the territories of the New Year.

"Tip, listen to the bells," said one of the two children, that were huddled beneath the grocery awning, speaking in a faint, though clear voice, like a bell heard in a fog, "listen. It is time for Kriss Kringle to come."

Tip's cold little lips opened, and nothing issued therefrom but a low, plaintive "I'm hungry, Binnie."

"So am I," said Binnie, with a sort of far-off cheeriness, as if his heart was at a considerable distance, and could communicate only very faintly. "But, let us wait. Perhaps Kriss Kringle will bring us something nice. What would you like most, Tip?"

"Coffee and cakes wouldn't be bad," said Tip, hesitatingly, as if rather afraid of the consequences if he allowed his imagination to run away with him.

"Or a plate of roast beef, rare, with potatoes and peach pie," suggested the more reckless Binnie, "just such as mother used to give us on Sunday. Poor mother!"

"What are we going to do tomorrow, Binnie, to get some money?"

"Shovel snow off the stoops," answered Binnie, resolutely. "We'll go into Union Square early, and ask all around at the houses whether they want the sidewalk cleared. Some of 'em are sure to give us a quarter; we might make fifty cents, and then wouldn't we have a time!"

"When we were living in the country with mother what fun we used to have on New Year's," said poor little Tip, creeping up closer to Binnie, with a shiver, for the night was getting very cold, and a few large snowflakes commenced falling straight down from the fleecy sky, white as the manna that fell in the desert, but alas! not so nutritious.

"O golly! yes. What a good mother she was to us, and what things we used to find in the old stocking that she gave us to hang up! Kriss Kringle don't come to us any more now that she's dead. I wonder if he really used to come down the chimney, Tip, or if 't was only make believe."

"I don't know," said Tip, "I watched ever so many nights, but somehow I always fell asleep just before he came, and then the things got into the stocking. I used to dream, though, that I saw him. A little man with a red coat all covered with gold lace, and a long feather in his cap and a little sword by his side. And he used to smile at me, and say, 'Tip, will you be a good boy if I put something into the stocking for you?' and then I used to promise, and when I had promised I used to hear music sounding all through the house, a great deal finer than the music we heard when we went to the circus, Binnie; and then Kriss Kringle would take off his hat to me, and make a jump, and go clean up the chimney out of sight, like a red cricket. Ah! how cold it is, Binnie, and how hungry I am. Tell us a story."

The wind arose in the north, and came down upon the city with a savage howl. The heavy snow-flakes fled before him into every angle and nook, like terrified white birds trying to hide themselves from some vast-winged, screaming falcon. They thrust themselves into the crevices of the windows, and between the slats of the window-blinds; they got under the sills of the doors. They left the centre of the streets, and flew madly into the gutters; they huddled themselves into the dark corner where Tip and Binnie were cowering, ran up the legs of their ragged trousers and slid down between their frail shirt-collars and their cold little necks. It was a fierce, biting, scratching wind of prey, and poor Binnie and Tip felt his talons digging into their flesh.

Just as the pair of vagrants had drawn closer together, and Binnie was trying to stop his teeth—which began to chatter—from biting in two the thread of the story that the patient little fellow was about to tell his brother, they heard a faint cry, something between a moan and a whistle, sounding close to them. Looking out into the dim twilight they beheld a dwarfish figure standing on the sidewalk, moaning and waving its arms. It seemed to be a little man about two feet high, clad in a red coat, covered with gold lace, and wearing a little cap, in which was stuck a long feather, that was bent nearly horizontal by the wind. A tiny sword, about the length of a lead-pencil, dangled at his side.

"O, Binnie," whispered Tip, "it's Kriss Kringle come again. I know him. He used to look exactly like that in my dream. I ain't afraid of him. Are you?"

"Not a bit," answered Binnie. "He looks a nice little chap. I hope he has brought us something."

The little man on the sidewalk seemed very uneasy. He waved his long arms continually, took off his little cap every now and then with a quick jerk, as if he were making a series of abbreviated bows to the two little vagrants, and then hopped about, moaning the same shrill and extraordinary moan.

"Binnie, I think he's cold; let us ask him to come and lie down with us and warm himself," said Tip. "You know, in all the fairy books, if you treat a fairy well, he's sure to give you three wishes."

Whatever Binnie may have thought of the suggestion of warming anything by putting it close to two such little icicles as himself and his brother, the latter part of the speech seemed to strike him as containing a felicitous idea. So, bracing his chattering teeth as well as he could, he said,—

"Kriss Kringle, will you come and lie down with us, and we will warm you?"

The little red-coated man made no reply to this hospitable invitation, but danced, and shivered, and moaned, and doffed his tiny cap many times in succession.

"Come, Kriss Kringle," continued Binnie, beckoning to the dwarf, "come in out of the snow."

"Maybe he don't speak English, Binnie," suggested the imaginative Tip.

This was a new view of the case, and Binnie began to consider within himself whether, by some inspiration of the moment, he might not suddenly master the particular foreign tongue with which their new friend was acquainted, when, suddenly, the little man made a swift leap and landed right in Tip's lap.

"Why, Binnie!" cried Tip, "it's not Kriss Kringle after all, it's only a monkey!"

Sure enough it was a monkey: a poor shivering little Brazilian, with pleading eyes and soft, silky hands, and a countenance that seemed to tell of a life of sorrow. A bit of broken chain dangling from a belt round his waist told his story. The eternal organ in the street; the black-bearded, heartless Italian; the little switch that scored his back at home; the cruel pinches to induce politeness, when wondering schoolboys proffered their hoarded coppers; the melancholy pantomime of sprightly gratitude which was taught with blows, and performed in fear and trembling. Poor little runaway! Poor little vagrant! He seemed to know that he had found brothers in misfortune when he thrust his timid, silky paw in Binnie's hand, and laid his little hairy face against Tip's bosom.

The children vied with each other in attentions to the poor little wanderer. I do believe that if Tip had an apple or a chestnut at that moment, hungry as he was, he would have given it to his red little Kriss Kringle. The boys placed him between them, and tried to snuggle him up in their tattered clothes. He clung to them as if he really loved them. His little hand found its way into Tip's shirt-bosom,—if that collection of

discolored tatters which he wore beneath his jacket could be called a shirt,
—and laid just over his heart. The poor vagrants kissed and fondled their
pet; and, God help them! were almost happy for the time.

Meanwhile the snow drifted and drifted right under the shed where the
vagrants lay. It began to pile itself up about them on all sides, and it clung
to every projection of their persons. The air grew colder and colder. The
wind swooped at them under the shed-still, like the wide-winged, shriek-
ing falcon,—as if it would take them up in its talons and bear them away
to its bleak nest to feed its unfledged tempests. Closer and closer the three
houseless creatures drew together, until a great drowsiness fell upon them,
and the sough of the storm sounded farther and farther off, and sleep and
snow covered them.

Then a dream came to Binnie and Tip. Red little Kriss Kringle jumped
up suddenly from his rest in their bosom, clad in the brightest finery. A
wondrous white egret's plume waved in his cap, and he wore a breastplate
of diamonds. His red coat was redder than the blossoms of the wild Lobe-
lia, and his sword was hilted with gold. Then he said to the boys, "Boys, ye
have been very kind to me, and sheltered me when it was cold, so now ye
shall come with me to the sweet land of the South, where ye shall idle in
the sunshine for ever and ever!"

Then he led them down to the wharf near by, where, moored among
the black hulls of the ships, they found a beautiful golden boat, so bright
with many-colored flags that it seemed as if her tall masts had swept the
rainbows from the sky. Fairy music sounded as the sails were set, and they
sailed and sailed and sailed until they landed on the sweet Southern shore.

There they found strange trees with leaves of satin and fruits of gold.
Wonderful birds shot like stars from bough to bough. The rivers sang like
musical instruments. From the limbs of the trees trailed brilliant tapestries
of orchideous flowers, which, with their roots in the air, sucked the sunlight into their secret veins, until their blossoms were covered with the
splendor of Day.

Here red little Kriss Kringle led them to the foot of a huge tree covered
with white flowers, and made them lie down while he fed them with fruits
of a magical flavor. The sun shone cheerfully on their heads. The birds
sang their pleasant songs. The huge tree rained its white blossoms on
them, as they dropped off to sleep, weary with delight, until they reposed
beneath a coverlet of scented snow.

When the first day of the New Year dawned, and the grocer's boy came from his bed behind the flour-barrels to take down the shutters, he saw a mound of snow close by the side of the coal-bin. He brought the shovel to take it away, and the first stroke disclosed the three little vagrants lying stark and stiff, enfolded in each other's arms.

Fantasies

From Hand to Mouth

I
How I Fell in with Count Goloptious

The evening of the 8th of November, in the present year, was distinguished by the occurrence of two sufficiently remarkable events. On that evening Mr. Ullman produced Meyerbeer's opera of "The Huguenots," for the first time in this country, and we were unexpectedly visited by a snow-storm. Winter and the great lyrical dramatist made their *début* together. Winter opened with a slow movement of heavy snow-flakes,—an andante, soft and melancholy, and breathing of polar drowsiness. The echoing streets were muffled, and the racket and din of the thoroughfares sounded like the roar of a far-off ocean. The large flakes fell sleepily through the dim blue air, like soft white birds that had been stricken with cold in the upper skies, and were sinking benumbed to earth. The trees and lamp-posts, decorated with snowy powder, gave the city the air of being laid out for a grand supper-party, with ornamental confectionery embellishing the long white table. Through the hoar drifts that lay along the streets peeped the black tips of building-stones and mud-piles in front of half-finished houses, until Broadway looked as if it was enveloped in an ermine robe, dotted with the black tails with which cunning furriers ornament that skin.

Despite the snow, I sallied forth with my friend Cobra, the musical critic of the New York Daily Cockchafer, to hear Meyerbeer's masterpiece. We entered a mute omnibus with a frozen driver, whose congealed hands could scarcely close upon our fares,—which accounted perhaps for a slight error in the change he gave us,—and so rolled up silently to Union Square, whence we floundered into the Academy. I listened to that wonderful picture of one of France's anniversaries of massacre, with bloody copies of which that "God-protected country" *(vide* speech from the throne on any public occasion) is continually furnishing the civilized world. The roar of Catholic cannon,—the whistle of Huguenot bullets,—the stealthy tread of conspiring priests,—the mournful wailing of women whose hearts foretell evil before it comes,—the sudden outburst of the treacherous, bloodthirsty Romish tiger,—the flight and shrieks of men and women about to die,—the valiant, despairing fighting of the stern Protestants,—the voice of the devilish French king, shouting from his balcony to his assassins the remorseless command, "Tuez! tuez!"—the ominous trickling of the red streams that sprung from cloven Lutheran hearts, and rolled slowly through the kennels;—all this arose before me vital and real, as the music of that sombre opera smote the air. Cobra, whose business it was—being a critic—not to attend to the performance, languidly surveyed the house, or availed himself of the intermission between the acts to fortify himself with certain refreshing but stimulating beverages.

The opera being concluded, we proceeded to Pilgarlik's,—Pilgarlik keeps a charming private restaurant at the upper end of Broadway,—and there, over a few reed-birds and a bottle of Burgundy, Cobra concocted his criticism on "The Huguenots,"—in which he talked learnedly of dominants, sub-dominants, ascending by thirds, and descending by twenty-thirds, and such like, while I, with nothing more weighty on my mind than paying for the supper, smoked my cigar and sipped my concluding cup of black coffee in a state of divine repose.

The snow was deep, when, at about one o'clock, A.M., Cobra and myself parted at the corner of Eighth Street and Broadway, each bound for his respective home. Cobra lived in Fourth Avenue,—I live, or lived, in Bleecker Street. The snow was deep, and the city quite still, as I half ran, half floundered down the sidewalk, thinking what a nice hot brandy-toddy I would make myself when I got home, and the pleasure I would have in boiling the water over my gas-light on a lately invented apparatus which I had acquired, and in which I took much pride; I also recollected with a thrill of pleasure that I had purchased a fresh supply of lemons that morning, so that nothing was needed for the scientific concoction of a nightcap. I turned down Bleecker Street and reached my door. I was singing a snatch of Pierre Dupont's song of *La Vigne* as I pulled out my night-key and inserted it in that orifice so perplexing to young men who have been to a late supper. One vigorous twist, and I was at home. The half-uttered triumphal chant of the Frenchman, who dilates with metrical malice on the fact that the vine does not flourish in England, died on my lips. The key turned, but the door, usually so yielding to the members of our family, obstinately refused to open. A horrible thought flashed across my mind. They had locked me out! A new servant had perhaps arrived, and cautiously barricaded the entrance; or the landlady—to whom, at the moment, I was under some slight pecuniary responsibility—had taken this cruel means of recalling me to a sense of my position. But it could not be. There was some mistake. There was fluff in my key,—yes, that was it,—there was fluff in the barrel of my night-key. I instantly proceeded to make a Pandean pipe of that instrument, and blew into the tube until my face resembled that queer picture of the wind in Aesop's fables, as it is represented in the act of endeavoring to make the traveller take off his cloak. A hopelessly shrill sound responded to my efforts. The key was clear as a flute. Was it the wrong key? I felt in every pocket, vaguely expecting a supernumerary one to turn up, but in vain. While thus occupied, the conviction forced itself on my mind that I had no money.

Locked out, with a foot of snow on the ground, and nothing but a three-cent piece and two new cents—so painfully bright that they presented illusory resemblances to half-eagles—in my pocket!

I knew well that an appeal to the bell was hopeless. I had tried it once before for three hours at a stretch, without the slightest avail. It is my private conviction that every member of that household, who slept at all within hearing of the bell, carefully stuffed his or her ears with cotton before retiring for the night, so as to be out of the reach of temptation to answer it. Every inmate of that establishment, after a certain hour, determinedly rehearsed the part of Ulysses when he was passing the Sirens. They were deaf to the melody of the bell. I once knew a physician who, to keep up appearances, had a night-bell affixed to his door. The initiated alone knew that he regularly took the tongue out before he went to bed. His conscience was satisfied, and he slept calmly. I might just as well have been pulling his bell.

Break the windows! Why not? Excellent idea; but, as I before stated, my pecuniary position scarcely allowed of such liberties. What was I to do? I could not walk up and down the city all night. I would freeze to death, and there would be a horrible paragraph in the morning papers about the sad death of a destitute author. I ran over rapidly in my mind every hotel in the city with which I was at all acquainted, in order to see if there was in any one of them a night-porter who knew me. Alas! Night-porters knew me not. Why had I not a watch or a diamond ring? I resolved on the instant to purchase both as soon as I got ten or twelve hundred dollars. I began to wonder where the news-boys' depot was, and recollected there was a warm spot somewhere over the Herald press-room, on which I had seen ragged urchins huddling as I passed by late of night. I was ruminating gravely over the awful position in which I was placed, when a loud but somewhat buttery voice disturbed me by shouting from the sidewalk: "Ha, ha! Capital joke! Locked out, eh? You'll never get in."

A stranger! perhaps benevolent, thought I. If so, I am indeed saved. To rush down the steps, place my hand upon his shoulder, and gaze into his face with the most winning expression I was capable of assuming, was but the work of several minutes,—which, however, included two tumbles on the stoop.

"Can it—can it be," I said, "that you have a night-key?"

"A night-key!" he answered with a jolly laugh, and speaking as if his mouth was full of turtle,— "a night-key! What the deuce should I do with a night-key? I never go home until morning."

"Sir," said I, sadly, "do not jest with the misery of a fellow-creature. I conjure you by the sanctity of your fireside to lend me your night-key."

"You've got one in your hand; why don't you use that?"

I had. In the excitement of the moment I had quite overlooked the fact that, if I had fifty night-keys, I would still have found myself on the wrong side of the door.

"The fact is—pardon me—but I forgot that the door was locked on the inside."

"Well, you can't get in, and you can't stay out," said the stranger, chuckling over a large mouthful of turtle. "What are you going to do?"

"Heaven only knows, unless you are in a position to lend me a dollar, which, sir, I assure you, shall be returned in the morning."

"Nonsense. I never lend money. But if you like, you shall come to my hotel and spend the night there, free of charge."

"What hotel?"

"The Hotel de Coup d'Oeil, in Broadway."

"I never heard of such an establishment."

"Perhaps. Nevertheless, it is what is called a first-class hotel."

"Well, but who are you, sir?" I inquired; for, in truth, my suspicions began to be slightly excited by this time. My interlocutor was rather a singular-looking person, as well as I could make out his features in the dusk. Middle height, broad shoulders, and a square, pale face, the upper part of which seemed literally covered with a pair of huge blue spectacles, while the lower portion was hidden in a frizzly beard. A small space on either cheek was all that was uncovered, and that shone white and cold as the snow that lay on the streets. "Who are you, sir?"

"I—I am Count Goloptious, Literary Man, *Bon vivant,* Foreign Noble-man, Linguist, Duellist, Dramatist, and Philanthropist."

"Rather contradictory pursuits, sir," I said, rather puzzled by the man's manner, and wishing to say something.

"Of course. Every man is a mass of contradictions in his present social state."

"But I never heard your name mentioned in the literary world," I remarked. "What have you written?"

"What have I not written? Gory essays upon Kansas for the New York Tribune. Smashing personal articles for the Herald. Carefully constructed non-committal double-reflex-action with escape-movement leaders for the Daily Times; sensation dramas for the Phantom Theatre. Boisterous practical joke comedies for Mr. Behemoth the low comedian; and so on *ad infinitum.*"

"Then as a *bon vivant*—?"

"I have been immensely distinguished. When Brillat Savarin was in this country, I invented a dish which nearly killed him. I called it *Surprise des Singes avec petite verole.*"

"Linguist?"

"I speak seventeen languages, sir."

"Duellist?"

"I was elected a Member of Congress for South Carolina."

"Philanthropist?"

"Am I not offering to you, a stranger, the hospitality of the Hotel de Coup d'Oeil?"

"Enough, sir," I cried; "I accept your offer. I thank you for your timely assistance."

"Then let us go," answered the Count Goloptious, offering me his arm.

II
The Hotel de Coup d'Oeil

The Count led me out of Bleecker Street into Broadway. We trudged a few blocks in silence, but whether towards Union Square or the Battery I could not for the life of me tell. It seemed as if I had lost all my old landmarks. The remarkable corners and signposts of the great thoroughfare seemed to have vanished.

We stopped at length before a large edifice, built of what seemed at first glance to be a species of variegated marble; on examining more closely, I perceived that every stone in the front of the building was a mosaic, in which was represented one of the four chief organs of the body. The stones were arranged in the form of a cross, with these designs depicted on them.

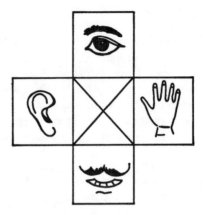

The effect of the entire front of this huge building, staring at you with a myriad painted eyes, listening to you with a myriad painted ears, beckoning to you with a myriad painted hands, and grinning at you with a myriad painted mouths, was inconceivably strange and bewildering.

"This is the Hotel," said Count Goloptious. "Let us enter."

We passed under a gigantic portal towards two gleaming doors of plate-glass, which voluntarily unclosed as we approached. A magnificent hall lay before us. The pavement was of tessellated marble, on every square of which the strange emblems which decorated the front of the establishment were repeated. From the centre of this vast chamber a spiral staircase arose, from each coil of which small bridges of delicate gilt iron work branched off, and led into what seemed to be the corridors of the building. At one end of the hall stood a curious Oriental-looking structure, within which, seated upon a sort of throne, I beheld a portly bearded personage whose breast was festooned with gold chains, and whose fingers were covered with rings.

"That is the night clerk," whispered the Count to me, pointing to this person. "Go and enter your name on the book."

I approached the Oriental temple, and, finding a hotel register with leaves of vellum and bound in silver and mother-of-pearl, open on a shelf close by, took up a pen and wrote down my name. The clerk did not even condescend to glance at me, while doing this.

"Would you like some supper?" asked the Count.

"No, no," I answered; "I want only to go to bed." The truth is, the whole scene so bewildered me, that I began to fear that I had gone mad. "Very well. I will call for your candle." So saying the Count approached a large model of a human ear, which was fixed in the wall of the Oriental temple, and putting his lips to it called out, "A bedroom light for 746."

In an instant a continuous murmur seemed to fill the hall and ascend towards the roof of the building. It appeared to me that ten thousand voices took up the words, "A bedroom light for 746," one after the other, until the sentence rolled along like the fire of a line of infantry. I turned, startled, towards the direction from which those echoes proceeded, and on casting my eyes upon the great spiral staircase beheld the cause.

III
Eye, Ear, Hand, and Mouth

The balustrades of the staircase on either side, and the sides of the different galleries branching off, were all decorated with two of the mystical emblems I had before seen so often repeated in this strange hotel. On the one side a line of human mouths ran up the edges of the staircase, while on the other a line of human hands occupied a corresponding position. There was, however, this difference between them and the symbols occupying the front of the establishment. They were all modelled in high relief. The balustrades seemed as if they had been decorated with the pillage of numberless anatomical museums. As I turned suddenly and glanced towards the staircase, I saw the lips of those ten thousand mouths moving, and whispering softly but distinctly the words, "A bedroom light for 746."

I had scarcely recovered from the astonishment with which this sight overwhelmed me, and the rolling whisper had hardly died away in the domed roof of the hall, when my attention was attracted by a speck of light which appeared far away up on the staircase, and seemed to be travelling slowly down the huge spiral. I watched it with a sort of stupid interest, and when it came nearer discovered that it was nothing less than a chamber wax-light in a silver candlestick, which the ten thousand hands that lined the edge of the balustrade opposite to the balustrade of the mouths were carefully passing from one to the other. In a few moments it reached the bottom, where the last hand, a huge muscular-looking fist, held it.

"There is your light," said the Count; "follow it up stairs, and it will lead you to your room. I will, for the present, wish you a good-night, as I have to go and take my before-morning walk."

I confusedly wished my strange friend good night, and walked towards the hand that held my candle. As I approached, the hand passed it to the hand next above, and the candle so began to ascend the stairs. I followed. After toiling up an interminable number of steps, the hands suddenly took the candle off into one of the side galleries, in which at last it stopped before a huge polished door, on the upper panels of which were painted again a huge eye and an equally gigantic ear. I could not help noticing that the eye had a demoniac expression.

I pushed the door open, and, taking the candle from the attendant hand, was about to enter the room, when my attention was attracted by that member giving my coat a gentle twitch. I turned, and there beheld the hand stretched out with an expression—if ever hand had an expression —which was inexpressibly pleading. I was puzzled. What could it want? I would follow the example of my friend Count Goloptious, and speak to the ear. Approaching my lips to the ear painted over my door, I put the question, "What does this amiable hand want?" In an instant a fusillade of whispers came rolling up the line of mouths, answering. "He wants a quarter for his trouble." My heart sank,—I had only five cents.

"Pshaw!" said I, trying to bluff the thing off, "I can't attend to it now"; and so saying, stepped towards my room. As I entered and hurriedly closed the door, I beheld every hand down the long coil of stairs simultaneously double up and shake at me in menace, while a horrid sardonic laugh ran down the line of mouths. I never beheld anything more devilish than that spiral smile of scorn.

On closing the door of my room, I was not a little annoyed to find that the eye and the ear, which were on the outside, were on the inside also, so exactly alike that they seemed to have come through for the purpose of watching me, and listening to my sleep-talk. I felt wretchedly uncomfortable at the idea of undressing before that eye. It was fixed on me wherever I moved in the room. I tried to pin a handkerchief over it, but the wood of the door was too hard and the pins would not stick. As the handkerchief fell to the ground, I beheld the horrid eye wink at me with a devilish expression of derision. Determined not to be overlooked, I put out the light and undressed in the dark, when I tumbled into bed in a state of confusion of mind not easily described. I had scarcely laid my head on the pillow, when I heard a distinct knock at my door. Cursing the intrusion, and not without some tremor, being uncertain what new enchantment might be brewing, I opened it. There was the hand outstretched, and pleading for its infernal quarter. The abominable member was evidently determined to keep me awake all night. There was but one thing to be done,—to bribe him with a promise. I put my lips to the ear and said: "If the hand does not disturb me, I will put a gold ring on his finger to-morrow."

The ten thousand mouths repeated with tones of approval, "He will put a gold ring on his finger to-morrow," and the ten thousand hands waved their thanks. I shut my door, congratulating myself on my escape, and, flinging myself on the bed, soon fell fast asleep.

IV
Dr. Kitchener in a Dream

A horrible heat seemed to surround my head. I suffered intolerable agony. Count Goloptious had unscrewed my caput just at the point known to anatomists as the condyles, and deliberately placed it in the centre of a ring of burning brands which he had laid on the floor. The Philanthropic Duellist then drew a volume from his pocket, which, even in my excited condition, I could not help recognizing as Doctor Kitchener's cookery-book, and commenced deliberately to read aloud the recipe for roasting a goose alive, which is contained in that immortal work. I now perceived with unutterable indignation that he intended to cook my head after Kitchener's inhuman instructions.

The flames leaped higher and higher around my blistering cheeks. My whiskers—whiskers on which countless barbers had exhausted the resources of their art—shrivelled into ashy nothings. My eyeballs protruded, my lips cracked; my tongue, hard and wooden, beat against the roof of my mouth. I uttered a half-inarticulate cry for water. The Count laughed a devilish laugh, and consulted his book.

"True," he said, "the worthy doctor says, that when the goose thirsteth let her be fed with water, so that the flesh shall be tender when cooked. Let us give the poor head a drink."

So saying, he reached towards my parched lips a pannikin fixed on the end of a long handle. I quaffed eagerly the liquor which it contained. Ah! how grateful was that draught of brandy-and-water! I drained the cup to the bottom. But the bliss was short-lived. The flames hissed and crackled. My hair caught fire, and my poor head blazed like a Frenchman's "ponchbol." The sparkles from the burning brands flew against my forehead and into my eyes, scorching and blinding me. My brain simmered in the arched cells of my skull. My anguish was insufferable, and as a last desperate resource I cried out to the Count: "Take me from the fire,—take me from the fire,—I am overdone!"

The Count answered to this: "Patience, patience, head of a heathen! You are roasting beautifully. A few minutes more, and I will pour some Worcestershire sauce over you."

Worcestershire sauce! That essence of every peppery condiment known to civilized man! Worcestershire sauce, the delight of East Indian officers on half-pay, and the horror of Frenchmen who encounter it in London restaurants, and return to "La Belle" with excoriated palates; this biting, inflammatory stuff to be poured over a wretched head, whose scalp was cracking like the skin of a roasted apple,—it was too much to endure, so I gave vent to my feelings in one unearthly shriek of agony and—awoke.

My head was hot, but, thank Heaven, it was not roasting. It was lying on a tumbled pillow across which a stream of the morning sunlight was pouring in a golden tide. There was no Count Goloptious,—no circle of firebrands,—no Worcestershire sauce,—I was in bed, and alone in the Hotel de Coup d'Oeil.

So soon as I had sufficiently recovered from the effects of my horrible dream, I sat up in bed, and inspected my apartment. It was large and lofty and sumptuously furnished. A touching attention to my necessities was visible as I glanced round the room. By my bedside, on a small buhl table, stood a large tumbler containing a creaming champagne cocktail. I drained it as a libation to the God of Morning. It was an appropriate sacrifice. The early sunlight itself seemed to flash through its amber globules. The white foam of dawn creamed in its effervescence. The tonic flavor of the fresh air that blows over the awaking earth was represented by the few drops of Boker's bitters with which it was tinctured. The immediate glow which it sent through every limb typified the healthy circulation produced by morning exercise.

I lay back on my pillow and began to speculate on the strange series of incidents which had befallen me. Who was Count Goloptious? What weird hotel was this, of which I had become an inmate? Were the days of enchantment indeed revived? or did I merely dream of those myriads of beseeching hands and whispering mouths and ever-wakeful eyes?

I glanced involuntarily to the door at this juncture, and lo! there I beheld the eye which seemed set in the panel of my door. A full flood of the sunlight that poured across my bed struck across that side of my room, and I saw the eye winking drowsily in the blaze,—drowsily, but yet wakefully, like one who is accustomed to watch between sleeping and waking; a sentinel which was never entirely somnolent.

The eye was watching me, despite the sleepy film with which it was overspread. Did I make any abrupt movement in the bed, its half-closed lid suddenly opened, and stared at me with appalling vigilance. There was no avoiding it. It commanded every corner of the room.

How was I to rise and attire myself, with so unpleasant a supervision? I had no longer the resource of extinguishing the light. The sun was beyond the reach of such a process. I meditated for a while, and at length hit upon the idea of constructing a species of wigwam out of the bedclothes, and dressing myself under its shelter. This I accomplished all the more easily, as I had laid my clothes, on retiring to rest, within easy reach of the bed; and as I constructed my impromptu tent, I thought I could discern an expression of drowsy disappointment shooting from underneath the half-closed lid of the Sentinel Eye.

V

How I Magnetized My Eye

Having finished my toilet sufficiently to justify my stepping from my bed, I was proceeding with my ablutions, when I heard a few chords struck upon a piano, in what seemed to be the next apartment. The moment after, a rich, luxurious contralto voice commenced to sing Schubert's beautiful serenade. I listened entranced. It seemed as if Alboni herself were singing. Those showers of rich, round notes falling in rhythmical sequence; that *sostenuto*, that, when first uttered, seemed a sound too weak to live, but growing and swelling every moment until it filled all the air with delicious sound, and then lessening and lessening till it almost died away, like distant music heard across the sea at night; those firm accentuations; the precision of those vocal descents, when the voice seemed to leap from the pinnacles of the gamut with the surety and fearlessness of a chamois-hunter leaping from Alpine peaks;—all told me that I was listening to a queen of song.

I ran to the window of my room, and, opening it, thrust my head forth. There was a window next to mine, but I could see nothing. The blinds were down, but I could feel the glass panes vibrating with that wondrous tide of song.

A woman,—a great singer,—the greatest I had ever heard, lived next to me. What was she like? That heavenly voice could never come from a lean and withered chest, from a skeleton throat. She must be young, must be lovely. I determined on the instant to form her acquaintance.

But there was the Sentinel Eye! How to evade the vigilance of that abominable optic? Its horrible magnetic gaze followed me in every motion that I made. Magnetic gaze! There was an idea. It was doubtless an enchanted eye; but was there any enchantment that could stand against the human will? I was strong, body and soul. My magnetic power I had frequently proved to be of the highest force; why not exercise it on my sentinel? I resolved to attempt to magnetize The Eye!

I shut the window, and, taking a chair, seated myself opposite the demoniac optic. I fixed my eyes upon it, and, concentrating all the will of which I was master, sent a powerful magnetic current straight to the centre of the glaring pupil. It would be a desperate struggle, I knew, but I was determined not to succumb. The Eye became uneasy. It glanced hither and thither, and seemed to wish to avoid my gaze. The painted eyelids drooped; the devilish pupil contracted and dilated, but still the orb always had to return and meet mine.

Presently the glaze of a magnetic sleep began to overspread it. The scintillating lights that played within grew dim. The lid drooped, and, after lifting once or twice, I beheld the long, dark lashes fall, and slumber veiled my sentinel.

VI

Fair Rosamond

No sooner was the Sentinel Eye fairly magnetized than I hastened to the window and flung it open. I possess a tolerable tenor voice, and as I thought vocalism was the simplest way of attracting the attention of the fair unknown, I sang the first verse of the charming serenade in the Knight of Arva; a melody full of grace and passion, for which Mr. Glover never obtained sufficient commendation. I had hardly concluded the first verse when I heard the neighboring window unclose. Unable to restrain my curiosity, I thrust my head out of my casement. Almost at the same instant a lovely face emerged from the window on the right. I had just time to get a flash of a glorious blond head, when the apparition disappeared. My head went in also. I waited a few moments, then cautiously, and after the manner of a turtle, protruded my caput once more. The Blond Head was out, but went in again like a flash. I remained with outstretched neck. After a brief pause I saw a gleam of fair curls. Then a white forehead, then a nose *retroussé*, then an entire face. I instantly withdrew into my shell. The Blond Head was timid, and I wished to encourage it.

Have you ever seen those philosophical toys which are constructed for the purpose of telling whether the day will be rainy or shiny? No? Then I will describe one to you.

There is a rustic house with two portals, one on either side. In the portal on the right a little man is concealed; in the portal on the left, a woman. They are both connected with a vertical coil of catgut, which runs from the base to the roof of the house, between the two. In dry weather the catgut relaxes, and the little man, by the action of such relaxation, is swung out of his portal into the open air. In wet weather the catgut contracts, and the woman enjoys the atmosphere. This toy has two advantages. One is, that it is infallible in its predictions, as it never announces fine weather until the weather is already fine; the other, that it affords an admirable illustration of the present social state of woman. When the day of storm arrives, in goes the man to his comfortable shelter, and out comes the woman to brave the elements. How many households does this typify! In sunshine and summer weather the husband is a charming fellow, and flaunts abroad in all his splendor; but when the clouds gather, when the fire goes out on the hearth for want of fuel, and duns are at the door, then poor woman is sent out to meet them, while the lord of creation hides in the cellar. I commend the toy to the consideration of Miss Lucy Stone.

Well, the Blond Head and myself played at weather-telling for five minutes. No sooner was one in than the other was out. It was a game of "tee to—tottering" performed after a new fashion. I resolved to put an end to it.

I gave three distinct hems.

There is a good deal of expression in a "hem." There is the hem of alarm, such as Alexis gives to Corydon, who is flirting in the garden with Phillis, when that young lady's mother is approaching. There is the hem of importance, such as that with which old Beeswax, the merchant, who is "worth his million, sir," prefaces a remark: the hem of confusion,—the hem of derision or unbelief,—the hem of satisfaction,—the hem of disappointment,—in short, a whole circle or hemmysphere of hems, each expressive in its way of a peculiar emotion. My hem was the hem of interrogation.

It was answered, and the next moment the Blond Head hovered, as it were, on the window-sill. It looked like a bird whose cage door has been opened after years of captivity, and who flutters on the threshold, not daring to advance into the free air.

I advanced my head boldly, and caught the Blond Head on the wing. It was retreating after the usual fashion, and with the usual rapidity, when I shot it with the word,—

"Stay!"

It fluttered for an instant, and then remained still.

"We are neighbors," I remarked to the Blond Head. It was a truism, I know, but still it was a remark. After all, what does it matter what you say to most women, so that what you say is a remark?

"So I perceive," answered the Head, still fluttering a little.

"May I have the honor of knowing—" I commenced.

"Certainly," interrupted the Blond Head, "I am Rosamond."

"The fair Rosamond, I see," I interposed, in my gallantest manner.

"Yes," replied Rosamond, with wonderful *naïveté*, "fair perhaps, but very unhappy."

"Unhappy! How? Can I relieve you,—be of any service?"

A glance of suspicion was shot at me from a pair of large, lustrous blue eyes.

"Are you not one of his satellites?" asked the Blond Head.

"I a satellite?" I answered indignantly,— "I am no one's satellite,— unless indeed it be yours," I added; "for I would gladly revolve round so fair a planet."

"Then you are not a friend of Count Goloptious?"

"No. I never saw him until last night. He brought me to this hotel, where I have been bewildered by enchantments."

"All my doing! all my doing!" cried Rosamond, wringing her hands.

"How your doing?" I inquired, with some astonishment.

"I am the artist,—the fatal, the accursed artist. It was I who painted, I who modelled."

"Painted, modelled what?"

"Hush! you can save me, perhaps. I will see you again to-day. Is not the Eye watching you?"

"I have magnetized it."

"Good! you are a clever fellow," and Rosamond's eyes sparkled. "You must help me to escape."

"From what?"

"I will tell you—but quick! shut your window. Count Goloptious is coming."

The Blond Head gave me a sweet smile, and retreated. I did likewise, and closed my window. The next moment my door opened, and Count Goloptious entered.

VII
Three Columns a Day

Count Goloptious entered. He seemed somewhat agitated, and banged the door to loudly. The shock dispelled the magnetic slumber of the Sentinel Eye, which suddenly opened its heavy lid and glared around with an expression which seemed to say, "I'd like to catch anybody saying that I have been asleep!"

"Sir," said the Count, "you have been misconducting yourself."

"I? Misconducting myself! What do you mean, Count Goloptious?"

"You have been singing love-songs, sir. In a tenor voice, too. If you were a bass I would not so much care, but to sing tenor,—it's infamous!"

The blue goggles of the Count seemed to scintillate with anger as he glared at me.

"What the devil is the meaning of all this mystery?" I demanded angrily, for I really was getting savage at the incomprehensibility of everything that surrounded me. "What do your infernal eyes and hands and ears and mouths mean? If you are a night-mare, why don't you say so, and let me wake up? Why can't I sing love-songs if I like,—and in a tenor voice, if I like? I'll sing alto if I choose, Count Goloptious."

"It is not for you to penetrate the mysteries of the Hotel de Coup d'Oeil, sir," answered the Count. "You have enjoyed its hospitalities, and you can go. You have sung tenor songs, sir. You know, as well as I, the influence of the tenor voice upon the female heart. You are familiar with the history of the opera, sir. You have beheld penniless Italians, with curled mustaches, and with no earthly attraction except a peculiar formation of the windpipe, wreck the peace of the loveliest of our females. There is a female in this vicinity, sir. A poor, weak-minded girl, who has been placed under my guardianship, and who is crazy on the subject of music. You have been singing to her, sir. Yes, with that accursed mellifluous voice of yours,—that vocal honey in which you tenors administer the poison of your love,—with that voice, sir, you are endeavoring to destroy the peace of mind of my ward. You have slept here, sir. You can go now."

"I have not the slightest intention of going now, Count Goloptious. This hotel suits me admirably well. It has certain little drawbacks to be sure. It is not pleasant to be always overlooked and overheard in one's privacy." Here I pointed to the Ear and the Eye. "But still one can grow accustomed to that, I suppose. By the way, I should like some breakfast."

My coolness took the Count completely by surprise. He stared at me without being able to utter a word. The fact was, that the Blond Head had bewitched me. Those clouds of golden hair that enfolded the wondrous oval of her face like a continual sunset had set my heart on fire. Never, never would I quit that hotel, unless I bore her with me. She had hinted at misfortune in our brief interview. She was a captive,—a captive of the false Count, who now pretended that he was her guardian. Meshed in the countless spells and enchantments that surrounded her, she was helpless as those fair creatures we read of in the Arabian Nights. I would be her rescuer. I would discover the charm before which the bonds should melt. It was Andromache and Perseus and the sea-monster over again, in the year 1858. The Count, it is needless to say, was the monster. I had no Medusan shield, it is true, but I felt powerful as Perseus, for all that. My blond Andromache should be saved.

"So you won't go, eh?" said Goloptious, after a long silence.

"No."

"You had better."

"This is a hotel. I have a right to accommodation here as long as I pay for it. Hotels belong to the public, when the public has money."

"I know I can't force you to go, but I don't think, young sir, that you will be able to pay for your board."

"How much do you charge here, by the day?"

"Three columns a day."

"Three what?"

"Three columns a day."

"I have heard of pillar dollars, but hang me if I ever heard of money that was called columns."

"We don't take money in pay at the Hotel de Coup d'Oeil. Brain is the only currency that passes here. You must write me three columns of the best literary matter every day; those are our terms for this room. We have rooms higher up which rent for less. Some go as low as a paragraph. This is a four-column room usually, but you can have it for three."

Was the fellow laughing at me? His countenance was perfectly serious the whole time he was speaking. He talked as deliberately as if he had been a simple hotel clerk talking to a traveller, who was about pricing rooms. The whole thing struck me so comically that I could not refrain from a smile. I determined to carry the thing out in the Count's own vein.

"Meals are of course included?" I said inquiringly.

"Certainly, and served in your own room."

"I don't think the apartment dear," I continued, inspecting my chamber with a critical eye. "I'll take it."

"Very good"; and I saw a gleam of gratified malice shoot through the Count's great blue goggles.

"Now," said I, "perhaps you will inform me, Count Goloptious, why a few moments since you were so anxious to get rid of me, and why now you so tranquilly consent to my remaining an inmate of the Hotel de Coup d'Oeil?"

"I have my reasons," said the Count, mysteriously. "You have now taken a room in the Hotel de Coup d'Oeil; you will never quit it unless with my consent. The Eye shall watch you, the Ear shall hear you, the Hands shall detain you, the Mouths shall betray you; work is henceforth your portion. Your brain is my property; you shall spin it out as the spider his web, until you spin out your life with it. I have a lien on your intellect. There is one of my professions which I omitted in the catalogue which I gave you on our first meeting,—I am a Publisher!"

VIII
The Blond Head

This last speech of the Count's, I confess, stunned me. He was then a publisher. I, who for years had been anxiously keeping my individuality as an author intact, who had been strenuously avoiding the vortex of the literary whirlpool of which the publisher is the centre, who had resisted, successfully, the absorbing process by which that profession succeeds in sucking the vitals out of the literary man, now suddenly found myself on the outer edge of the maelstrom, slowly but surely revolving towards the central funnel which was to swallow me.

An anticipation of unknown misfortunes seemed to overwhelm me. There was something sternly prophetic in the last tones of Goloptious's voice. He seemed to have had no turtle in his throat for several days. He was harsh and strident.

I determined to consult with the Blond Head in my extremity. It would, at least, be a consolation to me to gaze into those wondrous blue eyes, to bask in the sunshine of that luminous hair.

I raised my window, and hummed a bar of *Com'e Gentil.* In a moment the adjoining window was raised, and out came the Blond Head. The likeness to the weather-toy existed no longer: both our heads were out together.

"You have seen Goloptious," said the Blond Head. "What did he say?"

"Excuse me from continuing the conversation just at this moment," I replied. "I have forgotten something."

I had. The Ear and the Eye were in full play,—one watching, the other listening. Such witnesses must be disposed of, if I was to hold any secret conversation with Rosamond. I retired therefore into my chamber again, and set to work to deliberately magnetize the eye. That organ did not seem to relish the operation at all, but it had no resource. In a few moments the film overspread it, and it closed. But what was to be done with the ear? I could not magnetize that. If, like the king in Hamlet, I had only a little poison to pour into it, I might deafen it forever. Or, like the sailors of Ulysses, when passing the island of the Sirens—ah! Ulysses!—that was the idea. Stop up the ear with wax! My bedroom candle was not all burned out. To appropriate a portion of that luminary, soften it in my hands, and plaster it over the auricular organ on my door was the work of a few moments. It was a triumph of strategy. Both my enchanted guardians completely entrapped, and by what simple means!

I now resumed my out-of-window conversation with Rosamond with a feeling of perfect security.

"I have seen Goloptious," I said, in reply to her previous question, "and am now a boarder in the Hotel de Coup d'Oeil."

"Great heavens, then you are lost!" exclaimed Rosamond, shaking her cloudy curls at me.

"Lost! How so?"

"Simply that you are the slave of Goloptious. He will live on your brains, until every fibre is dried up. You will become a mental atrophy,— and, alas! worse."

"What do you mean? Explain, for Heaven's sake. You mystify me."

"I cannot explain. But we must endeavor to escape. You are ingenious and bold. I saw that by the manner in which you overcame the Sentinel Eye by magnetism. This hotel is a den of enchantments. I have been confined here for over a year. My profession is that of a sculptor, and I have been forced to model all those demon hands and mouths and ears with which the building is so thickly sown. Those weird glances that strike through the countless corridors from the myriad eyes are of my painting. Those ten thousand lips that fill this place with unearthly murmurs are born of my fingers. It is I, who, under the relentless sway of Goloptious, have erected those enchanted symbols of which you are the victim. I knew not what I did, when I made those things. But you can evade them all. We can escape, if you will only set your ingenuity to work."

"But, really, I see nothing to prevent our walking down stairs."

"There is everything. You cannot move in this house without each motion being telegraphed. The Hands that line the staircase would clutch your skirts and hold you firm prisoner, were you to attempt to leave."

"The Hands be—dished!" I exclaimed.

At this moment there came a knock. I hastily drew my head in, and opened my door. I beheld the Hand of the night before, pleadingly extended; and at the same moment a running fire of murmurs from the Mouths informed me that he wanted the gold ring I had promised him. It was evident that this infernal hand would dun me to all eternity, unless he was paid.

I rushed to the window in my despair.

"Rosamond! fair Rosamond!" I shouted. "Have you got a gold ring?"

"Certainly," answered the Blond Head, appearing.

"Stretch as far as you can out of your window and hand it to me."

"Alas, I cannot stretch out of the window."

"Why not?"

"Do not ask me—oh! do not ask me," answered the Blond Head, with so much anguish in her tones that I inwardly cursed myself for putting so beautiful a creature to pain.

"But," I continued, "if I reach over to you with a pair of tongs, will you give it to me?"

"O, with pleasure!" and the Blond Head smiled a seraphic smile.

A pair of tongs being adjacent, a plain gold ring was quickly transferred from Rosamond's slender finger to my hand. With much ceremony I proceeded to place it on the smallest finger of the Hand, not being able, however, to get it farther than the first joint. Even this partial decoration seemed however to meet with approval, for the ten thousand hands commenced applauding vigorously, so much so that for a moment I fancied myself at the opera.

"Good heavens!" I thought, "what a *claque* these hands would make!"

There was one thing, however, that puzzled me much as I reentered my room.

Why was it that Fair Rosamond could not lean out of the window? There was some mystery about it, I felt certain. I little thought in what manner or how soon that mystery was to be solved.

IX
Rosamond Makes a Green Bird

No sooner was my debt to the Hand thus satisfactorily acquitted, than, in the elation of the moment at having for the first time in my life paid a debt on the appointed day, I immediately applied my lips to the Ear on the inside, and communicated my desire for some pens, ink, and paper. In an incredibly short space of time, the Hands, doubtless stimulated by the magnificence of my reward, passed a quantity of writing materials up the stairs, and in a few moments I was at work on my three columns, being determined from that time not to fall into arrears for my board.

"It is of the utmost importance," I thought, "that I should be unfettered by pecuniary liabilities, if I would rescue Rosamond from the clutches of this vile Count. I feel convinced of being able to baffle all his enchantments. Yes, Hands, ye may close, Ears, ye may listen, Eyes, ye may watch, Mouths, ye may scream the alarm, but I will deceive ye all! There is no magician who can out-conjure the imagination of man."

Having mentally got rid of this fine sentence, I set myself regularly to work, and in a short space of time dashed off a stunning article on the hotel system of England as contrasted with that of America. If that paper was ever printed, it must have astonished the reader; for written as it was, under the influence of the enchantments of the Hotel de Coup d'Oeil, it mixed up the real and the ideal in so inextricable a manner, that it read somewhat like a fusion of alternate passages from Murray's guide-book and the Arabian Nights' Entertainments. Such as it was, however, it being finished, I folded it up and sent it by the Hand, with my compliments to Count Goloptious, begging that he should at the same time be informed that I was hungry, and wanted my breakfast. My message whirred along the ten thousand Mouths, and faded away down into the hall below.

I had scarcely re-entered my apartment when I heard the Blond Head open the window, and commence singing a strange wild sort of recitative, evidently with the view of attracting my attention. I listened, and found that it ran thus:—

Rosamond sings: "I have a bird, a bright green bird, who was born to-day.

"To-day the sunshine entered him through his eyes; his glittering wings rustled in the breath of the warm noon, and he began to live.

"He is merry and bold and wise, and is versed in the mysteries that are sung by the Unseen Spirits.

"Yet he knows not the mystical joys of the silently growing forests.

"No egg ever contained him.

"No down, white and silken, ever sheltered him from the cold.

"No anxious, bright-eyed mother ever brought him the oily grain of the millet to eat, or sat on the neighboring tree-tops, singing the holy hymns of maternal love.

"He never heard the sonorous melodies of the trees, when the wind with rushing fingers strikes the various notes of the forest, and Ash and Oak, Alder and Pine, are blent in the symphonic chords of the storm.

"Ten white fingers made him.

"The great sun—too far away to know what it was doing—hatched him into life, and in the supreme moment when his little heart just commenced to beat, and his magical blood to ebb and flow through the mystic cells of his frame, his maker cast from her lips, through his gaping golden bill, a stream of song, and gifted him with voice.

"This is the bird, bold and merry and wise, who will shake my salvation from his wings.

"Ah! until the hour of my delivery arrives, he shall be fed daintily on preserved butterflies, and shall scrape his bill on a shell of pearl!"

I opened my window as the last words of this strange song died away, and I had scarcely done so when a bright green bird, with an orange bill and cinnamon-colored legs, flew from Rosamond's window into my room, and perched on the table. It was a charming bird. Its shape was somewhat like that of the mocking-bird,—long, slender body, piquant head, and sweeping tail. Its color was of the most dazzling green, and its feathers shone like satin.

"Good morning, pretty bird," said I, holding out my finger to my visitor, who immediately flew to my hand and established himself there.

"Good morning," answered the Green Bird, in a voice so like Rosamond's that I was startled; "I am come to breakfast with you."

As the Green Bird spoke, a small bright feather dropped from its wing and fell slowly to the ground.

"I am delighted to have your society," I replied, with the utmost courtesy, "but I fear that I shall not be able to offer you any preserved butterflies. Nay, I have not as much as a beetle in pickle."

"Don't mention it," said the bird, with an off-hand flirt of his tail; "I can put up with anything. Besides, you know, one can always fall back on eggs."

To my surprise another bright green feather disengaged itself from the bird's plumage, and floated softly towards the carpet.

"Why, you'll lose all your feathers," said I. "Are you moulting?"

"No," answered the bird, "but I am gifted with speech on the condition that I shall lose a feather every time I use the faculty. When I lose all my feathers, which I calculate will not take place for about a year, I shall invent some artificial ornithological covering."

"Gracious!" I exclaimed, "what a figure—of speech you will be!"

At this moment the usual knock was heard at my door, on opening which I discovered a large tray covered with a snowy cloth, on which were placed a number of small porcelain covers, some bottles of red and white wine, a silver coffee-service, in short, everything necessary for a good breakfast.

X
Breakfast, Ornithologically Considered

In a few moments my repast was arranged on the table, at which I seated myself, the Green Bird perching on the edge of a pretty dish of scarlet fruits at which he pecked, occasionally moistening his golden bill in the slender glass of Barsac which I placed near him.

"Breakfast," said the bird, looking at me with a glance of undisguised contempt while I was devouring a plate of *rognons au vin de champagne,* —"breakfast is a meal utterly misinterpreted by human beings. What can be more unhealthy or more savage than the English or American breakfast? The latter is a miracle of indigestibility. The elastic, hot cakes. The tough, over-cooked meats. The half-boiled, muddy coffee. The half-baked, alum-tempered bread. Breakfast should be a light meal, invigorating, yet not overloading,—fruits to purify the palate and the physical system, and a little red wine to afford nourishment to the frame, and enable it to go through the work of the day. In the morning man arises refreshed, not exhausted; his frame needs but little support; it is only when the animal vitality has been used up by a hard day's labor, that the meal of succulent and carbonized food is required. The French make their breakfast too elaborate; the English too heavy; the Americans too indigestible."

"Am I to understand, then," I asked, "that birds breakfast more sensibly than men?"

"Certainly," replied the Green Bird. "What is more delicate, and at the same time more easy of digestion, than the mucilaginous Caterpillar? The

Dragon-fly, when carefully stripped of its corselet, is the lobster of the Insectivora. The green *acarus* is a dainty morsel, and the yellow roses sigh with relief when we gobble up their indolent enemy. The *coccinella*, or Lady-bird, is our turtle: with what dexterity is he stript of his upper shell and eaten palpitating!

"But the chief hygienic feature about the breakfast of us birds is, that we exercise in order that we may eat. Supposing the Blackbird, on withdrawing his head from under his crimson epaulet in the early morning, were merely to yawn, and stretch his wings, and, hopping lazily down branch by branch to the pool at the bottom of the tree on which he roosts, take his bath. That finished, we will suppose him retreating to his covert, when he rings a bell made of the blue campanula, and, being answered by an attendant Tom Tit, commands breakfast to be served. Tom Tit disappears, and after the usual absence returns with a meal of beetles, caterpillars, ripe cherries, and wild honey, neatly served on a satiny leaf of the Maple. Blackbird falls to and gorges himself. What an unhealthy bird he would be, compared with the Blackbird as he really is, stretching his wings at the first light of dawn, and setting off on a foraging expedition through the woods and fields! What glorious exercise and excitement there are in this chase after a breakfast! How all the physical powers are cultivated! The sight is sharpened. There is not a cranny in the bark of a tree, or a crevice in the earth, that the eye of the hungry bird does not penetrate. The extremest tip of the tail of a burrowing worm cannot remain undiscovered; he is whipped out and eaten in a moment. Then the long flight through the fresh air; the delicious draught of cool dew taken from time to time; the—"

"But," said I, interrupting the Green Bird, who I began to perceive was an interminable talker, "how is it possible for men to have the opportunity of pursuing their meals in the manner you describe? It would indeed present rather a ridiculous appearance, if at six o'clock in the morning I were to sally out, and run all over the fields turning up stones in order to find fried smelts, and diving into a rabbit burrow in the hope of discovering mutton chops *en papillotes*."

"If I were a man," said the Green Bird, sententiously, "I would have my meals carefully concealed by the servants in various places, and then set to work to hunt them out. It would be twice as healthy as the present indolent method."

Here he took another sip at the Barsac, and looked at me so queerly that I began to have a shrewd suspicion that he was drunk.

A brilliant idea here flashed across my mind. I would intoxicate the

Green Bird, and worm out of him the reason why it was that the Blond Head was never able to stretch farther out of her window than the shoulders. The comicality of a drunken bird also made me favorable to the idea.

"As far as eating goes," said I, "I think that you are perhaps right; but as to drinking, you surely will not compare your insipid dew to a drink like this!" and, as I spoke, I poured out a glass of Richebourg, and handed it to the bird.

He dipped his bill gravely in it, and took one or two swallows.

"It is a fine wine," he said sententiously, "but it has a strong body. I prefer the Barsac. The red wine seems to glow with the fires of earth, but the white wine seems illumined by the sunlight of heaven."

And the Green Bird returned to his Barsac.

XI
Leg-Bail

"So the fair Rosamond made you," I said carelessly.

"Yes, from terra-cotta," answered the Green Bird; "and, having been baked and colored, I came to life in the sun. I love this white wine, because the sun, who is my father, is in it"; and he took another deep draught.

"What induced her to construct you?" I asked.

"Why, with a view of escaping from this place, of course."

"O, then you are to assist her to escape?"

"Not at all,—you are to assist her. I will furnish her with the means."

"What means?"

"With the wings."

"The what?" I asked, somewhat astonished.

"The wings!"

"What the deuce does she want of wings? She is not going to escape by the window, is she?"

"Ha, ha, ha! Ho, ho, ho! He asks what Rosamond wants of wings!" And the bird, overcome with laughter at the ludicrousness of some esoteric jest, tumbled into his glass of Barsac, from which I rescued him draggled and dripping, all the more draggled as during our conversation he had been continually shedding his feathers.

"Well, what does she want of wings?" I asked, rather angrily, because a man does not like to see people laughing at a joke into the secret of which he is not admitted.

"To fly with," replied the Green Bird, nearly choking with the involuntary draught of white wine he had swallowed during his immersion.

"But why does she want to fly?"

"Because she has no legs,—that's the reason she wants to fly," said the bird, a little crossly.

"No legs!" I repeated, appalled at this awful intelligence,—"no legs! O, nonsense! you must be joking."

"No, I'm choking," answered the Green Bird.

"Why, she is like Miss Biffin, then, born without legs. Heavens! what a pity that so lovely a head shouldn't have a leg to stand on!"

"She wasn't born without legs," replied the Bird. "Her legs are down stairs."

"You don't mean to say that they have been amputated?"

"No. Count Goloptious was afraid she would escape; and as he wanted only her bust, that is, her brain, hands, and arms, he just took her legs away and put them in the store-room. He'll take your legs away some day, too, you'll find. He wants nothing but heads in this hotel."

"Never!" I exclaimed, horror-stricken at the idea. "Sooner than part with my legs, I'd—"

"Take arms against him I suppose. Well, *nous verrons*. Gracious! what a lot of feathers I have shed!" suddenly continued the Bird, looking down at a whole pile of green feathers that lay on the floor. "I'm talking too much. I sha'n't have a feather left soon if I go on at this rate. By the way, where is your mirror? I must reproduce myself."

XII
Holding the Mirror Up to Nature

I handed the Green Bird a small dressing-glass which lay on the bureau, —I mean, I placed it before him, for the impossibility of *handing* a bird anything will strike even the most uncultivated mind,—and seated myself to watch his proceedings with a considerable amount of curiosity.

I wish, before proceeding any further, to make a few random remarks on the looking-glass in America.

I take a certain natural pride in my personal appearance. It is of no consequence if my nose is a trifle too long, my chin too retreating, or my head too angular. I flatter myself that the elegance of a man's appearance does not depend on his individual traits, but upon his *tout ensemble*. I feel, when regarding myself in a well-constituted mirror, that, in spite of any trifling defects in detail, my figure on the whole is rather *distingué*.

In the matter of mirrors, I have suffered. The hotel and boarding-house keepers of this country—actuated doubtless by a wholesome desire to crush that pet fly called "vanity," with which the Devil angles for human souls—have, I am convinced, entered into a combination against the admiration of the human face divine by its owner.

Like Proteus, I find myself changing my shape wherever I go. At the Bunkum House, I am a fat boy. At the St. Bobolink, a living skeleton. Once I was seriously alarmed on inspecting myself for the first time in the glass,—on an occasion when I had just taken possession of a new boarding-house,—at discovering that one of my eyebrows was in the middle of my forehead. I had been informed by a medical student,—since plucked,—from whom I derived most of my chirurgical information, that paralysis not unfrequently produced such effects. I descended in some trepidation to the parlor, where I had an interesting interview with my landlady, who succeeded in removing the unpleasant impression from my mind that I was a victim to that unbecoming disease.

The glass was not, however, changed, and I never looked in it and beheld that eyebrow in the middle of my forehead, without the disagreeable sensation that in the end I should die a Cyclops.

The glass which I placed before the Green Bird possessed, I regret to say, certain defects in the plane of its surface, which rendered self-contemplation by its aid anything but an agreeable occupation. I know no man egotist enough to—as the novels say—"spend hours before" such a mirror.

The Green Bird, as soon as he beheld himself in this abominable mirror, uttered a scream of disgust. I must say, that, on looking over his shoulder, the image formed by him in the glass was not a graceful one. He was humped, one leg was shorter than the other, and his neck looked as if it had just been wrung by a school-boy.

What attracted my attention most, however, were certain peculiarities in the reflected image itself. It scarcely seemed a reflection. It was semi-substantial, and stood out from the surface of the glass in a sort of half-relief, that grew more and more positive every moment. In a few seconds more, the so-called image detached itself from the mirror, and hopped out on the table, a perfect counterpart of the Green Bird, only humped, with one leg shorter than the other, and a wry neck. It was an ornithological caricature.

The Green Bird itself now sidled away from its position before the mirror, and the Caricature Bird took his place. If the image cast by the former was distorted, no words can convey the deformity of the image cast by the latter. It was a feathered cripple. It was all hump. It stood on one long attenuated leg. Its neck was tortuous as the wall of Troy.

This rickety, ornithological image produced itself in the mirror, in precisely the same fashion as did its predecessor, and, after gradually growing into substance, detached itself from the polished surface, and came out upon the table, taking its position before the mirror, *vice* the first humpback resigned.

What the image cast by the third bird was like I cannot at all attempt to portray. It was a chaos of neck and humps and feathers. The reproduction, nevertheless, went on, and the prolific mirror kept sending forth a stream of green abortions, that after a little while were no longer recognizable as belonging to any species of animal in the earth below, or the heavens above, or the caverns that lie under the earth. They filled my room. Swarms of limping, wall-eyed, one-legged, green-feathered things hustled each other on the floor. My bed was alive with a plumed mass of deformity. They filled the air, making lame efforts at flight, and blindly falling to the floor, where they tumbled about in inextricable confusion. The whole atmosphere seemed thick with green feathers. Myriads of squinting eyes glittered before me. Quintillions of paralytic yellow bills crookedly gaped at me.

I felt myself treading on a thick carpet of soft, formless life. The fluttering of embryonic wings, the twittering of sickly voices, the ruffling of lustreless plumages, produced a continuous and vague sound that filled me with horror. I was knee-deep in the creatures. From out the distorting mirror they poured in a constant stream, like a procession of nightmares, and the tide-mark of this sea of plumage rose higher and higher every instant. I felt as if I was about to be suffocated,—as if I was drowning in an ocean of Green Birds. They were on my shoulders. Nestling in my hair. Crooning their loathsome notes into my ear. Filling my pockets, and brushing with their warm fuzzy breasts against my cheek. I grew wild with terror, and, making one desperate effort, struggled through the thick mass of life that pressed like a wall around me to the window, and, flinging it open, cried in a despairing voice: "Rosamond! Rosamond! Save me, Rosamond!"

XIII
A Stupid Chapter, and I Know It

"What's the matter?" cried the Blond Head, appearing at her window, with all her curls in a flurry.

"Your Green Bird," I answered, "has been misconducting himself in the most abominable manner. He—"

"You surely have not let him get at a mirror?" screamed Rosamond.

"Unfortunately I have; and pretty things he has been doing with it. My room is full of Green Birds. If you don't call them away, or tell me how to get rid of them, I shall be killed, as the persons suspected of hydrophobia were formerly killed in Ireland, that is, I shall be smothered by a feather-bed."

"What a wretch of a bird to waste himself in such a foolish way, when he was so particularly wanted! But rest a moment. I will rid you of your unpleasant company."

So saying, Rosamond withdrew her head from the window, and in a second or two afterwards a long shrill whistle came from her room, wild and penetrating as the highest notes of the oboe. The instant the Green Birds heard it, they all commenced jostling and crushing towards the open window, out of which they tumbled in a continual stream. As scarcely any of them could fly, only a few succeeded in reaching the sill of Rosamond's casement,—the goal towards which they all struggled. The rest fell like a green cataract on the hard flags with which the yard underneath my window was paved. In this narrow enclosure they hustled, and crawled, and limped, and writhed, till the place, filled with such a mass of feathered decrepitude, resembled an ornithological *Cour des Miracles*.

So soon as my room was cleared of the bird multitude, I commenced sweeping up the mass of green feathers which lay on the floor, and which had been shed by the original Green Bird, during his conversation with me at breakfast. While engaged in this task, I heard a laugh which seemed to come from my immediate neighborhood. I turned, and there sat the Green Bird on the mantelpiece, arranging what feathers he had left with his bill.

"What," I said, "are *you* there? Why, I thought you had gone with the rest of them!"

"Go with such *canaille* as that set!" answered the Green Bird, indignantly. "Catch me at it! I don't associate with such creatures."

"Then, may I ask, why the deuce did you produce all this *canaille* in my room, Green Bird?"

"It was your own fault. I intended to produce a few respectable and well-informed Green Birds, who would have been most entertaining society for you in your solitude, and materially aided you in your projects against Count Goloptious. But you presented me with a crooked mirror, and, instead of shapely and well-behaved Green Birds, I gave birth to a crowd of deformed and ill-mannered things, of no earthly use to themselves or any one else. The worst of it is, they will build nests in the yard underneath, and bring forth myriads of callow deformities, so that unless they are instantly destroyed you will have no peace from them."

"I'll shoot them."

"Where's your gun?"

"Well, then, I'll fish for them with a rod, line, and hook, as the Chinese fish for swallows, and then wring their necks."

"Pooh! that won't do. They'll breed faster than you can catch them. However, you need not trouble yourself about them; when the time comes I'll rid you of them. I owe you something for having caused this trouble; besides, your Barsac was very good."

"Will you take another glass?" I said.

"No, thank you," politely replied the Green Bird. "I have drank enough already. About those feathers" (I had just swept the green feathers up into a little heap),—"what are you going to do with them?"

"To burn them, of course. I can't have them littering my room."

"My dear sir," said the Green Bird, "those feathers are immensely valuable. They will be needed to make Rosamond's wings. Put them into one of the drawers of the bureau, until they are wanted."

I obeyed.

XIV
On the Advantages of Marrying a Witch

"Now," continued the bird, "what are your plans for escape?"

"I haven't any, except a general idea of throttling Goloptious the next time he comes in here, gagging the Mouths, handcuffing the Hands, and bunging up all the Eyes, and then bolting somewhere or other with the Blond Head,—that is, if we can recover her legs,—say to Grace Church, where, with the blessing of Brown, we can become man and wife."

"Are you not afraid to marry a sorceress?"

"Why should I be? Haven't I been continually calling every woman with whom I have been in love an enchantress; and writing lots of verses about the 'spells' with which she encompassed me; and the magic of her glance, and the witchery of her smile? I'm not at all sorry, if the truth must be confessed, to meet an enchantress at last. She will afford me continual amusement. I need never go to see Professor Wyman, or Herr Dobler, or Robert Houdin. I can get up a little Parlor Magic whenever I choose. Fancy the pleasure of having Genii for servants, just like Aladdin! No Irish Biddies, to over-roast your beef, and under-boil your potatoes; to 'fix' her mop of capillary brushwood with your private, particular hair-brush; to drink your brandy and then malign the cat; to go out on Sunday evenings, 'to see his Reverence Father McCarthy,' touching some matter connected with the confessional, and come home towards midnight drunk as an owl; to introduce at two in the morning, through the convenient postern of the basement, huge 'cousins,' whose size prevents you from ejecting them with the speed they merit, and who impudently finish their toddies before they obey your orders to quit. Genii have no cousins, I believe. Happy were the people in the days of Haroun Al Raschid.

"On these grounds I esteem it a privilege to marry a witch. If you want dinner, all you have got to do is to notify your wife. She does something or other, kills a black hen, or draws a circle in chalk, and lo! an attendant Genius, who lived four years in his last place, appears, and immediately produces an exquisite repast, obtained by some inscrutable means, known only to the Genii, and you dine, without having the slightest care as to marketing, or butcher's or baker's bills.

"Then again, if your wife knits you a purse, what more easy for her than to construct it after the pattern of Fortunatus's? If she embroiders you a pair of slippers, they can just as well as not be made on the last of the seven-league boots. Your smoking-cap can possess the power of conferring invisibility like that of Fortunio.

"You can have money when you want. You can dress better at church than any of her acquaintances, because all the treasures of Solomon are at her disposal, to say nothing of those belonging to Jamshid. You can travel faster than any locomotive. You can amuse yourself with inspecting the private lives of your friends. You can win at cards when you desire it. You can at any moment take up your drawing-room carpet, and make it sail away with you and all your earthly possessions to Minnesota, if you please. You can buy a block on Fifth Avenue, and build a palace in a night, and, in short, be always young, handsome, wealthy, happy, and respected.

Marry an enchantress! why, it's even more profitable than marrying a Spirit Medium!"

"So you intend to marry Rosamond," remarked the Green Bird, with the slightest sneer in the world.

"Certainly. Why not?"

"I don't see how you're to do it. She has not got any legs, and may not be able to get away from here. You won't have any legs in a day or two. You are both in the power of Count Goloptious; and, even if you were to escape from your rooms, you would not be able to find the way out of the Hotel de Coup d'Oeil."

"If I were forced to walk on my hands, I would bear Rosamond away from this cursed den of enchantment."

"An excellent speech for Ravel to make," replied the Green Bird, "but I fancy that your education as an Acrobat has been neglected."

"I think I see at what you are aiming," I answered. "You want to make terms. How much do you want to assist Rosamond and myself to escape? I learn from her song that you know the ropes."

"I know the stairs and the doors," said the Green Bird, indignantly, "and that is more to the purpose."

"Well, if you show us the way to get free, I will give you a golden cage."

"Good."

"You shall have as much hemp-seed as you can eat."

"Excellent."

"And as much Barsac as you can drink."

"No," here the Green Bird shook his head; "I won't drink any more of your wine, but I want every morning a saffron cocktail."

"A what?"

"A saffron cocktail. Saffron is our delight, not only of a shiny night, but also of a shiny morning, in all seasons of the year. It is the Congress Water of birds."

"Well, you shall have a saffron cocktail."

"And fresh groundsel every day."

"Agreed."

"Then I am yours. I will give my plot."

THE GREEN BIRD MAKES A PLOT WHICH DIFFERS FROM ALL
OTHER CONTEMPORARY PLOTS IN BEING SHORT AND SWEET.

"Sir," said the Green Bird, "you wish to escape."

"Undoubtedly."

"The chief enemies which you have at present to fear are the Hands
that clutch, and the Mouths that betray."

"I am aware of that fact."

"It is necessary that you should visit Rosamond's room."

"I would give my life to accomplish such a call."

"All you want to enable you to accomplish it is a couple of lead-pencils
and a paper of pins."

"Well?"

"Well, that's my plot. Order them at the Ear, and when you get them I
will show you how to use them"; and the Green Bird ruffled out his
feathers and gave himself airs of mystery.

I immediately went to the Ear, and, removing the wax with which I had
deafened it, ordered the articles as prescribed. I confess, however, that I
was rather puzzled to know how with the aid of two lead-pencils and a
paper of pins I was to baffle the spells of Goloptious.

XV

Preparations for Flight

While awaiting the arrival of the desired articles, I heard Rosamond
calling me through the window. I immediately obeyed the summons.

"An idea has just struck me," said the Blond Head. "I am exceedingly
anxious, as you know, to get away from here, and I have no doubt with
your aid might succeed in doing so, but how am I to take my trunks?"

"Your what?"

"Trunks. You did not suppose, surely, that I was staying here without a
change of dress."

"I always thought that imprisoned heroines contrived in some miraculous manner to get along without fresh linen. I have known, in the early
days of my novel-reading, a young lady run through six volumes, in the
course of which she was lost in forests, immersed in lakes, and imprisoned
in dungeons, in a single white skirt and nothing on her head. I often

thought what a color that white skirt must have been at the end of the novel."

"O," said Rosamond, "I have quite a wardrobe here."

"Well, I'm afraid you'll have to leave it behind."

"What! leave all those ducks of dresses behind! Why, I'd rather stay here forever than part with them. It's so like a man to say, in the coolest manner in the world, 'Leave them behind.'" And the Blond Head here agitated her curls with a certain tremulous motion, indicative of some indignation.

"My dear, you need not be angry," I said soothingly. "Perhaps, after all, we can manage to get your trunks away also. How much luggage have you got?"

"I will read you the list I made of it," answered Rosamond.

This is her list,—I jotted it down at the time in pencil. The remarks are my own:—

One large trunk, banded with iron, and containing my evening dresses.

One large square trunk containing my bonnets, two dozen. (The excusable vanity of an individual having nothing but a head.)

One cedar chest containing my furs. (At this point I ventured a joke about a cedar chest being a great deal too good for such minkses. I was promptly suppressed by the dignified statement that they were sables.)

One circular box for carrying the incompressible skirt. (Doubtless an expansive package.)

A bird-cage.

A case for artificial flowers.

A feather case. (Containing the last feather which is supposed to be fatal to the Camel.)

A willow basket for bonnets. (More bonnets!)

Three large trunks. (Contents not stated,—suspicious circumstance.)

Four small trunks. (What male who has ever travelled with a lady does not remember with terror her *small* parcels? The big ones gravitate naturally to the baggage-car; but you are requested to see after the little ones yourself. You carry them in your arms, tenderly, as if they were so many babies. What lamentations if they slip,—and they are always doing it,— and fall in the street! Something very precious must be inside. In the cars, you have to stow them away under the seat so that you have no room for your legs. Woe to you if one is lost or mislaid. It always contains *the* very thing of all others which the owner would not have lost for worlds.)

A bandbox. (The bandbox is the most terrible apparatus connected with the locomotion of females. It refuses utterly to accommodate itself to travel. Its lid comes off. It will fit into no shaped vehicle. Of its own accord it seems to place itself in positions favorable to its being sat upon. When crushed or in any way injured, it is capable of greater shabbiness of appearance than any other article of luggage.)

A dressing-case.

A portable bath.

An easel. (Easily carried.)

Three boxes of books. (A porter who was once removing my luggage called my attention to the weight of the box in which I had packed my books. They were certainly very heavy, and yet I had selected them with the greatest care.)

Here Rosamond stopped, and then proposed going over the list again, as she was sure she had forgotten something.

I respectfully declined the repetition, but asked her by what possible means she expected to transport such a quantity of luggage out of the Hotel de Coup d'Oeil.

"You and the Green Bird can manage it, I suppose," she answered; "and I wish you would make haste, for I am getting very weary of not being able to walk. I shall enjoy so having my legs back again."

"Have you any idea where Count Goloptious put them?"

"O yes. They are in some cellar or other in a bin, with a number of other legs."

"Are the bins numbered?"

"Certainly."

"Do you know the number of your bin?"

"No. How should I?"

"It strikes me as rather awkward that you do not. For supposing that the Green Bird and myself succeed in getting down stairs in search of your legs, if we don't know the number of the bin we shall have some difficulty in finding the right ones, and it would be very disagreeable if you had to walk off with another person's legs."

"I never thought of that," said Rosamond, gravely. "A misfit would be horribly uncomfortable."

XVI
A Thrilling Chapter

We were certainly in a very unpleasant fix. To go down stairs on a wild-goose chase among the bins in search of the legs of the Blond Head would be anything but agreeable.

"Can you not make any pair do for the present?" I asked.

"Any pair? Certainly not. Could you get along with any other head but your own?"

The question rather took me aback. I confessed that such a change was not at all to be desired.

"Then go," said the Blond Head, "and search for them."

"Faint heart," etc.; a musty adage came into my head, and I answered, "I will do so." Turning to the Green Bird, I asked, "Will you come to the cellars?"

"Yes, at once," was the answer.

"Lead the way, then; you must be better acquainted here than I am."

The Green Bird led the way down the stairs, with all the hands before us; but not one moved now. Down! down! at least an hundred flights, then through a hall, and into a vast chamber black as midnight.

"How are we to find the legs in this plutonian darkness?" I asked.

"Silence!" said the Green Bird, and a falling feather aroused an echo that sounded like the beating of an hundred drums; "speak not if you would succeed!"

In silence I followed on through the cavernous chamber with its pitchy walls,—on, still on. At last a small blue light appeared burning in the distance like the eye of a tiger. As we approached, it gradually increased in size, until, at last, as we neared it, it became magnified into an opening some sixty feet wide. Beyond, burned a lake of deadly blue sulphur, shedding a pale unearthly light. As we passed through the opening, a figure suddenly appeared before us. It was that of an old man. He carried a stick in his right hand, and walked with a feeble gait, but, what struck me as rather peculiar, his head, instead of being on his shoulders, he carried under his left arm.

"Who are you?" he asked, speaking from the head under his arm.

"I am an author," I replied.

"Look there?" he said, as he pointed to the burning lake.

I looked, and beheld what I had not before noticed. It was inhabited.

Hundreds of poor wretches were there, burning and writhing in the seething flame.

"Who are those wretched beings?" I queried, in terror.

"Ha! ha! ha!" laughed the old man. "Those are authors!"

"Why doomed to a residence here?"

"Because, when on the earth beyond, they failed to fulfil their mission. They lost sight of their goal. They digressed from the path of honor. They—"

"I see. They went it blind."

"Exactly."

"There," and he pointed to a floating head near the edge of the lake,— "there is a plagiarist. His is the A No. 1 degree. There," and he pointed to another, "is one who published and edited a newspaper."

"His offence?" I asked.

"Black-mailing. There is one who wrote flash novels."

"Jack Sheppard. The Bhoys," I muttered.

"Ay; you be wise; avoid the broad path; keep faith; be true. And now what seek you here?"

I told him my errand.

"And you hope to find the legs?"

"I do."

"Come, then, with me. Here, carry my head."

I took the head, and, with the Green Bird by my side, followed the singular old man. He led us round by the lake, so close that, at times, the heat seemed to scorch my clothing. Presently he stopped opposite a great door of blue veined marble. Pushing that open, we entered a large and brilliantly lighted apartment. Here, upon every side, countless legs protruded from the wall. As we entered, the legs all at once commenced kicking as though they would eject us from their abode.

The old man took his head from us, and, putting it under his arm, commanded the legs to desist from their threatening attitudes. In an instant they all fell dormant.

"Here," he said, "are the legs of all who have ever slept in the Hotel de Coup d'Oeil, and here you will find those of the Blond Head."

"But how am I to know them?" I said.

"That I cannot tell you."

"I can tell them," said the Green Bird, now speaking for the first time since we left the darkness; and it flew around the room, stopping to look at now one pair of legs, now another. At last it stopped opposite a remarkably crooked pair of limbs. "Here they are," he said.

"Nonsense! it cannot be. Such a beauty as the Blond Head never propelled on such pedals as those."

"It is true," answered the bird. "Take them down, and see."

I seized the legs, and with a sudden jerk pulled them from their place. What was my surprise on finding Count Goloptious before me. The legs were his.

"Ha!" he exclaimed, "you would trick me, but I have watched you. The Blond Head is safe."

"Safe!" I echoed.

"Ay, safe, safe in my stronghold, the Hotel de Coup d'Oeil."

" 'T is false!" cried the Green Bird. "She is here!" As it spoke, it flew to a small door in the wall which I had not before noticed. Tapping with its beak against it, it opened instantly, and, looking in, I beheld the Blond Head complete. Never did I behold a being so beautiful as she seemed to me at that glance. Grace, beauty, voluptuousness,—well, imagine all the extensive descriptions of female loveliness you have ever read in two-shilling novels, put them all altogether, and pile on as much more, and then you have her description.

"Fair Rosamond," I exclaimed, as I started forward to gain her,—"Fair Rosamond, you shall be saved."

"Never!" cried Count Goloptious,—"never! Beware, rash youth! You have dared to criticise Italian opera, you have dared write political leaders, you have dared theatrical managers, you have dared a fickle public,—all this you have done, but brave not me. If you would be safe, if you value your life, go, depart in peace!"

As he spoke, I felt the chivalric blood fast coursing through my veins. Go, and leave the fair being I loved in the power of a monster? No, I resolved upon the instant that I would die with her, or I would have her free.

"Count," I exclaimed in passionate tones, "I defy thee. I will never forsake yon wretched lady."

"Then your doom is sealed." He stamped three times upon the floor, and instantly the Green Bird disappeared. The place was wrapped in darkness. I felt myself borne through the murky, foul air of the cavern through which we had first passed, with the rapidity of a cannon-ball. Emerging from it, I found myself in the arms of the Count; by his side stood the old man with his head under his arm.

"Here," cried the Count, "is the nine hundred and twentieth. Eighty more, and we are free."

A demoniacal laugh burst from the old man as he took me, unable to resist him, from Goloptious. "Go, go to your brother authors, to the blue lake of oblivion. Go," he exclaimed with a sardonic bitterness, as he pitched me from him into the burning lake.

A wild shriek. The burning sulphur entered my ears, my eyes, my mouth. My senses were going, when suddenly a great body, moving near, struck me. The liquid opened, and closed over me. I found myself going down, down. At last, I struck the bottom. One long scream of agony, and—

XVII
How It All Happened

"Good gracious! is that you? Why, how came you there?"

"Dunno."

"Bless me, you've almost frozen. Come, up with you."

"What! Bunkler, that you? Where's the Blond Head?"

"Blond what? You've been drinking."

"Where's Count Goloptious?"

"Count the deuce; you're crazy."

"Where's the Green Bird?"

"You're a Green Bird, or you wouldn't lie there in the snow. Come, get up."

In an instant I was awake. I saw it all. "What's the time?" I asked.

"Just two!"

Could all that have happened in an hour! Yes. The Hotel de Coup d'Oeil. The Blond Head. The Green Bird. The Count. The Blue Lake. The Hands. The Legs. The Eyes, the every-thing singular, were the creations of Pilgarlik's Burgundy. I had slipped in the snow at the door, and was dreaming.

The cold had revived me, and I was now shivering. I arose. My friend and fellow-boarder, Dick Bunkler, who had been tripping it on the light fantastic toe at a ball in the Apollo, was before me; and lucky it was for me that he had gone to that ball, for had I lain there all night, the probability is Coroner Connery would have made a V off my body, next day.

"How came you to lie there *outside* the door?" asked Dick.

"The door is fast; my night-key wouldn't work."

"Night-key! ha! ha! night-key!"

I looked at my hand, and beheld what? My silver pencil-case,—the only piece of jewelry I ever possessed.

Dick opened the door, and in a very short time was engaged in manufacturing the "Nightcap" which I had promised myself an hour before. Over it I told my dream in the snow, and we enjoyed a hearty laugh at the effect of the bottle of Burgundy which passed from Hand to Mouth.

The Wonderful Adventures
of Mr. Papplewick

I

Mr. Papplewick kept a hardware store in Maiden lane. He was a man of grave demeanor, and was much respected by his neighbors, both for the probity of his conduct and the sobriety of his manners. He was well to do in the world, and was more than usually blessed in the domestic relations of life, as he had the happiness to possess an affectionate spouse and two lovely children. This social felicity which he had enjoyed uninterruptedly for eleven years was, however, soon to be shivered, and the very ties which once constituted his entire enjoyment were about to add keener pangs to his misery. One day, after dining with a friend, Mr. Papplewick felt a little unwell, and happening to mention this to an old lady who was just then paying a visit to his wife, she immediately advised him to send to the next apothecary for some Magnesian Pills, which medicine, she said, was an infallible specific for all dyspeptic affections. Having great faith in the old lady's knowledge in all matters relating to the healing art, Mr. Papplewick did as she recommended, and at once despatched the female servant, Bridget, to the nearest apothecary's, with directions to get him a small box of the Magnesian Pills. Now, Bridget misunderstanding the directions given to her, went to the apothecary and asked him for a box of *Magnetic Pills*, which she brought to Mr. Papplewick, who, without considering the label, swallowed as many of them as he considered would constitute a dose. Now these pills, as their nature indicates, possess the terrible power of rendering whoever swallows them magnetic in the highest degree, and were intended by the inventor to be used solely for the destruction of rats and mice, which vermin on devouring the pills find themselves (owing to the magnetic power) suddenly attracted to the nearest steel rat trap, where they meet the usual fate of their race. The wondrous powers of these pills had never yet been tried on a human being, until Mr. Papplewick became the unhappy victim of the inventor's well meant science. Immediately after he had swallowed the fatal potion, he felt a sort of cold vibration run through his veins, and his extremities became like ice and seemed to move independent of his will. The next moment he observed that a strange vitality appeared to have infused itself into several articles of furniture in the room. The fire-irons suddenly began to move slowly from their places within the fender, and advance towards him. Terrified at what he believed to be some diabolical sorcery, Mr. Papplewick retreated rapidly into a corner of the room, where he remained a picture of terror. But all attempt at escape seemed vain. The fire-irons followed him with increasing speed, and he now saw several other metallic articles in his vicinity gradually putting themselves into motion and advancing in the same direction as their companions. Firmly believing that he was a victim to some deep laid scheme of the Evil One, Mr. Papplewick shouted loudly for assistance and began to utter his prayers lustily, but just at this moment the fire-irons having approached more nearly, suddenly flew up in the most wonderful manner and attached themselves to his person, while all the metal furniture of the apartment was rushing rapidly towards him, preparatory to following their example. It was then, for the first time, that the terrible truth burst upon him, that since the moment he had swallowed the pills he had become a *living magnet!* He rushed towards the table, through much incommoded by the strange additions the last minute had made to his person, and taking up the box read upon the label in large letters, LYONS' MAGNETIC PILLS!

"Gracious Heaven!" he cried, "I am doomed for the rest of my existence, to be nothing more than a human loadstone. Why was I ever born to have such a fate pursue me? Better, a thousand times better, that I had perished before these eyes had ever opened upon the light of day!"

Overpowered with this terrible prospect, he sank with a groan into a rocking chair that was near, and covering his face with his hands continued to inveigh against Providence which had so wantonly persecuted him.

"What have I ever done" said he, "that I should be thus punished? I have never wronged a neighbor—neither have I forsaken a friend when he wanted my assistance. I have been a faithful husband, an indulgent father, and a conscientious employer. I owe not any man, and out of my superfluous wealth I have given largely to the poor. But in spite of all this, Heaven has cursed me with a misfortune which is of too terrible a nature to be visited on the worst of sinners."

In this way did the unhappy man rail against Providence, and with sighs and tears contemplate the horrible future which stretched out so drearily before his mental vision. He was aroused from these bitter reflections by the opening of the door, and his wife, who had been attracted by his cries for help, entered and approached him. As soon as she beheld the condition in which he was, she was struck with the most profound grief and astonishment.

"Good God!" she exclaimed, "what sight is this I behold? Speak, Hezekiah, speak, and in mercy to me explain the meaning of this frightful mystery."

"Alas! Jemima," he replied, "Your Hezekiah no longer belongs to himself or you. He is an outcast from society; a curse to himself and a burden to his friends."

So saying, he related to the weeping Jemima the history of the strange events which had befallen him, telling her how he had swallowed the wrong pills in mistake, and how in consequence he had been immediately transformed into a human magnet, with the power of attracting every metallic substance which came within his sphere. "And now, dear Jemima, I have told you all"—he concluded, pointing to the fire shovel which had attached itself to his nose—"You have a magnet for a husband, and behold the result."

Though nearly overwhelmed by this astounding misfortune, Mrs. Papplewick still maintained that presence of mind which, in cases of sudden difficulty, renders woman so superior to man. She instantly began to revolve in her mind whether there was not some means of ridding her husband of this unhappy attribute, and at last came to the resolution of taking him without further loss of time to a celebrated foreign physician, who possessed a great reputation for dealing successfully with uncommon cases. She proposed it to her husband, who having implicit confidence in his wife's judgment, instantly prepared to accompany her. A new and unforeseen difficulty however arose. On making an attempt to rise from the rocking chair into which he had flung himself in his first paroxism of grief, he found himself held back by an irresistible power. The chair was unhappily constructed of iron, and the magnetic power now inherent in his body gaining strength by contact with the metal, became so powerful that he found he must either remain always where he then was, or carry the chair along with him in its present position. The latter, from its weight, was impossible, and all his efforts to extricate himself proved unavailing. He was again sinking into a state of utter despondency, and calling on death to release him from his sufferings, when the quick intellect of Mrs. Papplewick suggested a remedy. She sent out instantly and hired a number of strong laborers. A powerful machine was then introduced through the window, like the cranes used on wharves, and the chair in which Mr. Papplewick was imprisoned was firmly screwed to the floor. A rope was now passed through a pulley at the end of the machine, and fastened strongly under Mr. Papplewick's shoulders. The other end of the rope was held by six powerful men who pulled at it with all their might. The operation was highly painful to Mr. Papplewick, because being clung to the chair at one end and dragged towards the ceiling at the other, his body naturally became gradually elongated and his joints cracked horribly. He endured it all, however, without a murmur, and after some minutes hard pulling he had the satisfaction of finding himself gradually lifted out of the chair, and then suddenly propelled against the ceiling with considerable violence. A cry of joy burst from his wife's lips at the success of her experiment, but her enthusiasm was considerably damaged when on his being lowered she perceived that her husband, who had always been a man of very ordinary stature, had been considerably lengthened in the process of extrication, and from being rather short and stout had grown to be exceedingly tall and proportionately slender. Happy, however, at loosing him from bondage under any circumstances, she embraced him affectionately and sent for a carriage to convey him to the foreign physician's— taking, however, the precaution to oil his body all over, so that in case he stuck to any of the iron work of the vehicle the slippery surface would render his release less difficult.

II

The foreign Physician lived at the upper end of Broadway, close to the New York Hotel. He was a very famous man and had a great number of grand titles prefixed to his name, all of which he declared had been conferred on him by the principal potentates of Europe for distinguished services he had rendered them in extreme cases. Mrs. Papplewick had great faith in him on account of a certain wonderful cure he was said to have performed on a poor boy with distorted limbs. The youth came to Dr. Baron Splashassco (such was the physician's name) in order to have his legs straightened. The Baron declared the cure to be quite possible, and having obtained the usual fee, he ordered the boy to keep his legs in boiling water until the misshapen bones softened, when nothing was easier than to remould the legs into a symmetrical form. The poor boy, unfortunately for the interest of science, lacked the moral courage necessary to enable him to undergo the operation. "But," as Mrs. Papplewick afterwards said, "there can be no doubt but that the boy would have been cured, if he only did what the Doctor told him."

By a lucky chance the Baron was at home when Mr. and Mrs. Papplewick arrived—he met them at the door with a respectful inclination of the head and ushered them into his private study, the walls of which were decorated with the portraits of celebrated cripples he had cured, one picture representing the unfortunates in a state of unnatural distortion, the other portraying them restored to a symmetrical form by the wondrous art of the Physician.

When Mrs. Papplewick had fully described the unhappy events which had brought them, and explained the terrible destiny which pursued her husband, she paused with intense anxiety for the Baron's reply. That gentleman, however, did not seem to have any intention of speaking. At first Mrs. Papplewick imagined that he was ruminating profoundly over her husband's case, but presently perceiving his eyes directed scrutinizingly towards her hands she instantly recollected that it was the invariable custom of this great Physician to receive his fee in advance, and he was now, no doubt, waiting to have the established usage complied with. Producing her purse she at once handed him a note for fifty dollars, and it was wonderful to see the effect which the transfer had on the hitherto grave countenance of the Baron. He lost all his lugubrious aspect, and proceeded with much animation to examine Mr. Papplewick.

"This is a strange case indeed," said he, as soon as he had completed his investigation, "there is only one similar case on record, and that occurred at St. Petersburgh, in Russia. The man was an officer in one of the Cossack regiments, and the magnetic disease attacked him very suddenly. The first intimation he had of it was one day on parade, when the lances of his men suddenly escaped from their grasp, and flying towards him with the velocity of an arrow, pierced his heart with a hundred wounds."

Mr. Papplewick groaned audibly.

"There is but one mode of treating this malady," continued the Baron, "and that is unhappily a severe one. The magnetic power has by this infused itself into our friend's blood, and of this infected blood it will be absolutely necessary to drain him ere we can hope to rid him of the disease. As soon as his veins are thoroughly exhausted of all sanguine matter they contain, we can easily refill them with the blood of some young healthy animal—a lamb for instance."

At this horrible picture of what was before him, Mr. Papplewick's brain whirled. He saw himself stretched on a board wounded with a hundred lancets, and counting the tickings of the Doctor's watch as his tide of life ebbed slowly away. Then he saw people holding a nasty bleeding quadruped, from whose impure veins his were supplied with an unnatural circulation. Who knows then, but that with the blood he may imbibe the habits of the animal—and ever after bleat or bray through the world. Oh! it was too much. His brain grew hot as fire, and with a wild shriek he rushed from the room into the street. He sped down Broadway like a mad man. There was but little fear of his friends' recognising him, as his figure had become greatly elongated in his extrication from the rocking chair, and the wild terror now painted in his features rendered such a chance still more improbable.

For a long time he wandered about not knowing where to go, and industriously avoiding every place where he might appear to meet those he knew. His distress of mind was terrible, and he thought with anguish upon the happiness of the home from which a cruel destiny had driven him. He was likewise much annoyed in his passage through the streets, by the numerous bits of old iron and broken horse shoes scattered about, all of which would instantly attach themselves to his person and cause considerable trouble in the removal. At the corner of Fulton street, and only a few doors from the Lantern office, while he was in the act of detaching a piece of rusty hoop which had clung to his leg, a gentleman accosted him, attracted no doubt by the singularity of his movements. The gentleman spoke so kindly that Papplewick felt irresistibly attracted to him, and it was not long before he unbosomed himself to the stranger, giving him a detail of all his misfortunes. His new acquaintance seemed greatly interested in his sad history, and evinced a strong desire to assist and comfort him.

"Come!" said the benevolent stranger, "thou can'st not wander about the streets all night—come with me, my house is near and right gladly will I give thee shelter; we will treat thee well and make thee as one of the family."

Touched to the heart by this disinterested offer, Papplewick gladly accepted it, and his smooth-spoken acquaintance bidding him follow led the way to his abode.

It seemed a strange house to Mr. Papplewick. It was very large, and covered outside with paintings. There was a band playing on the balcony, and crowds of people were continually passing in and out. On remarking this, the stranger replied that owing to his being a public man he had a great many visitors. Pushing through the crowd, the stranger led Papplewick up a private stair-case into a large room in which were some half dozen persons of very singular aspect. There was a boy so enormously tall that his head nearly touched the ceiling—there was an old withered man not more than three feet in height, who was sitting on the mantle-piece, while at the farther end of the room was what appeared to be a large bath, in which was swimming some animal with a human head and the tail of a fish. The stranger now bid Papplewick remain where he was, and promising to be back presently he left the room.

Papplewick's reflections were anything but pleasant in the curious company in which he found himself, and he wondered seriously at the strange taste of his new friend, who could fill his house with such a number of monstrosities. While he was thus cogitating upon this and his own melancholy prospects, a door at the farther end of the room was thrown open and a crowd of people entered eagerly. Papplewick was surprised to find himself almost immediately the object of their undivided attention. They walked around him and stared at him, until he began to feel both indignant and uncomfortable, and he actually saw one man sketching him on the leaf of his tablets. Several little boys present annoyed him greatly by presenting penknives at his person, and crying out with delight when they stuck to him. Totally at a loss to imagine what was the reason of all this curiosity, Papplewick began to wish heartily for the return of the stranger. Just then two gentlemen entered, who came up to him and regarded him with great attention. After a little time one of them opened a small packet and taking a handful of iron filings out of it, threw them towards Papplewick, to whose person they immediately adhered. Both the gentlemen cried "how very singular! what a curious phenomenon!" and Papplewick, full of indignation was about to resent so unprovoked an insult, when his eye fell on a bill which one of them carried in his hand. There, to his horror, he saw in large letters—BARNUM'S MUSEUM—MR. PAPPLEWICK, THE HUMAN MAGNET!!! ADMISSION 25 CENTS.

Overpowered at this discovery he sank into a chair. All was now clear to him. His hospitable friend was no other than the Arch-Speculator himself, and for the future he was to be exhibited at 25 cents a head, in company with a giant, a dwarf and a mermaid.

III

As soon as Mr. Papplewick had recovered from the stupor into which his appalling discovery had thrown him, he burst into the most bitter reproaches against his false friend who, under the guise of hospitality, had converted him into a degrading exhibition.

"Oh! my Jemima," he cried in heart broken accents, "how foolish was I ever to leave your affectionate bosom to wander madly through the world a prey to the designing, and an object of pity to none, Heaven is my witness that if I ever again find myself by your side, no misfortune, however great, shall tempt me to abandon it, for there is no pang which cannot be alleviated by the tender cares of those that love us."

While he was thus bitterly inveighing against his destiny, the giant approached him and endeavored to console him in his own rough fashion.

"Bless you!" said he, "its nothing when you're used to it; at first I didn't like it but as little as you, but now I take it all easy and the people may stare as much as they like for all that I care. So cheer up old fellow, there's no use in being down in the mouth about it. It isn't every man whose figure is a fortune to him like yours and mine."

Papplewick made no reply to this well meant address, but to groan bitterly and rock himself to and fro in his chair; while he was indulging in these sombre reflections, he heard a noise behind him and turning round, to his horror discovered that the mermaid had got out of her bath and was making advances towards him of a character not to be mistaken. Completely upset by this new discovery, he sprang from his chair and rushed violently towards the door, which before he had reached it opened inwards and the Arch-Speculator, accompanied by two gentlemen, stood before him.

"Save me, save me!" gasped Papplewick, seizing the speculator by the arms.

"What's the matter? what has happened?" demanded his friend.

"Th-th-at thing th-th-e-re wanted to kiss me," stammered Papplewick, pointing to the mermaid who was floundering back to her bath in a great hurry.

"Oh! is that all," they exclaimed, and the three gentlemen fell to laughing violently at Mr. Papplewick's distress. The Arch-Speculator then took him on one side and told him that the two gentlemen whom he saw with him were celebrated philosophers, who had been attracted by the strange magnetic phenomenon which he, Mr. Papplewick's person, exhibited. That they had made a proposal to him relative to Mr. Papplewick, which he trusted, for the interest of science and for the sake of the world at large, that gentleman would not hesitate to accept. This was nothing less than that Mr. Papplewick should undertake a voyage of discovery to the North Pole—the magnetic power which was inherent in his system fitting him peculiarly for such a task. At the bare mention of this proposition, Mr. Papplewick's heart sank within him, and he saw himself undergoing all the perils of an Arctic winter, blocked up in the ice, hunted by Polar bears and probably in the end reduced to the extremity of subsisting for weeks together upon a pair of boots. In vain, however, did he decline this honorable but dangerous office. The scientific gentlemen talked so much and so loudly, and painted in such a lively manner the immortality which would encompass his name in case of success, that Papplewick's resolution melted before their arguments as snow before a kitchen fire, and it was not long until home, Jemima, children and all were forgotten in the gorgeous and golden dreams of Fame. As soon as his consent to the expedition had been obtained, the scientific gentlemen immediately undertook to put it into instant execution. A liberal merchant volunteered the use of one of his condemned ships for the voyage, and a promise of liberal payment soon secured the services of an active and valuable crew. As to Mr. Papplewick, he spent all the time previous to his departure in preparing for the exigencies of his undertaking. Tailors measured him for Polar suits, Navy Contractors presented him with casks of preserved meats that could not be smelt farther than half a mile, and a celebrated Chemist bestowed on him a box of life preserving pills, one of which was sufficient to sustain existence for a month without the aid of any other nourishment. All arrangements having been completed, Mr. Papplewick arrayed himself in a nautical suit, purchased a telescope with a leather sling, put on a yachting hat and prepared for his departure. Previous to this, however, he had an affecting interview with his wife and children, which was of too harrowing a nature to inflict upon the reader.

At ten o'clock, on a fine April morning, Mr. Papplewick sailed in the schooner Bam, amid the acclamations of the assembled multitude, which he gracefully acknowledged from the poop, bowing and waving his little hat repeatedly.

Despite the perils he was about to encounter, and the agony of parting from his country and relatives, Mr. Papplewick did not feel so well since the fatal hour when he imbibed the magnetic dose. He was growing accustomed to his fate, the novelty was wearing off and with it much of the anguish, and nothing now filled his mind but magnificent visions of glory. Sebastian Cabot, Vespucius, Columbus, Cortez, all sank into insignificance before the illustrious Papplewick, who, single handed, was about to solve the great mystery of the world and drag away with daring hand the icy veil with which it was shrouded by the spells of nature? Papplewick indicated the greatness of the thoughts that were passing through his soul by standing treat that night to all the crew, which liberality elevated him considerably in the opinions of the sailors, and towards the end of the evening he was on such good terms with them that he was heard to pronounce them to be "cabilalset of fellows." Thus passed Papplewick's first night at sea.

Days, weeks went by and the weather became colder and colder. The Bam though an old vessel was a fast sailer, and every day enormous icebergs might be seen floating by with a look of placid but mighty majesty. The crew being chosen almost at hazard were mutinous and reckless, and the days and nights were spent in carousal and debauch. Several times the Captain was observed to look at the compass with a strange and puzzled air, and he took many solar and lunar observations but still seemed to be at fault. The first mate was heard likewise to declare that something extraordinary must be the matter with the needle, or their charts must be false, as they could not determine the ship's position by the usual course. This state of things continued for several days until the crew, which had hitherto left the vessel very much to herself, began to gather in knots on the forecastle, and whisper and point at Mr. Papplewick mysteriously. Papplewick never dreaming of any machinations against his safety, was standing one evening on the quarter deck watching the numberless icebergs which surrounded the ship on all sides, and which glowed in the light of the setting sun like mountains of opal. As he was dreaming of his future glory and wondering who would write his life, the Captain stepped up to him and begged to speak with him. He then told him that the crew had declared that Mr. Papplewick's magnetic power had caused such a variation in the needle, that the ship had lost its bearings and that they were not safe as long as he remained on board. They had, therefore come to the resolution of disposing of him as a second Jonah, and throwing him into the sea. Horrified at this termination to his expedition, Mr. Papplewick threw himself upon his knees before the Captain and begged for mercy. But the crew rushed forward in a body, and regardless of his tears and entreaties they were preparing to throw him over the side, when an appalling cry issued from the Captain's lips. Everybody turned and looked at the ship's bow, where his finger was pointed. There, hastening towards the vessel with a smooth and awful rapidity, they beheld a vast mountain of ice whose cold summits glowing with reflected fire, towered far above the mast. Every heart grew still. Papplewick was forgotten. Not a cry was heard, but every man stood face to face with death. On came the giant of ice, his chilly breath swept across the pale faces of the crowd, and they heard the waves rippling around his sharp and jagged base. Majestically,

swiftly, noiselessly it swept on to the devoted vessel, the very incarnation
of silent but resistless power—then came a grating sound, every one shut
his teeth and held his breath—then a dull soft crash, the frail timbers of
the vessel split asunder like water, there was a sound of swelling waves and
the schooner swaled downwards with a sickening motion. Every soul on
board looked to heaven for the last time and beheld a tall glittering spire
of ice, that seemed to reach to and pierce the skies, then the planks sank
beneath their feet. The iceberg moved majestically on, and there was not
a trace of the Bam upon the ocean!

IV

Ingulphed in the foaming surge, hollow, gurgling sounds swelled in
Papplewick's ears, and a horrible sense of suffocation pressed, like a load of
iron, on his chest. He struck out wildly in all directions, but still seemed to
sink downwards with a swift and easy motion. Flashes of many colored
fires danced before his eyes, and by a strange mental operation, a continuous vision of his entire life from childhood up to the present hour flitted
before him like a panorama, and impressed him with all the vivid sensations of reality. Then a black mist came over all—his breath was suspended; he could feel the blood rushing through his brain with the noise
of some vast waterfall, and the same instant consciousness entirely forsook
him. When Mr. Papplewick recovered his senses the sun was shining
brightly, and gilding with the most gorgeous hues a host of lofty icebergs
that floated on every side. He looked around for the schooner, but there
was no sign to tell that she ever had been—not even a broken plank or a
hencoop floated on the waves. Next, his thoughts naturally reverted to
himself, and what was his astonishment at finding that he was self-sup-
ported in the water, and floated there as buoyantly as a piece of cork.
Though entirely at a loss to account for this singular phenomenon, (unless
it was that his magnetic powers had, through some mysterious operation
of nature, diminished his specific gravity,) he nevertheless felt considerably reassured by the discovery that he was, at all events insured from the
chance of being drowned. But as he looked around him and saw the cold
icebergs floating gradually onwards, without a trace of vegetation upon
their glittering spires, and as his eyes wandered over the trackless fields of
ice that stretched away in the distance, without a single living thing to
break the awful desolation, the conviction flashed upon him that although
he might not drown, still there was every possibility of being starved. The

prospect of so horrible a fate made him exceedingly melancholy, and as he was inwardly bemoaning his situation, he suddenly recollected his life-preserving pills which the great chemist had given him previous to his departure in the ill-fated Bam. Trembling with eagerness, he anxiously sought, in all his pockets, and, to his great and inexpressible joy, discovered the invaluable box which contained the treasure, carefully stowed away in an inner one. He opened the box and counted the pills. There were exactly twelve, and as each pill was capable of sustaining existence for a month, he calculated on being able to subsist for one year, before the expiration of which it was more than probable that some vessel, bound on a polar expedition, would pick him up. Strange to say, Papplewick did not experience the cold generally so keenly felt by voyagers in these regions. It would seem as if his frame, on becoming magnetic, had also acquired a singular power of retaining caloric. On the whole, therefore, Mr. Papplewick was rather comfortable under such adverse circumstances, and having discovered a little pocket pistol, which was filled with the best *eau de rie* in the left hand pocket of his nautical jacket, he paid such marked attention to it that, in a short time, he rather began to like the ice, and absolutely went so far as to ask one of the tallest icebergs "if it would take a drink?" Night, or rather twilight, closed in, and Mr. Papplewick, to use the language of poetry, "slept, like a bird upon the waters."

Next morning he was awakened by strange, hoarse cries and gruntings, and a great splashing in the water; lifting up his head from the billow, (which served him as a pillow,) he was astonished to find himself close to the sharp edges of a large iceberg, on the smooth edges of which a number of strange hairy animals, with fierce black eyes and long tusks, were grunting hoarsely, and floundering about in a state of great excitement. They looked so very large and savage that Mr. Papplewick began to get seriously alarmed at his position, and guessing from their appearance, which much resembled the woodcuts of the seal in the book on natural history which he read at school, that they belonged to the same tribe, though infinitely larger and more dangerous looking; he wished himself anywhere but where he was, as he had a vivid recollection of a passage which stated that "animals of the seal tribe, when they catch hold of a man's limb with their powerful jaws, never relinquish their hold until they hear the bones crack; on which account, the fishermen that hunt them fill their trousers with cinders which of course, on being bitten, crack easily, and deceive the seal, so far as to induce him to let go, when he is immediately knocked on the head." These reminiscences of his early studies were not at all calculated to allay Papplewick's apprehensions, and he already imagined he felt his *tibia* breaking beneath the remorseless jaws of the savage animals.

"I wonder what it is?" ejaculated Papplewick to himself, as he saw one of the animals, an immense fellow, covered with long gray hair, advancing towards him with a peculiarly awkward motion.

"I'm a walrus," replied the hairy individual.

Papplewick nearly jumped out of the sea with astonishment at hearing the animal answer him distinctly. He thought he must be dreaming.

"A what?" he demanded with staring eyes.

"A walrus," repeated the gray-haired old fellow, "you're a very ignorant old dog not to know what we are. I thought everybody had heard of us, now that so many ships come out here looking for the North Pole, and then go home and write a parcel of lies about our attacking boats and killing sailors, and what not. However, I'm very glad to see you. It was getting very dull here, and your society will be an advantage."

Papplewick thanked the walrus for his hospitality, and to say the truth, he was very much rejoiced to find that he was not going to be eaten. Still, he could not help thinking it very odd that a walrus should talk such good English, and he sighed as he thought that if he was spared to return to his own country, this part of his story would certainly never be believed.

"Now," said the walrus, "you'd better get out of the sea, and come in here, for I see that you aren't used to much swimming. We've got a nice, comfortable cave in this iceberg, and there are some capital whale-calf steaks for dinner to-day."

So saying, with the assistance of the rest of the walruses, the old fellow, landed Papplewick safely on the iceberg.

"By the way," said this old walrus, who appeared to be the chief of the party, as soon as Papplewick was settled comfortably, "By the way, how is Sir John Parry?"

Papplewick had never heard of Sir John Parry, but fancying, from this question that he must be some polar voyager, he answered at hazard that he was "very well."

"And my old friend Ross—I hope he's all right?"

Papplewick replied, confidently, that he was "quite right."

"I remember, as well as if it was only yesterday," continued the walrus, "when old Ross knocked this left eye of mine out. I had been fishing all day, and was rather tired, when I saw Ross coming towards me in a small boat; so I thought that I would rest myself a little, if he would let me. Accordingly I swam up to the boat, and was going to hold on by my tusks, when one of the sailors cried out that I was trying to upset the boat—an act that I would not have been guilty of for the world; but Sir John Ross, who was then rather a young man, got up in the stern-sheets the moment he heard the cry, and drawing a pistol from his belt, fired at me, and wounded me in the left eye. I don't blame him for it," continued the walrus mildly, "for he acted under a false impression, but I have lost the sight of that eye ever since."

Just as the walrus had concluded his tale, Papplewick heard a peculiar cry uttered, and the old gray beard, starting up, said—

"Our dinner is ready. Come with me, and I will show you the way to our cave."

So saying, the walrus, followed by his comrades, jumped into the water, and directing Papplewick to lay hold of his long fur, swam rapidly along the shores of the iceberg. After proceeding for about five minutes, the walrus told Papplewick to hold on fast, and then suddenly dived. The latter thought at first that the walrus was playing him false, and that this was a stratagem to suffocate him; but after a few seconds submission, he felt himself rising; and on reaching the surface of the water, a most singular scene met his view. They were at the entrance of a large Gothic arch, which led into a vast grotto of ice, at the farther end of which were congregated round a large fire about a hundred and fifty walruses, of all sizes and ages. They appeared to be enjoying themselves very pleasantly, and the young ones were playing a variety of antics, which, from their unwieldy forms, appeared doubly comical.

"This, you perceive, is our cave," said walrus to Papplewick, "and I can assure you we are tolerably comfortable here. The only drawback upon our residence is that frequently that portion of the iceberg which is below water, and which is, of course, the heavier end, is continually melting away from the higher temperature of the sea, until, at last, the upper portion becomes the heavier, when the entire iceberg turns over; the ends are reversed, and, of course, we are obliged, on such occasions, to seek another cave. But come. The whale calf steaks are nearly done, and it is time that we eat something."

As soon as Papplewick's companion was perceived by the rest of the walruses, they set up a great cry of applause, and it was evident by the way in which he was welcomed, that he was a walrus of considerable dignity.

Notwithstanding the delicacy of the whale-calf steaks, Papplewick did not eat much of them. He was lost in amazement at the state of civilization to which walruses had arrived. He listened, too, with great interest to their stories about encounters with white bears, which savage animals they considered to be their most deadly enemies, and several of their skins were hanging in the grotto as trophies of the courage of the walruses.

While this conversation was going on, Papplewick, who was much wearied with all that he had lately undergone fell into a deep slumber, in which we will for the present leave him.

V

When Papplewick awoke it was broad daylight, and the cavern was deserted, the walruses having departed on a fishing excursion. While our hero was ruminating on the strange events which had befallen him lately, and cogitating whether it was possible to enlist his friend the walrus in his scheme for the discovery of the North Pole, his attention was attracted by a low growl, proceeding from a remote corner of the cavern. Thinking that the walrus had, perhaps, returned, he advanced in the direction from whence the sound proceeded, and as the light was somewhat obscure, he saw nothing, until he suddenly discovered himself face to face with an enormous white bear, who was eagerly sniffing up the foetid odour of last night's feast, which still lingered in the cavern. On seeing Papplewick, the bear, who doubtless had never expected to light on such a dainty morsel, opened his terrible jaws, that seemed like a real cavern, hedged round with pillars of glittering ivory. Papplewick started back, horrified at this appalling sight, and, almost mechanically thrusting his hand into his pocket, drew forth his snuff-box; and as the hungry animal was just in the act of springing upon him, threw the entire of its pungent contents into his face. The next instant the ponderous icicles that hung from the roof were shivered by a succession of the most stentorian sneezes, and Papplewick, taking advantage of Bruin's discomfiture, and without having the courtesy even to offer him a pocket handkerchief, fled swiftly up a narrow passage which was near, and seemed to lead in an upward direction. After proceeding for some time, slipping upon the icy path, mounting over huge frozen flocks, and squeezing through narrow crevices, Papplewick emerged into the open air upon a ledge of ice, which jutted from the main body of the Berg, and overhung the sea. It was a glorious Polar summer's day. The sunbeams played brilliantly upon the lofty spires of the Berg, until it seemed like a cathedral, built of splendid jewels; and a whole army of detached masses of ice floated solemnly on the calm waters. While Papplewick was enjoying the beautiful prospect, and watching the evolutions of the icebergs, he heard a loud crackling noise above his head, and before he could turn to see what it proceeded from, a large fragment of ice, which had been loosened by the heat of the sun, slid down rapidly, and catching the ledge on which Papplewick was standing, toppled inwards, fairly enclosing that gentleman in a solid prison of ice, through whose semi-transparent walls his figure was dimly visible.

Our hero had now become so unured to extraordinary and unforeseen casualties, that he had ceased to be astonished at them; and so far conquered the fear natural to his nature, as to bear with a considerable degree of philosophy even the most distressing calamities. When he found himself, therefore, suddenly immured in this transparent dungeon, he resigned himself to his fate, and with the more equanimity when he reflected, that having the life-preserving pills in his possession, he could not starve for at least a twelvemonth. Besides, he trusted to an accidental thaw releasing him before then. Deliverance, however, came sooner than he expected. After he had been several hours imprisoned, he heard a peculiar whistle, which he recognised as the property of his friend the walrus. Presently that worthy individual scrambled up on the ledge, and uttered an exclamation of joy at seeing Papplewick, for whom he had conceived a great affection. Perceiving the dilemma in which his friend was, the walrus made signs expressive of sympathy, (because the ice interrupted all sound,) and telegraphing, in this way, that he would soon return, he plunged into the water. In about half an hour he returned, accompanied by a herd of walruses, and three strange animals. These were evidently not amphibious animals, for they staid in the water while the walrus was making his arrangements on the ice-berg for Papplewick's deliverance. All these animals had some strange appendage to their noses. One had a long ivory saw, with sharp teeth, projecting from his snout; another's nose terminated in a gigantic spear of black polished bone; while the third bore before him a sort of ivory javelin, which grew just above his upper lip. Papplewick thought he had seen pictures of the saw-fish, and the narwhal, or sea unicorn, in natural histories, which much resembled the new arrivals; but these latter were so much larger in size, that they could only be a gigantic variety of the species. Now, by order of the walrus, the saw-fish raised himself out of the water, and commenced sawing away the wall of ice which surrounded Papplewick; while the narwhal and sword-fish dug away with their ivory spears, until large splinters of the ice flew about, like chips of marble beneath the stone-cutter's chisel. In a very short space of time the ice wall was completely sawn through, and separated into two pieces, both of which fell with a great splash into the sea, and Papplewick once more emerged into the free air.

As soon as this was fully accomplished, the walrus dismissed the saw-fish and his companions, having ordered them to be rewarded with a considerable gratuity of bear's liver for their services, Papplewick and he then proceeded in triumph to the cave, where they had a great feast in honor of the former gentleman's deliverance.

Towards evening the walrus produced some pipes, made out of a narwhal's tusk, and tobacco, which had been found in a vessel deserted by some Polar voyagers, and asking Papplewick whether he ever blew a cloud, he lit one himself, and the two friends retired to a quiet corner of the cave, to enjoy a smoke.

Finding the walrus in an amiable humor, Papplewick thought this a good opportunity to broach his favorite scheme of the North Pole discovery to his friend. He accordingly asked him whether he had ever been there?

At this question the walrus looked very mysterious, indeed, and appeared anxious to evade any reply; but Papplewick pressing it on him, he said—

"You are now treading on dangerous ground. The sights and scenes that exist at the North Pole are mysteries, to which no man has ever yet been admitted; but as I have conceived a regard for you, I will, if you are willing to brave the danger consequent upon the attempt, take you to-night to a grand meeting of the Dodos, the wisest birds in the world. They have deserted the surface of the earth, and it is thought by men that the race is extinct; but they live many miles northward, in a subterranean cave, heated with volcanic fire. They will, perhaps, gratify your curiosity; and if the Chief Dodo takes a fancy to you, we will try and get him to introduce you to the Living Loadstones."

At the mention of the Living Loadstones, Papplewick's heart bounded with joy, for he felt that they must have some connection with the great mystery which he was seeking to solve. He found it was in vain, however, to question the walrus any further on the subject, that individual preserving a profound silence on the topic, so that Papplewick was fain to content himself with listening to the walrus' stories of Sir John Ross and Captain Parry, and waited very patiently until the time should arrive for his introduction to the Dodos.

Where night fell in the walrus, having finished his pipe, asked Papplewick whether he was ready to go, as the Dodos were already assembled. Our hero prepared himself for the expedition with the greatest alacrity, and the walrus, taking from a pouch made of the skin of a sea serpent, a small fragment of some brown substance, told Papplewick to swallow it. He obeyed the command, and had scarcely put it to his lips than he became totally insensible.

When he recovered his recollection he found himself in a lofty chamber, the roof of which seemed to be lost in distance. Large spiral jets of fire spouted up through apertures in the floor at regular distances, illuminating the chamber to its remotest corners. The walls were formed of solid rock, against which hung files of every newspaper which was ever published. There Papplewick could discern the familiar features of the New York Herald, the Tribune, and the Lantern. At the upper end of this subterranean chamber sat a number of grave-looking unwieldy birds, with large bills, which our hero conjectured could be none other than the famous Dodos. Every Dodo had a book or newspaper in its claw, and on a sort of dais in the centre sat one Dodo, larger and wiser looking than any of the rest. This bird was intently perusing a late number of the Lantern, and, by the frequent shaking of his short wings, Papplewick could see that the pungent wit of that periodical was not lost upon him.

The walrus, who was close by, now whispered to Papplewick, and the pair advanced towards the Chief Dodo, making respectful obeisances. That grave dignitary, as soon as he perceived them, arose, and greeted the walrus very warmly, acknowledging Papplewick's salutation with a condescending smile. After the usual preliminaries of conversation, the Dodo, turning to Papplewick, said—

"What a bad accident that was on the Erie railroad the other day!"

Papplewick stared. The Dodo, seeing his confusion, continued—

"Ah! no doubt you have not heard of it, as you have been some time from home; but I get all the daily papers here. The account is in yesterday's Herald. Would you like to see it?"

Papplewick, whose mind was intent only on one object, declined respectfully; but could not help wondering how the Dodo got the newspapers so soon.

"My friend, the walrus," resumed the Dodo, "tells me you are anxious to be introduced to the Living Loadstones."

"I am, indeed, very desirous to meet with them," replied Papplewick.

"They are strange persons," said the Dodo, "and are not over fond of strangers. They are also very dangerous at times. However, if your curiosity is strong enough to overcome your fear, I will introduce you to them tomorrow."

Papplewick thanked the Dodo with a grateful heart.

"Now," said the Dodo, "you are about to see the trial of one of our body. We are very exclusive, and are bound by certain laws never to visit the upper earth, where we once endured so much persecution from hunters, under the penalty of death. A young Dodo, not more than three hundred years old, has been detected not alone in a breach of this law, but we have also discovered that he has married an albatross, whom he visits very frequently on the surface of the earth. For this offence he is to be tried this night, and, if convicted, he must die."

It seemed then to Papplewick that the Chief Dodo, and all the other Dodos, suddenly changed into big unwieldy judges, clothed in black and white feathers. And the Chief Dodo took his seat upon the highest bench, while the others sat round him. Two rather shabbily feathered Dodos then dragged forward the prisoner, who appeared to be sinking with terror. His feathers were all brushed up the wrong way, and there were heavy fetters upon his legs. The Chief Dodo then recapitulated the charge brought against him, and asked him what he had to say in his defence? The poor fellow acknowledged his guilt, but pleaded his extreme youth as a reason for his punishment being mitigated. The Chief Dodo, after having consulted with his brother judges, put on a cap made of the skin of a black albatross, and proceeded to pass sentence of death upon the prisoner, commenting at the same time severely upon the degradation he had brought upon the race of Dodos by intermarrying with an Albatross. After the awful sentence had been pronounced, and the court had resumed their seats, the two jailor Dodos took the fetters off of the prisoner's legs, and left him panting with terror in the centre of the cave.

The Chief Justice then gave a signal, by striking the tusk of a narwhal against the skull of a whale; and, as the gong-like sound rolled along the cave, Papplewick beheld the jets of fire that sported up through the floor, suddenly leave their places, and advance towards the unhappy Dodo prisoner. In vain did he flap his short wings, and run round the cave, seeking to escape. The fountains of fire encompassed him in every direction, casting upon him spouts of lurid flame, until his feathers were scorched to cinders, and he sank gasping on the floor. Then all the fires suddenly rushed together, and formed a belt of flame around his expiring body. Papplewick heard a faint shriek, a hissing crackling sound; and then what with the foetid odour of burnt feathers, and the sickness consequent on beholding such a death, he fell back from his seat, and swooned away.

The Comet and I

I

I was walking down Broadway on last Tuesday night—after having taken dinner with a sick friend—and on looking up at the clear blue sky, sown with such myriads of silver stars, I became filled with disgust at my ignorance of the noble science of astronomy. There were constellations distributed generally on all sides of me, and aristocratic stars of the first magnitude, and eccentric stars, remarkable for some peculiarity of form or habit, as Horace Greeley is remarkable for his boots, and yet I did not know the name of one of them. The Great Bear, Orion, Sirius, the Southern Cross, the Plow, and all the rest of them, might have been right over my head without my knowing any thing at all about it. The fact is, that, with all due deference to astronomers, whenever any of these constellations were pointed out to me by some friend who was just learning the use of the globes, I never could detect the slightest similarity between them and the objects after which they were named.

"I know so little about astronomy," I muttered to myself, "that I must certainly write a book about it."

At this moment I found myself opposite the New York Hospital, where the patient man with the long brass telescope is always ready, for a small remuneration, to sweep the sidereal heavens. While I was gazing upon this forlorn astronomer, and wondering whether a first-class star paid him as well as Miss Heron must have paid her enterprising New York manager, the idea of the comet, which is so soon to smash into us, crossed my mind.

"By Jove!" thought I, "I'll have a look for him. Who knows but he may be within sight? So that, having a little warning of his coming, I may go into New Jersey in order to be out of the way."

I suppose I must have given utterance to these thoughts aloud, for just as I was putting my hand in my pocket to feel if I had the necessary coin to entitle me to a peep through the telescope, I felt a tip on my shoulder, and, turning round, saw a queer, rubicund-looking little old man standing beside me. He was dressed in an odd flame-colored suit, a red cap, and I declare most solemnly that I beheld, protruding from underneath his Raglan, a long, fan-shaped tail. This last, though, seemed more phantasmal than real; for when I tried to tread on it my foot passed as through vapor.

"Well, Sir! what do you want?" I demanded, angrily; for I felt annoyed at being tapped on the shoulder by so ridiculous a personage.

"Put up your money," answered the stranger; "don't spend it foolishly!"

"I'll spend my money if I like, Sir!" I replied, with dignity. "Besides, I wish to see if there is any sign of Charles the Twelfth's comet, which is expected every day."

"It won't be here till the evening of the eighteenth of June," said the stranger.

I own the preciseness and confidence of his assertion struck me as being remarkable.

"Pray, Sir, how do you know this so positively?" I demanded, with a half sneer.

"How do I know it? Because I am the Comet! Stay, here's my card." And so saying, he pulled a steel card-case out of his pocket, and presented me with a small square of linen, on which was printed:

> ### THE COMET
>
> **OF CHARLES THE TWELFTH**
>
> **At Home.**
>
> *Thursday,* 18*th June,* 1837.

"I hope I shall have the pleasure of seeing you on that evening," continued the Comet, with an air of elegant politeness, such as a Marquis of the time of Louis XIV, would have exhibited in inviting me to a grand *fete.* "My cards, as you perceive, are of linen. The reason is, that I have them made of asbestos in order to insure their being incombustible. Otherwise they would take fire in my pocket."

I now remarked that the card was warm!

"Then you are really going to destroy the world on the day mentioned?" I said, inquiringly, feeling a decidedly uncomfortable feeling in my heart and throat.

"Not at all," answered the Comet. "My devastation will be only partial. I have come to cleanse rather than to destroy. Purification by fire is what will be accomplished by my advent; and I will, as it were, cauterize all the sores of the world."

"But what brings you on in advance of your arrival—if you will excuse the apparent Hibernicism?" I asked.

"Ah! simply in order to know where to strike. I wish to see for myself. For instance, I don't want to run a muck through New York, killing blindly. I wish to gain such information as will enable me to extirpate nuisances, and leave uninjured whatever I find good and pure."

"Heaven protect us!" I ejaculated. "Then New York is a total ruin!"

"Not so—not so!" repeated the Comet. "Let me see for myself. You can assist me. I know you; you are the Man about Town, and you can guide me through this labyrinth. If you will give me the information that I want, I will give you a ticket of safety, insuring your preservation from any of the effects of my visit."

"It's a bargain!" I cried, much relieved in my mind by this proposition. "Let us take a drink on it."

The bar-room that we entered was one of the most splendid in Broadway. Its walls were hung with seductive colored prints; its ceiling was frescoed with loose designs, while the bar itself glittered with a magnificently-decorated machinery for the distribution of poisoned liquor. A thick cloud of tobacco-smoke floated through the room; the click of billiard-balls jarred sharply from the farther end; and the place was swarming with knots of youth—few of them more than twenty years—whose flushed faces were dimly lit by heavy, dissipated eyes, and whose pale lips were jaded with drink and smoke, and blasphemous with constant oaths.

"Here," said I, as the Comet and myself quaffed our lager-bier—a drink to which my erratic friend seemed to take very kindly—"here is one of a class of places of amusement which I think we might dispense with. It is not because young men spend their dollars here that I object to it. It is because across that bar something more than money is taken. Youth, and health, and vigor; innocence, good feeling, and refinement; all senses of social decency pass across that counter invisibly night after night, and their owners go on none the wiser for their loss, until, in some hour of self-examination, they awake to the consciousness of all that they have squandered."

The Comet nodded his head approvingly, and taking out a black notebook, traced some memoranda on it with his finger, which left a glittering mark like phosphorus. We then went out into the town.

"Where are we now?" asked the Comet, after we had walked some time, stopping suddenly under the façade of a large building.

"This is the celebrated Wall Street," I answered; "the paradise of adventurers. Sweep it, my dear Comet, from top to bottom. Don't leave a trace of it. A single fragment of it, if left floating around, will, like the polypus, become an independent settlement, and grow to its original size. It is here that speculation fattens as a bubble grows, swelling and swelling, until suddenly, piff! paff! the thing bursts, and all that remains is a little dirty water. This is the great central habitation where a colony of spiders have fixed their abode, and from which they spread their nets over the whole city. Unlike the ordinary spider, they rarely fight among themselves, and generously assist each other when in distress. It is against the poor outside insects that their machinations are chiefly directed. There is a fraternity of brigandage among these brokers that forbids them devouring each other; but woe to him who, belonging not to their band, ventures with full pockets into their domain. Here many lofty hopes have died. Here many honorable shields have been stained forever. Here is what may be considered the great centre of the floating capital of New York. Yet there is not a prison in the city that has not had its ranks of malefactors recruited from the Board of Brokers."

Out came the Comet's note-book, and down went a memorandum fatal to Wall Street. Heaven help the Exchange on the 18th of June!

"What order of architecture does that building belong to?" asked the Comet, as we were passing the City Hall, a short time after.

"That," said I, "is what is commonly called the Dutch Corinthian. That noble edifice, of which our city is so proud, is the Hotel de Ville of New York; in other words, the City Hall. You should see it, my dear Comet, on the 4th of July, when the front is decorated with an imposing effigy of the Father of his Country, and ten thousand dollars worth of fire-crackers testify the patriotic enthusiasm of our newly-imported citizens. There is a fine field for a sweep of your tail in the corridors of that edifice, most noble Comet! Street-contractors that don't do their work; Mayors that make a job of politics; policemen that are appointed because they are good shoulder-hitters at primary elections; together with a thousand corruptions which I have no time to name. Make a note, most noble Comet!"

"That tall, rickety building, but of which I see a crazed-looking man in a white hat and old boots issuing, what is that?"

"That is the office of the *Rostrum*, the great philanthropical journal of America, which, like the Baron Spolasco, or any other gentleman of his kidney, earns a living by being eccentric. Every thing is determinedly turned topsy-turvy by the employés of that paper. They want to make men of women, and women of men. Their trowsers are always too short and their hair too long. They employ Russians to write their English, and musicians to instruct the public on politics. They keep a parson who reviews their profane literature, and a layman who writes sermons on popped corn. They attack every body, and bellow like the Bulls of Bashan if they are attacked in turn. They profess to be intensely democratic, and their building is a sort of caravanserai for foreign noblemen who bivouac among the desks and exchanges. They have their fine eyes, like Mrs. Jellyby, always fixed on Africa, and do not see the civic sores that fester at their very feet. In short, their eccentricities and 'isms' are as wide as the brims of their hats, and, like them, shut them off from the light of heaven!"

"I guess we'll let the *Rostrum* building stand," said the Comet. "It is a harmless institution, and affords the public amusement. I like to see a comic newspaper thrive."

From the Park we passed upward, and I pointed out many shams to the Comet, which he promised to attend to on the 18th of June. He said that he would most particularly wait upon the Central Park Commission, on Coroner Connery, on Mr. Russ, and on the gentleman who has been promising the public a catalogue of the books in the Astor Library ever since that institution opened.

We were now opposite to the Cooper Institute, and while I was explaining to my friend the Comet that this noble gift to the people should be held sacred, not alone on account of the amiable donor, but for the benefit which the rising generation would derive from it, I suddenly heard a whizzing noise in the air. I looked up, and behold the Comet was shooting away into space like a rocket, leaving a long, luminous wake after him. He kissed his hand and smiled to me as he soared upward.

"Oh criky!" cried a little boy behind me, "ain't that a jolly rocket!" and I saw a number of people look aloft. They all saw only a fire-work. I alone knew it was the Comet.

II

I am horribly disappointed! The tiger who misses his spring; the young lady who, hoping for a proposal from a certain swain for her own hand, receives one for her younger sister; the salmon-fisher, at the moment that the rod straightens with a jerk, and he knows that "he is gone"—all these are but faint types of the agonizing disappointment I experienced when I found that the Comet did not strike the earth.

The case, I submit, was very hard. I had met, as I conceived, a well-bred, gentlemanly Comet—a Comet of his word—who made me certain promises, in which I blindly believed, and on the faith of which I made certain arrangements. The apparent sincerity with which he spoke of his impingement on the earth, did not allow me room for a doubt. He seemed calm and self-assured—and now, after all this, he has not come! The earth still revolves in its accustomed orbit; the City Hall—I regret still more to say—still lifts its proud chimney-pots over the adjacent buildings!

But the predicament in which this breach of faith on the part of the Comet has placed me is very lamentable. When I was assured at that memorable interview related in a previous "Man About Town," that such a body was really about to visit us, I immediately commenced to reflect on certain consequences which must inevitably result from such a catastrophe.

"If the earth is smashed up," I thought, "debt must certainly be abolished; therefore I have nothing to fear from that infuriated class of acquaintances known to me as creditors. Likewise, if there is a general collision to take place in the course of a week or so, I see no crime in running still farther into debt. Before the bills can by any possibility become due, debtor and creditor will be involved in common ruin. *Dum vivimus vivamus!*—'A short life and a merry one!' as Epictetus says in his 'Enchiridion.' Let us, without delay, run into debt!"

Accordingly, I proceeded on the most approved principles. For the last fortnight I have exhausted every pleasure. Dinners, suppers, horses, clothes, jewelry, cards. What boots I ordered! what entrancing coats! what seraphic waistcoats! My convivial parties have been the talk of the town. My friends and myself have exhausted the supply of several of the finest wines that come to this market. The epicures of the city wander wildly from restaurant to restaurant calling in vain for *Vieux Ceps*, for *Clos Vougeot*, for *St. Peray*. "It is all gone!" reply the proprietors. " 'The Man About Town' has drunk it all up!" I bought a yacht; purchased a picture-gallery and a library; gave a thousand dollars for a gold dressing-case, mounted with turquoises (there were a pair of dress boot-hooks in it made of amber, that took my fancy); ordered twenty thousand cigars, at a hundred and twenty-five dollars a thousand—in short, indulged in all the luxury of buying.

What is the consequence? The Comet has not kept his word, and I am besieged. My bell is going all day, and creditors are ten deep round my door. Tailors' boys, bending under loads of trowsers and waistcoats, are continually coming to my room, with long bills in their hands, and departing threatening and unpaid. I can not go into a single respectable restaurant without being dunned for dinners, suppers, and breakfasts obtained during the brief period of my luxury. As I walk down Broadway ravenous tradespeople spring at me, and demand their money. I have had enough of executions served on me to paper my walls with. Sheriffs' officers assail me before I rise in the morning with legal documents, the terrors of which are quadrupled in magnitude from my not understanding them. I am growing thin and pale. My life is forever rendered wretched by this ungentlemanly conduct of the Comet. If the wealthy and respectable firm of publishers with whom I am connected do not immediately advance me twenty thousand dollars on account of literary matter to be hereafter furnished, I see no resource left me but to take Prussic acid, or go back with General Walker to Nicaragua.

I sometimes wonder why it was that the Comet did not come. I am afraid he was disgusted at the disparaging manner in which our scientific man spoke of him in the *Weekly*. If I thought that this was really the case, I would challenge our scientific man.

What am I to do?

Oh, faithless Comet!

The Man Without a Shadow

Fortunate fellow that I am! I have lost my shadow!

But do not imagine that, like the poor Peter Schlemihl, I have sold it to the Devil! Heaven forbid that any Devil should be stupid or extravagant enough to buy such a Shadow!

No; as it came, so it has departed, a thing of mystery, an awful bore.

It is not my natural shadow I speak of; but an unnatural, an impertinent Shadow, which of late attached itself to my person, and could not be shaken off whether in the glare of sunshine or the pale moonlight, in the rays of volatile gas or of explosive camphine.

I first observed it about six weeks ago. I knew it was a shadow, for I never could detect anything real or true about it; nevertheless, to look at it, one would have taken it for a man, or, at the least, a monkey. I have had my doubts in the latter point. But no! I will not insult monkeydom by the suspicion. I was only a Shadow—no more.

When I first observed it at a friend's house, I tried to find out what it was; but my friend knew as little as myself. It had followed him from another friend's, and that friend said it had followed him from somewhere else. Of its origin nothing was known. Like all Shadows, its nature was involved in obscurity. At any attempt to throw light upon it, it disappeared entirely—like other Shadows.

Still it was a very troublesome Shadow, and very different from my own dear aboriginal Shadow which so closely resembled me in outline, that no one would fail to detect my relationship; but this new strange Shadow was not a bit like me. It was my opposite in every respect—even at dinner. And it was not only a troublesome, but an expensive Shadow; for when I dined, it dined with me, and when the bill came, the waiter charged for the Shadow as if for a human being—and truly it had a most astonishing semblance of eating and drinking about it! Whatever I took it took, when

I drank wine it drank wine—nay, it drank even more than I drank myself, for Shadows are generally larger than the objects which shun them. I should almost have questioned whether it was a Shadow, had it not in all respects aped my movements and reflections. If I said it was a hot day, the Shadow said it was a hot day, or I fancied it said so. If I wiped my forehead, the Shadow seemed to do the same. If I put my hand in my pocket to pay for cigars, the Shadow did the same—only being a Shadow, it never brought out any money to pay for them, which is a peculiarity of Shadows.

When I praised anything the Shadow praised, and when I condemned the Shadow condemned—at least so its attitude seemed to imply. When I was going up town the Shadow was going up town, and when I inclined towards the Battery the Shadow was likewise attracted thither. Wherever I went, the Shadow went too. What I did, the Shadow did. What I thought the Shadow thought, and what I swore the Shadow swore. Of its Shadowy nature, there could surely be no question.

It is now a whole week since it left me. When I last saw it I was dressing to go out, and the Shadow of course had precisely at that epoch occasion to dress too; so it put on one of my clean shirts (as I did myself), and went out with me. At the door it borrowed a five dollar bill, and— vanished. It is the nature of Shadows to vanish. I have since heard that the same Shadow has vanished from more than one boarding house in the most shadowy manner.

May the reader never be haunted by Shadows!

I have a scientific theory, by the way, with reference to these visitors from Shadow-land. It is, that they are the spiritual manifestations of departed (i.e. emigrated) Do–dos. I mean to suggest the idea at the next meeting of the Royal Society, in London.

An Arabian Nightmare

It came to pass, some years ago, that I went to the fair of Nishin, Novogorod, which is in the land of the Muscovites, who are unbelievers, and worship the pictures of created things. And, lo! I took to the fair fur caps and cloaks from Thibet, and woollen garments from Cashmere, and also the dates of Bokhara. And our Lord the Prophet, whose tomb I have visited (and whose name is blessed), gave me a ready sale for my merchandise, so that I had soon a girdle full of roubles, which are coins of the Muscovites. And, behold! I made acquaintance with one of the unbelievers, whose name was Demski, and who had brought to the fair garments of white fur and garments of seal-skin. And, of a truth, before the fair was over, I was greatly troubled in my body by reason of the noise and the crowd, and the anxieties of buying and selling; and also by reason of the unwholesome food, wherewith the Muscovites (may God enlighten them!) are wont to fill themselves. And I was afflicted with a great trembling of the limbs, so that walking fatigued me—although I am one who had journeyed to Mecca (the riches of which place may God increase). And whereas, when I was in Khiva, my girdle caused a shortness of the breath, and a constriction of the ribs: it would now have fallen over my waist, if the good roubles, whereof our Lord the Prophet had permitted me to despoil the Muscovites, had not kept it in its place. And when Demski saw that I walked with difficulty, and was even as a peeled wand for thinness, he said, "Verily, oh Hamet! the way to Khiva is long, and the motion of camels, I have heard, is an affliction to the limbs: it were better for thee to go with me and my merchandise unto Berezow, which is a town on the river Obb, in the province of Tobolsk; for though the winter is long and cold; yet, when we roll thee up in furs, and give thee the warmest corner of the stove, and cause the pores of thy skin to be opened by means of the sweating house, thou wilt not think of the snow or of the long night." And I said, "Of a truth, oh my friend! the words of the poet are exemplified in thee, saying,

'In a brother I have found no love, but a stranger
    hathshown me affection.
And a stranger has been to me more than the son of
    my mother.' "

But he answered, "These are foolish words! When I come to Khiva,
thou wilt prepare the kabobs and the pilaff for me. And now, oh Hamet,
make ready thy goods; for on the second day we shall harness the horse to
the sledge."

And on the second day Demski loaded his sledge with merchandise,
even with dried meat and fish, and with brandy, and with stewed pears
(may Allah confound them and exterminate them!), for of such things do
the Muscovites eat. And he spread fur cloaks upon the merchandise, and
we sat thereon, and he struck the horse with a whip having three lashes,
and we went like the horses of the Kurds, and like the camels of the
Bedawee.

And, lo, the journey was long; but the novelty thereof sustained me, for
from my youth up, I have loved to see strange places, and to hear of the
people who dwell therein. And when we came to Berezow, we found there
Petrovna, the wife of Demski, and Alexandrovitch, their little son, and I
gave to her a handkerchief of bright colours, and to him a tarboosh of red
cloth; so that they were glad to see me, and I abode with them during the
winter. And, verily, I saw a strange thing; for the sun appeared not for the
space of five months. And when I saw this, I said, "Of a truth this is a land
forsaken of God. And it is because the people thereof worship the pictures
of created things."

And I abode much in the house, going only from the stove to the
sweating-house, and from the sweating-house to the stove. And in the
sweating-house they took from me my clothes, and set me on warm stones,
and poured water on stones heated in the fire, until the house was filled
with the steam thereof, and beat my body gently with the twigs of birch,
until the perspiration ran from me; and indeed this is of great convenience
in so cold a land. And in the house we talked of the countries we had seen,
and of the wonderful works of God: and Demski taught me the game of
chess, and I taught him that of Ahama, which I had learned of an Os-
ruanlee when I journeyed to Mecca, (which may God establish!).

And, lo! one evening I noticed that Alexandrovitch, the son of Demski,
was cutting out the bits of bone wherewith the game of chess is played,
and fashioning them into the images of created things. And I saw that the
bone wherefrom he was cutting them was that of a large animal; and I

said, "Oh Demski! whence is that bone for I have seen here no animals whose bones are of such a bigness, but only a few hares and foxes, with white fur. For in this accursed land, God has withdrawn the light of his countenance from the animals, and there is no colour in them." And Demski told me that the bone was found in the ice; and that also whole animals were found therein, with the hair and flesh on them; and that amongst them were the bones of the elephant, and even entire elephants, which are animals that I have seen in the land of the Mogul, where the inhabitants (may Allah instruct them!) worship cows. And I said, "Oh Demski! how came these animals in the ice? for they are animals that inhabit hot countries, and could not live in this cold place, which causeth the blood to stand still, and maketh the fingers like those of dead men." And he said, "Thy question is that of a man of understanding; and verily there was a learned man here, whom the Czar (whom God preserve!) sent to us, a man of the nation of Franks, who examined these bones, and looked at the creatures as they lay in the ice, and said to me and to others, that this land had once been warmer and fit for such creatures, and that these frozen rivers and seas had once flowed like the great rivers and the ocean which thou hast seen." And I said, "Oh Demski! this is but foolishness; and God will confound these Feringees, who pry into the origin of things. For these are works of Eblis and of the Jân, and these creatures are shut up here by enchantment, even as Gog and Magog were shut up by Iskander, in the mountains near the Caspian Sea. And Gog and Magog are always digging through the mountain to get out; but cannot, by reason of the strong enchantment wherewith they are enchanted; nor shall they, because they cannot say, 'Inshallah!' which means 'God willing.' But one day there shall be a boy amongst them, called 'Inshallah;' and one of them shall say to him, 'Inshallah, I will dig through the rock;' and straightway they shall dig through the rock, and overspread the world, and Deijal shall come forth to lead them. And who knows but these creatures are shut up here by like enchantment, and will one day come forth?"

And Demski and Petrovna, and Alexandrovitch, their son, allowed that I had spoken wisely, and praised me much; so that when supper came I was elated, and eat of the dried meat and of fish, and of stewed pears, which I had never before tasted (may Allah confound them!); and drank of the brandy until I shouted and sang, as one should not shout and sing who has travelled to Mecca—(may God establish it and maintain it!) And, behold, when I lay down on the stone to sleep, I was much pleased that I had spoken so wisely about Eblis and the Jân, and Gog and Magog, and

Iskander; for it beseemeth a schereef to instruct the ignorant, and one who hath wisdom to impart it to one who hath not. So I slept.

But about the middle of the night I felt a heavy hand upon my breast, and I awoke; and, lo! when one of the evil ones stood by me, even a Jin, having the face of a bull, and a hand like the foot of an elephant, and his hand was upon my breast. And he said, "Oh Hamet, arise and go with me!" And I answered, "Oh Bull Face! whither?" And he said, "Unto the shores of the Frozen Sea, and to the palace of Eblis, and to the abode of the enchanted creatures of whom thou spakest before supper."

Then said I, "Now are the words of the poet accomplished, for he said:—

> " 'Speak no evil of the Jân, for they are always about
>   thee,
>   And one of them shall carry thy words to the rest
>   in the palace of Eblis.' "

And the Bull Face grinned. And I arose, and went with him out of the house; and he took me by the hand, and we ran swiftly, like the Mahry, on which the Tonarick rides forth to plunder. And when I saw that he meddled not with Demski, nor with Petrovna, his wife, neither with any of the people of Berezow, I said, "See, now! what it is to worship the pictures of created things; for the Jân regard these people as brothers." And the Bull Face snorted. And by this time we had come to the shores of the Frozen Sea; but the ice was not all of equal strength, nor was the sea covered by it; but great shapes of ice sailed down it, which were of a blue colour, by reason of the moon. And the Jin would have carried me over; but when he essayed it, I was too heavy for him; so that he said, "Of a truth, this wretch must have some holy thing about him, that I cannot lift him." And I remembered with joy that I had on my heart a piece of cloth wherewith I had touched the Holy Stone at Mecca, and I repeated the verses:—

"Keep holy things about thee, and gird thee with sacred spells: that thy wickedness may be forgiven for the sake of that thou wearest."

And the Jin struck the ice with a stone, and made it crack; and, lo! I heard it cracking and splitting all across the sea, until the sound thereof was louder than that of thunder. And the Jân who were in the palace of Eblis heard it; and straightway three of them, having the faces of hawks and the claws of eagles, came flying to us. And the Bull Face said: "Oh

Hook Noses! Eblis sent me to bring this wretch to him, but he is too heavy for me, by reason of some holy thing which he hath about him. Help me to carry him." And they took me in their arms, and flew. And when I felt the swiftness of our motion through the air, and reflected that the evil ones might let me fall on the ice, or into the cold sea, I resolved to entreat them courteously; and I said to one of the Hook Noses who bore up my right shoulder, "Wherefore, oh my aga! doth my lord Eblis abide in this desolate place with creatures forsaken of God?" And he said: "Not choice, but necessity, brought us hither, thou abandoned one; for Eblis was once lord of the morning star, and God had given him a brightness well nigh equal to that of the sun, and permitted his star to be seen of men, even till the third hour of the day; but Eblis wished that his light might be greater, and that his star might be seen of men all the day long; wherefore God banished him from the morning star, and shut him up here with forsaken creatures; and as for us, we are even as he is." And the Bull Face and the Hook Noses howled for grief, and I was sorry that I had questioned them, for I thought, they have a sore burden to bear, and I have reminded them of it. And now they flew down to the land, whereon the palace of Eblis stands; and, verily, it is a land of ice, for there are neither trees nor plants in it, nor any living herb, nor any running water, but only great rocks and columns of ice; even pillars like those of Tadmor, which Solomon built in the desert. And in these columns I saw what will scarce be believed; for I saw all manner of animals, entire and perfect, even elephants bigger than any that I ever saw in the land of the Mogul, and great deer, and crocodiles, such as live by the Nile. These were all shut up in the ice, as flies and straws are enclosed in the amber of the merchants; and the expression of their countenances was that of animals which have died in pain. And I said to them who were with me, "Oh Jân! how came these creatures here?" And one of them said, "Of a truth, this was once a land with rivers of water, and with trees and plants, both great and small, and these creatures lived therein; but when God sent Eblis hither, he caused the Sun to shine on other parts of the world and not on this, so that these creatures were all frozen up here, and the breath went out of them."

Then thought I, "Lo! now this is what the Frank said to Demski and to others. Surely God has cursed these Franks, for they speak like the Jâns." But though there was no sun in this land, there was a light, such as I never saw before or since; for it proceeded from no visible cause, but resembled the reflection of a lamp upon a wall; and verily the ice was luminous, and I saw pale flames on the top of every rock and pillar of ice, and they resembled the mist which surrounds the moon when rain is about to be sent. And the flames were everywhere, even in the ground whereon I walked, and in the air which I breathed; but there was no heat in the flame. And, lo! we came into the hall where Eblis sat, and it was all of luminous ice, and the inhabitants thereof were of ice also; and as I looked at the Jân who had brought me, behold! they were all of ice, and pale flames were around all their heads, and at the ends of all their fingers, and their bodies were luminous, so that I could see their hearts beat. And Eblis sat on a frozen throne, and his body looked like a pure opal without flaw, and his face was like unto a milk-white cornelian. And there was no light in the palace, or in all that land, but that which came from the ice, and from the inhabitants thereof.

And they set me in the midst. And Eblis said, "What present has my servant Hamet brought to his lord?" And I answered, "Nay, my Sultan; I was taken in the night, and have brought nothing, and, moreover, I am not the servant of my Sultan; but if he will send me back to Berezow, to the house of Demski, I will give him, as a present, fur caps of Thibet, and woollen garments of Cashmere, inasmuch as he needeth them sorely." And thereat the men of ice laughed, until their joints cracked horribly. And Eblis said, "Yea! but thou hast served me often; even at the fair of Novogorod, when thou didst sell fur caps for two roubles, that were not worth one; and again, no later than last night, when thou didst drink brandy and eat stewed pears." And I said, "Of a truth, the fur caps were not good, and the stewed pears are an accursed food; but I am a poor man, and my Sultan will take a small present from me." And he answered, "Yea! I will take even what thou hast with thee;" and turning to a blue Jin, who stood near him, he said, "Take from him the girdle of roubles which is about his waist." And when I heard this, I thought, "It were better for me to die than to let these accursed ones have my roubles; as man can only die once, but poverty is an abiding affliction." So I took courage, and cried, "Oh! Frozen Ones, accursed are your mothers and your sisters; but my roubles ye shall not have." And I held up my garments and ran; and the men of ice ran too, and slid round about me on the ice, and caught at me with their slippery hands, and chilled me with their icy breath. And the rocks, and the pillars, and the frozen ground, shot out pale flames at me as I passed; and the creatures in the pillars, the expression of whose countenances was that of creatures which had died in pain, writhed themselves in the ice, and grinned at me horribly. And all the men of ice shouted, "Hamet! Stop, Hamet! Thy roubles, Hamet! Thy roubles!" And their words struck against the rocks, and ran along the frozen ground, and along the surface of the sea, until all that desolate place repeated "Hamet! Stop, Hamet! Thy roubles, Hamet! Thy roubles!" and my foot slipped. And as I strove to save myself from falling, behold! I was on my back on the stove in the house of Demski, and he and his wife and their son were shouting to me. And they said that I had slept long: but how I escaped from those frozen ones, I know not; but I suppose the bit of cloth, with which I had touched the Holy Stone, redeemed me from them, even from the power of the Jân; by which one may see that it is good to go to Mecca, and that Mohammed is the Prophet of God.

And when the spring came I departed from Demski and his wife, and returned to Khiva, both I and my roubles, whereof those evil ones had wished to rob me.

The King of Nodland
and
His Dwarf

Chapter I
Some Little Account of Nodland

Far away in the wide tracts of the southern seas lies a country called Nodland. If any of my readers are geographically inclined, I fear that I shall be quite unable to answer the usual question as to latitude and longitude. But when I say that its shores were lashed by the waves of the Pacific ocean, I settle its position quite as definitely as the objects of this little story require. Nodland was a strange but beautiful country. The soil was rich and fertile, and the land sometimes rose into soft, green hills, with their summits crowned with fragrant trees, whose blossoms never faded. In other districts the surface of the soil was dotted all over with numberless small lakes, belted round and hidden from the world by tall sombre trees, until they looked like myriads of beautiful blue eyes, shaded by their long, dark lashes. There were some portions, too, covered with wild, savage forests, where the panther and hyena roared their lives away, and splendid birds with wings of gold and azure fluttered amid the trees, until it seemed as if the blue stars and yellow sunbeams had come down from heaven to make a holiday among those lonely woods. Yet with all this beauty there was a lifelessness around the land. The air seemed heavy with sleep; the tall corn-stalks in the fields, and the orange trees on the sunny slopes, bowed their heads and nodded drowsily. The very wind was lazy, and seemed to blow only on compulsion.

The inhabitants of Nodland shared in this universal torpor. Sleep appeared to be the great object of existence, and sleep they did all through the day, and far into the night. Life with them had but two alternations—from the bed to the table; from the table to the bed. In this way a Nodlander was very happy. He had a king who was not worse than the general run of monarchs; the soil was fruitful, and a good nap was always to be had at will. Possessing these things, he wished for nothing more. In such a drowsy state of society, it may be supposed that the people were not much given to work. A Nodlander would as soon have thought of committing suicide as digging a hole, or planting a carrot. A potato furrow would have been a Rubicon impossible to get over, and all the corn in Nodland might have rotted in its fullness, ere one sheaf of it would have fallen before the scythe of those destined to consume it. Now though the soil of Nodland was fertile, it was not sufficiently generous to produce, unaided, all that was requisite for the support of so lazy a nation. It was necessary to plough, manure and sow it with the requisite seed, and as it was quite out of the question that this could be done by the Nodlanders, it was equally obvious that somebody else must be got who would do it, otherwise the consequences to the nation at large might be excessively unpleasant. This was the great principle on which the constitution of Nodland turned. Too lazy to labor themselves, the Nodlanders must have people to labor for them. But where were these to be had? Once every year, in the early spring, when the winter-hidden flowers were bursting joyously up through the soil, to meet their old friend the sunshine, the people of Nodland cast off for a brief while the constitutional lethargy which enchained them, and donned the sword and buckler of the warrior. They formed themselves into a great army, and like most lazy people they were brave when they were thoroughly aroused, and marched with much martial pomp across the borders of their own kingdom into the heart of the neighboring country. This country was inhabited by a peaceful and industrious race called the Cock-Crow Indians, who, amid the fertile valleys of their lofty hills, cultivated the soil and lived a life of pastoral innocence. They knew little of the use of warlike weapons, and though they were brave, were unhappily defenseless. The Nodlanders therefore found them an easy conquest. It was in vain that they fled to the summits of their mountains, and hurled huge crags upon the heads of the invaders; it was in vain that they sought refuge in the dark caverns among the rocks, and shot their feeble arrows from thence against the foe: their simple strategy was of no avail, when opposed to the art of the more cultivated Nodlander, and every year brought sorrow and desolation amid the steep hills of the Cock-Crows. The captives which the Nodlanders brought back from these expeditions served to supply all their agricultural wants, and fill the industrial gap which their own indolence left unoccupied. The unhappy Cock-Crows were sold by the government as slaves, and the honest mountaineers found themselves reduced from the proud independence of their alpine farms, to the degrading drudgery of tilling the soil for their ungrateful tyrants. Historians who relate these facts, state that it was a piteous sight to behold the army of Nodland returning from one of these recruiting expeditions with a long and melancholy rank of captives in its train. None but the most stalwart Cock-Crows were selected as slaves, and it frequently happened that whole families were dependent upon the labor of these youths for subsistence. What then could be more heart-rending than to see aged mothers, helpless fathers, and tender sisters weeping bitterly as they saw their only support torn from them? What a terrible sight to behold a wife convulsed with an agony of grief, at the prospect of losing her husband, in the very dawn of wedded happiness! Along the road for many a mile, even to the very borders of Nodland, the army would be accompanied by crowds of lamenting and despairing relatives, weeping and invoking curses upon the heads of those who had wrecked the happiness of their country, and scattered the ashes of desolation upon their hearth. Once reached the limits that separated the two countries, the train of mourners stayed their steps, and then, after a moment of brief agony, those that they loved best in the world were torn from their gaze and borne off into slavery. Then the unhappy destiny of the Cock-Crow captives commenced. Some tilled the soil from morn till night; some breathed the heavy air of towns, where they manufactured goods; others subdued their free mountain step into the hushed and stealthy tread of the trained domestic. All were employed, but it was not the free, unshackled toil which strengthens soul and body. They were slaves, and they knew it; and that knowledge made even the lightest task of their servitude seem heavy, and poisoned their every enjoyment. Thus did the Nodlanders supply their necessities, and force others to do for them what they were too lazy to do for themselves. And having accomplished this inroad upon their quiet neighbors, and carried sorrow and desolation into a thousand peaceful homes, they relapsed into their usual lethargic state, until the returning spring warned them again that the time was come when it was necessary that they should recruit their slave ranks.

King Slumberous of Nodland was a great king. History proclaims the fact, and it must be true; besides, it would have been very unsuitable if he had not been, for Nodland was a great country. King Slumberous's claims to distinction were many and well founded. He never taxed the people, except when he was in need of money. He spent the public funds right royally, and gave the people occasional glimpses of his august person with unparalleled condescension. He made war upon a grand scale, and was never known to retire from the field without leaving a mountain of corpses behind him. Most of those, to be sure, were his own soldiers; but that mattered little: they lost their lives, but the nation gained a battle, and who would cavil at such an exchange? He built the finest palaces in the world, and it did the people's hearts good to go on a fine summer's evening, between nap-times, and look at the outside of these gorgeous edifices. The Nodlanders would slap their pockets at the sight, and cry proudly, "Bless King Slumberous! I helped to build him that palace, and I'm as proud of it as if it was my own. How kind of him, to be sure, to allow us to come and look at it every day!"

King Slumberous did the nation credit by the way in which he entertained foreign potentates when they paid him a visit. Entertainments of the most magnificent description enlivened the palace night and day. Gorgeous *fêtes*, wondrous illuminations, and delightful hunting excursions occupied the royal leisure, that is waking moments, and the delighted people cried, "Bless our good King Slumberous for showing us all these beautiful things!" There were some discontented spirits in Nodland, who said that the King was a humbug, and that the people were taxed tyrannically; but they were low, demagogical fellows, and no one paid any attention to them. There was one thing, however, which above all endeared the monarch to his subjects. King Slumberous was beyond all question the heaviest sleeper in the kingdom. This stamped him at once as a remarkable man, and the people would have done any thing for a sovereign who could sleep fifty-six hours on a stretch.

It may be supposed that with these somniferous habits, King Slumberous had little time or inclination to attend to the affairs of state. But while the gracious monarch snored and dreamed, there was one man in his kingdom who was always wide awake—a man who, though born to the usual drowsy inheritance of his countrymen, had by training so far conquered his nature as to require scarcely any sleep at all. This ever watchful individual was the Lord Incubus, prime minister to King Slumberous, and the most hated man in all Nodland. Lord Incubus was a dwarf; probably the most successful epitome of ugliness that nature ever published. With a swarthy and misshapen countenance, and long spidery arms, he seemed to be a combination of the beetle and the monkey, and possessed all the malicious cunning of the one, with the repulsive loathsomeness of the other. Even his ability was distorted. He was exceedingly clever, but it was a very unpleasant kind of talent. No man could devise a new and oppressive impost better than he. No one could cook up the public accounts into a plausible shape, or avert popular indignation by some apparently liberal, but really worthless concession, more successfully than he. When nature bestowed upon him the faculty of telling a lie better than any other man in the kingdom; when she made him cruel, unscrupulous, and dishonest, she seemed to have designed him for a prime minister, and her end was fully answered.

Incubus managed the affairs of state, as Slumberous gently nodded in an intermittent slumber; but while conducting money from the pockets of the people into the royal treasury, he had a little private syphon off the main tube, which terminated in a certain strong box in the minister's own palace. The people did not like Lord Incubus; they feared him much and hated him more. Popular perception was sufficiently acute to perceive that good King Slumberous had little hand in the oppressive system of taxation with which they were overwhelmed. They also saw pretty clearly that Incubus was making a good profit out of the concern, and murmurs of indignation arose through the land against the dwarf minister. This brooding spirit was shortly brought to a head by a movement on the part of Incubus, which shook the constitution of Nodland to its foundation. It had been a long time a matter of grave deliberation with Incubus and his ministers, as to what was the best means of imposing a fresh tax upon the people. Imposts already existed upon every available article in the kingdom, and as there was a serious need of money for the royal treasury, it became a question of vital importance how it was to be raised. Many and grave were the councils held upon the matter. The ministers racked their brains in order to discover some commodity as yet untaxed, but in vain, and the royal treasury stood a very fair chance of being bankrupt. At length a young Secretary of State (whose fortune was made by this one suggestion) hit upon a bright idea. It is a well-known fact that the inhabitants of Nodland are distinguished by a wonderful passion for high heels to their shoes. No Nodlander of any position whatever would condescend to appear in public unless his heels were removed at least four inches from the surface of the earth. Fashionable people went still farther, and elevated themselves to five and sometimes even six inches; and to such a pitch was this fashionable eccentricity carried, that at the coronation of King Slumberous one of the ladies attached to the court was severely hurt, in consequence of her having the misfortune, to get a fall off of her heels. Now the young Secretary argued very properly, and with much discrimination, that as the Nodlanders would almost as soon lose their heads as their heels, heels were a legitimate object for taxation. The more necessary a thing is, said he, the more it ought to be taxed. Superfluities can be dispensed with, but if you want to be sure of a man's money, tax something that he cannot possibly do without. This proposition met with great applause, and the tax was finally resolved on. The ministers, however, did not include in their calculations the popular indignation which so sweeping a measure would excite; and when it was proclaimed that all persons wishing to wear heels above one inch in height must pay a tax for every inch by which they exceeded the proposed standard, all Nodland was aroused. A spirit of anarchy, which had been for some time past brooding in the breasts of certain demagogues, now seized the occasion to break out in full force, and the country flamed with rebellion. Meetings were held, and banners flaunted with the devices of "Down with Incubus!" "High heels for ever!" and one represented pictorially a great giant, allegorical of public opinion, crushing the dwarf minister beneath a heel of Titanic proportions. Strangely enough, the leader of all this anarchical confusion was not a Nodlander by birth. He was a native of a neighboring island on the coast called Broga, and having been expelled from his own country for his misconduct, he sought the friendly shelter of Nodland, which was always open to the stranger. The first return he made for this hospitality was to stir up ill-feeling and disunion through the land that he lived in. He possessed a certain species of vulgar, brazen eloquence, that was very effective with a particular class. His effrontery was dauntless, and his conscience, from systematic stretching, had become so large that it was capable of embracing any set of opinions from which the most profit was to be derived. He blustered largely about an article he called "patriotism," but which in reality meant self-interest; he was, in short, one of those bold, bad men who was sufficiently elevated above his own low class to be regarded by them as a leader, but who was too far beneath any other to be looked on in the light of any thing but an unpleasant pest. This man was called Ivned. Ivned seized the opportunity offered by the heel-tax, with great avidity. He talked largely about the interests of his country, forgetting that he was not even a citizen by adoption, and with his unscrupulous speeches, and impudent attacks on the government, raised a flame in the land which it took a long time to extinguish. King Slumberous grew alarmed at this unusual demonstration from his subjects; and when one day a sacrilegious wretch, supposed to be in the pay of Ivned, flung a rotten egg full in the face of the gracious monarch, when he was engaged in taking the air, he remonstrated seriously with Incubus as to his policy in taxing so necessary a portion of a Nodlander's person as his heels. The dwarf promised to calm the tumults, but refused to abolish the tax. He must have money, he said, and money could only come from the people. The riots meantime grew more serious; monster meetings were held throughout the land, and the nation seemed on the eve of a convulsion.

Ivned was in high spirits, for there was nothing in which he delighted so much as anarchy and confusion. At this juncture, Incubus put in practice one of those expedients for which he was celebrated. He caused it to be publicly announced, that in consequence of the consideration which his Majesty King Slumberous had for the opinions of his people, the odious heel-tax would be abolished. The people were in ecstasies. Incubus was a god, the preserver of the nation, and Slumberous was the greatest king that ever reigned. Votes of thanks were resolved on all over the country to the dwarf premier, and a grand banquet was given to him by the citizens of the metropolis. Ivned was overwhelmed with confusion, for in the general excitement no one would listen to his insidious speeches. But amid this popular phrensy, no one observed the birth of a little edict which slipped into the world immediately on the heels of the proclamation repealing the tax. Astounded by the magnitude of the concession, the people were blinded to every thing else; and it was only when they awoke from their dream that they discovered that they had all the while been quietly submitting to a similar impost, if possible more oppressive than the heel-tax. It was nothing less than a duty levied upon every body who wore their own hair. The Nodlanders, being rather a vain people, scarcely liked to disfigure themselves with wigs, and the people began to murmur. But the reaction which Incubus had calculated on was taking place. The people had exhausted their indignation in the previous riots, and a general apathy overspread them. Even Ivned could not get an audience, and in a few months the tax was paid as willingly as any other. Thus the royal treasury was filled, the feuds between the citizens and the government were healed, and the people were sold.

I have given this little history of the events that happened in Nodland previous to the opening of my story. It is dry and tedious, but was necessary in order to understand perfectly what follows.

Chapter II
The Way to Build a Palace

It was noon. A dead silence reigned in the King's chamber, while he himself slumbered amid billows of down. Two Cock-Crow slaves waved fans made from the feathers of the grochayo noiselessly above his head, and a cool breeze, perfumed in passing through the flower-clad lattices, wandered through the room. It was a luxurious apartment. The floor was paved with a peculiar granite of a delicate purple color, and susceptible of the highest polish. The walls were lined with slender pillars, carved and stained in imitation of palm trees, from whose lofty crowns long pendent leaves of green satin waved in the fragrant breeze. In the centre of the hall an elegant fountain threw a silver stream of water into the air, that fell back again in light showers upon the rich lilies and sleepy water plants that were twined around the basin's edge. A low, subdued, murmuring music wandered fitfully through the place; this was produced by a species of water-organ which was concealed beneath the fountain. Graduated streams of water trickled upon sonorous plates of metal, and produced a series of mournful but soothing sounds. At one end of this luxurious apartment, King Slumberous lay sleeping. He did not snore. An air of calm, torpid enjoyment, glassed over his smooth features. His breathing was low and regular, and he lay in an attitude of conspicuous ease. He knew how to sleep. At the other end of the room, perched on a high stool, with no back to lean against, or no cushion to repose on, sat the restless Incubus, his Majesty's Prime Minister. The small black eyes of the dwarf were fixed with a glittering uneasiness upon the form of the sleeping King. He fidgeted on his stool, and endeavored to make a necklace of his long, thin legs, and twisted his misshapen form into every imaginable attitude. He was evidently suffering all the pangs of impatience, and grunted occasionally very intelligible signs of his dissatisfaction. At last, as if his patience was completely exhausted, he suddenly sprang like a squirrel off his high stool, and alit with a tremendous clatter on the granite pavement. The Cock-Crow slaves, startled at the sound, let their fans fall; the music of the water-organ was drowned in the rude echoes that reverberated through the hall; the down pillows that encircled royalty were suddenly disturbed, and King Slumberous awoke. He raised himself on his couch, and rubbing his eyes like any other man, demanded what the—no, no—simply, "what *was* the matter?"

Incubus advanced and made a profound obeisance to the King.

"Ah! Incubus, is that you?" said his Majesty, drowsily; "what do you want?"

"Money, your Majesty," replied the dwarf laconically.

"Money? impossible! What has become of the last hundred thousand bloodrops* which came in from the tax on ringlets?"

"Spent, your Majesty; every ounce of it—spent."

"Hum! is there nothing in the treasury then?"

"Yes, your Majesty, there is one thing."

* The name of a Nodland coin, equal to five dollars of our money.

"What is that?"

"Invention. When every thing else has fled from the treasury box, invention, like hope, remains at the bottom."

"What! a new tax, Incubus? Do you think they'll stand it?"

"Oh! they'll make a noise about it, and hold meetings, and probably attempt to assassinate your Majesty; but they'll pay it—oh! they'll pay it in the end."

King Slumberous wriggled a little among his down pillows at this allusion of the dwarf to his life being imperilled, but it did not make much impression on him apparently, for he laughed in a drowsy kind way, and said:

"Well, let us have a new tax, Incubus; I leave it all to you, only let me have enough of money to build my new palace;" and he lay back seemingly with a strong intention of going off to sleep again.

"It is easy to say, let us have a tax," said the dwarf impressively; "but what are we to tax?"

"Oh! any thing—every thing—something that the people can't do without."

"All the necessaries in the kingdom are taxed to the utmost."

"Then we must bring something into fashion, and when the people come to want it we will tax it."

"Your Majesty is ingenious," said the dwarf with a sneer; "but the people are cunning."

"It's a very hard case," said the King, mournfully, "that a man has nothing left in his kingdom on which he can raise a little ready money. Couldn't we put a tax upon life, Incubus? couldn't we make the people pay for the privilege of existing?"

"We might do that, certainly, your Majesty; but what if the people refused to pay?"

"Kill them!"

"True! if they will not pay the tax, we kill them. But recollect that when we kill them, they are not bound to pay the tax. The idea is ingenious, your Majesty, but I am afraid it is not practicable."

"What are we to do?" asked the King, sitting up amid his pillows with an air of ludicrous bewilderment. "We can't get on without money, you know, Incubus. There's the Prince of Fungi, whom I have invited to a great hunting party next week, and we must have funds, or we shall be positively disgraced. Incubus, you must raise the money or lose your head."

"But, your Majesty—"

"I have said it; I give you an hour for reflection. Meanwhile, I will enjoy that of which, thank Heaven, no tax can deprive me—sleep!"

The dwarf made three bounds as the King uttered these words, and at the third his head almost touched the pendants that hung down from the lofty ceiling.

"Are you mad, Incubus! Are you distracted?" asked the King, angry at this apparently disrespectful conduct.

"Yes, with joy, your Majesty; mad with sheer joy! I have found a tax; I have found such a beautiful impost."

"Ah! let us hear it; what is this tax? Come, I am all impatience, Incubus."

"You let it slip yourself, your Majesty, not a moment since. We will instantly lay a tax on sleep."

"What! on sleep? tax a Nodlander's slumbers? Oh! Incubus, it will never do; it would be too tyrannous. They could not exist without it."

"They can have it by paying for it."

"But they will rebel, Incubus!"

"Oh, your Majesty, leave that to me. I'll manage them, I warrant you."

"But really, Incubus, such cruelty!"

"Recollect the palace, and the Prince of Fungi, your Majesty: we must have money."

"True, true," muttered the King; "we must have money. Well, Incubus, I leave it all to you; but be gentle, be gentle. Certainly, when one comes to think of it, sleep is worth paying for."

Two minutes after this the King was fast asleep.

Incubus laughed a low, silent, malicious laugh, as he left the royal chamber, and betook himself to the office of the Secretary of State.

"There is but one man," he muttered to himself, "who is at all to be feared. We must muzzle Ivned."

The next morning Nodland was in commotion. A royal edict had been published during the night, and which was found at day-break in all conspicuous places, to the effect, that inasmuch as it was the sovereign will and pleasure of his gracious Majesty King Slumberous the First, that his well-beloved subjects should be subject to a certain tax, duty and impost, which was to be levied on sleep. The edict, after some further preamble, went on to say, that the maximum of sleep to be allowed to each individual was four hours. All transgression of these limits was to be taxed as a luxury, according to a scale which was therein laid down. It may be imagined what the sensation must have been in a place like Nodland, where every man consumed at least fourteen hours out of the twenty-four in slumber. Every city in the land convened public meetings as soon as the oppressive edict was made known. Speakers ranted on platforms, and patriots began to make money. Ivned was in his glory. He wrote diatribes against the King. He foamed at the mouth in public with virtuous indignation. There was no word so foul, that he hesitated to fling it at the government. He denounced Incubus as a public pest, and all monarchs as hereditary evils. "What," he would cry at some public meeting, flinging his arms aloft with frenzy, "deprive us of our natural rights? contravene the immutable and wise designs of Providence? Base and bloody tyranny! wretched and besotted King! wicked and distorted Minister! The seasons change. To the summer succeeds the winter, and earth veils in rest the quickness of her bosom; she recruits her strength with a three months slumber, but we are not to rest, save by Act of Parliament! Our sleep must be legal, or not at all. For aught we know, our dreams may be contraband! Fellow-citizens, shall we suffer this? Shall we be trampled under foot, and have our slumbers measured out to us with an ell wand? No! rather let our sacred constitution perish, than have it made the hobby-horse of such tyrants."

In this way, and with such addresses as these, Ivned raised a flame through the land. Some people, to be sure, said that, not being a Nodlander born, he had no earthly right to talk; nay, that he even did not require the quantity of sleep which a Nodlander required. But the mass of the people did not care who spoke, if his discourse was well seasoned with popular blashemy and sedition. The state of the country grew alarming; revolt menaced the government on every side. But Incubus was inexorable. He appointed officers under the late act, and styled them sleep-wardens. It was the duty of these men to enforce the payment of the tax, and see that no person in their district enjoyed more sleep than the law allowed, without paying for it. Offices were established in every townland to grant certificates of sleep, to those who chose to buy them, and these places were thronged from morning till night with a crowd of discontented, murmuring citizens, who, although they were plotting treason against the State, preferred buying their certificate in the interval, to being martyrs to the cause of independence. Rebellion was brooding. A vast scheme to dethrone King Slumberous, murder the dwarf minister, and establish an elective monarchy, was on foot. Of course Ivned was at head of it, and hoped, no doubt, to win the suffrages of the people, and be elected King. The day was fixed for the first demonstration, and the drowsy King Slumberous stood, without knowing it, on the edge of a volcano.

The evening before the day appointed for the breaking out of the rebellion a strange sight met the eyes of the bewildered Nodlanders. It was nothing less than a bulletin in the Court Journal, announcing that Signor Ivned had, by the gracious will of his Majesty, been appointed to the office of Lord Chamberlain. The people could not believe their eyesight. They hastened to Ivned's house, but that gentleman sent them word that he was too busy to see them just then, but if they had any complaint to make, they might put it in the form of a petition. His disappointed adherents went away muttering threats of vengeance. The whole conspiracy was paralyzed at a blow. Ivned was no longer there to stir the sediment of public wrongs, and it began to settle down. The day appointed for the revolution arrived. A few undecided groups of people were seen in the public squares. One or two enthusiasts endeavored to address the crowds, but were promptly arrested, and the conspirators, seeing that it was useless to proceed with the affair after the treachery of Ivned, went back to their homes in silence. Thus was the great sleep-tax established. Henceforth Nodlanders slept according to law; the King built his palace and entertained the Prince of Fungi, and Lord Incubus added another blossom to the crown of public hate which he already wore.

Chapter III
A Hunting Expedition by the Lake of Dreams

It was a glorious autumn morning; the tall shadowy trees that belted round the dark Lake of Dreams were gemmed here and there with spots of ruby and gold; the small, white clouds floated in the clear blue sky like sleeping sea-birds. The wood-wind murmured to the wave-wind an invitation to forsake the monotonous lake, and come and play among the leaves.

The Lake of Dreams, usually so silent and solitary, on this morning seemed to have actively cast off its gloomy torpor. Bugle notes rang through the rocks and the forest. The deep bay of the hounds echoed through the sonorous aisles of trees, and horsemen gaily attired flashed through the green vistas of the woods. King Slumberous gave a great hunting party that day to his guest and neighbor, the Prince of Fungi.

In the middle of a large green circle, which had been artificially cut in the forest for the accommodation of royalty, stood King Slumberous and his suite, accompanied by the Prince of Fungi. Ivned was there too, gorgeously dressed, but bearing the vulgar impress of the plebeian on his countenance, and which all his splendor of attire could not disguise. Incubus was there, perched on the top of a tall horse, and looking more like a wood-gnome who had dropped from the branches above upon the saddle, than any thing human. The dwarf's principal amusement was plaguing Ivned with allusions to his low origin, and unexpected rise in the world, the topic of all others which wounded the Lord Chamberlain most deeply. The rest of the group was composed of the young nobility of the court, and no less than five of King Slumberous's wives were present in palanquins to see the hunt. The rivalry between these ladies amused the court not a little. Their palanquins were borne on the shoulders of Cock-Crow slaves, and it was a great point with each of them to endeavor to have her palanquin held a few inches higher from the ground than the rest. Accordingly, the poor Cock-Crows were forced by the rival owners to hold the heavy vehicles as high above their heads as was possible, and even then each lady might be seen leaning out, and striking her slaves on the head with little sticks, in order to force them to lift her half an inch higher.

"May I never sleep again," said King Slumberous impatiently, "if we have not been here over half an hour without finding even a wild boar. This will never do."

"Here is a tame one, your Majesty," replied Incubus, pointing to Ivned, who looked as if he could swallow the dwarf, horse and all.

"He does not look active enough to promise good sport," said the King, laughing heartily at the dwarf's old wit.

"How should he be active?" said Incubus with a sneer; "he has been used the greater part of his life to lying in the mire."

Ivned grew as red as the fallen leaves around him, at this bitter allusion to his birth. He raised himself in his stirrups, elevated his right arm, and assumed the menacing attitude he was once so famous for, when he rose to reply to some assailant at the demagogical meetings. But suddenly remembering where he was, and his altered position, he let his arm drop, and glancing maliciously over the dwarf's deformed person, said:

"Whether I lay in the mire, or whether I led the people, I always left a better impression than you could make, Lord Incubus."

"Ha! you have it there, Incubus," said the Prince of Fungi, who always thought it necessary to explain other people's jokes. "He alludes to your being so ill-made."

"And I," said Incubus, darting a glance full of malice at Ivned, "alluded to his being so ill-begotten."

"Ha! you have it now, Signor Ivned," said the Prince; "he means that you are low-born."

"Better that, your Highness, than—"

What this retort would have been was never known, for just at this moment a loud cry broke from a thicket close by, and every body's attention was instantly drawn to the place from which it proceeded.

"Let us see what all this is," said King Slumberous, spurring his horse into the thicket; "it sounded like the snarl of a hyena."

The rest of the party forced their way after the King, and as they plunged deeper and deeper into the wood, the cries became louder, and were apparently mingled with the low, ferocious growl of hounds at combat. Full of curiosity, the King and his suite hurried on, as fast as the thick brush-wood would allow, and bursting through a thick screen of low trees, found themselves suddenly the spectators of a very curious scene.

In the centre of a small glade, two huge hounds belonging to the royal pack were engaged in fierce combat with a beautiful leopard. The latter, though attacked on both sides, defended itself with equal dexterity and courage. Its eyes gleamed like the wood-flames at night, and its white teeth were flecked with the blood of its assailants. It used its long, graceful tail as a weapon of defense, and dealt the hounds heavy blows with it whenever they came within its reach. Its attitudes were so full of grace, its bounds so supple and elegant, and its courage so indomitable, that the King could not restrain an exclamation of admiration.

"Hold off! hold off!" he cried to the hounds; "where is our master of the hunt? We must have that leopard alive. He is a beautiful creature."

The hounds, awed by the King's voice, ceased their attacks, and drew off to a little distance, where, with bleeding flanks, they stood and glared at their enemy. The leopard, as soon as he found himself free, glanced disdainfully at the crowd of spectators, and walked slowly towards the edge of the thicket.

"Why, look, brother," cried the Prince of Fungi, pointing to him as he retreated, "what an extraordinary circumstance! he has a steel collar round his neck. He must be a tame beast."

"So he has, by Somnus!" cried the King. "Let us follow him. I must have him for my menagerie."

The leopard, when he saw himself pursued by the King, turned round and showed his teeth as if expecting an attack; but finding that the King stopped too, he again went his way towards the thicket. When he arrived at the edge, he stopped at what seemed to be a heap of dead leaves, and smelled carefully all round. He then lay down.

"I see a man!" cried Incubus; "I see a man half covered with leaves, near to where the leopard is lying. The beast has killed somebody."

"If he has, he shall suffer for it." said the King, dismounting. Then, drawing his sword, he cautiously approached the spot indicated by the dwarf. The leopard did not move, and as the King drew nearer he saw that the animal was lying with his head resting on the chest of a man whose form was half concealed in the dry leaves. He never took his eye off of the King for a moment, and was ready in an instant to act on either the offensive or defensive. The King gazed curiously at the man thus strangely guarded, and then beckoned to some of his suite to come closer.

"The man is asleep," said he, as Incubus cautiously drew near.

"What! a man asleep in the royal forest!" cried the dwarf. "We must see whether he has got his certificate."

So saying, the dwarf stooped down, and flung a small pebble at the sleeping man, who awoke with a sudden start, and gazed round with a bewildered air at finding himself in the centre of so brilliant a throng of people.

"What is your name; and what do you here?" asked Incubus, in a tone of authority.

The man—or rather youth, for he did not seem more than nineteen years of age—stared in astonishment for a few moments, and said in a weak voice:

"I was faint with travel, and lay down to sleep. Pina, here, promised to watch over me while I slumbered, but she has betrayed her trust;" and he looked reproachfully at the leopard, which still lay in the same position. The animal, as if it understood its master, gave a low moan, and turned its large eyes pleadingly towards him. "What ails thee, Pina?" he continued, laying his hand gently on its head; "what ails thee? Do not grieve; I am not angry with thee; but stay—what is this? Oh! how did this happen to thee, dear Pina?"

This exclamation was the result of a slight movement on the part of Pina, thereby disclosing a maimed and shattered leg, which easily accounted for her apparent breach of trust. The youth seemed as much grieved as if it had been his own limb that had been wounded, and hung over his pet with an air of touching grief.

"The animal defended you bravely," said the King. "It was in a combat with two of my bloodhounds that she received that wound."

"Poor, faithful Pina!" muttered the youth.

"But you have not answered for yourself," persisted Incubus, who smelled a mystery as a beagle would a hare. "What do you here; and what is your name?"

"I am called Zoy," said the youth suddenly.

"Zoy! why, that must be a Cock-Crow name. Are you one of that nation?"

"I am."

"Whose slave are you?"

"I am no man's slave!" and the youth looked at Incubus with a proud glance.

"A Cock-Crow in Nodland, and not a slave? By my faith, this is strange. Where is your sleep-certificate?"

"What certificate? I have none."

"Do you not know that any man sleeping without a certificate is liable to be imprisoned for life? at least according to the act passed by his gracious Majesty the King here;" and Incubus nodded at King Slumberous as he spoke.

The youth caught at the word.

"Is this the King?" he asked eagerly, and quite forgetting poor Pina's wounded leg in his anxiety to learn.

"I am the King," said his Majesty; "what want you?"

"Justice! your Majesty, justice!" cried the youth, throwing himself at the King's feet. "I ask for justice."

"A downright insult to the King's prime minister," said Ivned to the Prince of Fungi, in a tone loud enough for Incubus to hear it.

"Ha! there's at you, Incubus," cried the Prince, explaining as usual; "he means that while you are at the head of affairs, there is little use in asking for such a thing."

"In what way have you been aggrieved, young man?" asked the King gently.

"I had a bride, your Majesty, a dear bride, the only creature in life I cared for, except Pina there; we lived together in a little cottage in our own country; we were very happy and knew no care; I hunted for our living, and we had plenty of venison drying over our chimney, and Pina— poor Pina there, used to hunt down a deer or two for us whenever we were out of meat."

Pina waved her tufted tail gently, as if she took some pleasure in these reminiscences of her sporting exploits.

"Well, your Majesty, we were very happy, as I say, until one day we saw a great army coming up the mountain, and a bugle was blown, and I saw my neighbors hurrying away to hide themselves, and then I knew that the Nodlanders were on us. Well, I caught up my bride in my arms, and tried to escape to a cavern hard by, where I might remain concealed, but I was intercepted by twenty or thirty soldiers, who fell upon me; and though

Pina there and I fought hard, we were overpowered and both left for dead, and when I recovered my senses I found my bride gone—torn from me—torn off into slavery; she that had never soiled her hands with work in her life! Oh! your Majesty! give me back my bride, give me justice, or let me work by her side. It is a cruel, cruel system!" and the youth wept bitterly.

"My friend!" said King Slumberous solemnly, "the Cock-Crow question is one that we never discuss. What was your bride's name?"

"She was called Lereena, your Majesty; but she would be easily known by her beauty."

"Lereena!" exclaimed Incubus starting; "that was her name then?"

"Yes! Lereena. Oh! do you know any thing of her, sir? is she still alive?"

"No, no, the name merely struck me as being a strange one, that is all. I know nothing of her, I assure you. Your Majesty had better send this fellow to prison, for being without his sleep certificate," whispered the dwarf in a low voice to the King. "The example is worth making."

"I leave all these things to you, Incubus," replied the King; then turning to Zoy: "You will have to be a slave, young man. It is the law. But I will cause inquiries to be made after Lereena, and if she can be discovered, you shall be placed in the same household."

"Heaven bless your Majesty!" cried poor Zoy, as much delighted as if he received a court appointment instead of being doomed to captivity. "I will work better than any Cock-Crow in Nodland, if I am near my Lereena."

"Your leopard there?"

"Poor Pina!" said Zoy, turning tenderly to her, "she has broken her leg. Your Majesty will let her remain with me—will you not? She is the only one now that loves me."

"Pina shall be cared for," answered the King, "but she cannot remain with you. She shall be attached to the palace. My favorite wife wants a pet, and this beautiful leopard will be sure to please her. Incubus, attach this young man to your body of slaves; and, in the interval, institute inquiries about his bride Lereena."

"But, your Majesty! I have not room;" and the dwarf looked any thing but pleased at this arrangement.

"I have said it," rejoined the King, with oriental significance.

Zoy, when he heard that Pina was to be separated from him, turned sadly away, and large tears rolled down his smooth, youthful cheeks. He stooped down and kissed the wounded animal, while his chest might be seen heaving with suppressed sobs. "Pina," he whispered, as if he fancied that she was imbued with intelligence equal to his own; "Pina, you will be free, when I am in captivity; make use of your liberty, Pina, as I would make use of mine, if I had it. Seek out our Lereena!"

Pina raised her large, soft eyes to his face, as if she fully understood what he said, and accepted the task which he had assigned to her.

Incubus, who, for some reason best known to himself, did not appear at all obliged to King Slumberous for giving Zoy to him as a slave, but was of course obliged to obey the royal mandate, gave his new acquisition in charge to two of his attendants, with whispered directions that the moment they reached his palace, they were to confine the youth in the eastern dungeon, and on no account to allow him to be seen by any one about his residence. So Zoy, after making a profound obeisance to the King, and giving a farewell glance at poor Pina, whose broken leg the huntsman was binding up, set off for the dwarf's palace between his two ferocious-looking guards.

Then the bugle sounded once more; the hounds bayed through the deep woods, the King mounted his horse, Incubus commenced his verbal attacks on Ivned, while the Prince of Fungi continued his explanations, and the whole cavalcade swept from the scene, leaving the spot, which was a moment before brilliant with golden trappings and waving plumes, to its original silence. And the leaves that dared not fall before in the presence of majesty, now rained down in brown myriads from the boughs; the wild birds peeped forth from their coverts, lost in wonder at the strange beings who had just disturbed their solitude, and the timid heart of the hidden deer regained its usual pulse, as it heard the frightful voice of man no longer.

Chapter IV
Lereena

The palace of the dwarf minister was situated in the suburb. A more delightful spot can scarcely be imagined. Beautiful grounds extended about the house, which was built of the finest red and white marble. Fountains hidden among the trees sent a soothing murmur through the shadowy walks with which the place was traversed, and all through the domain were scattered the most luxurious apparatus for slumber that the ingenuity of a people who made sleep the principal object of their existence could contrive. Sometimes it was a swing which hung from the summit of some sturdy oak, and which oscillated gently with the breeze that played among the branches. Another was a cool grotto, where couches of moss and fragrant herbs invited the indolent and the weary to a perfumed repose. Or it might be a delicious arbor cunningly contrived, in the very heart of some great tree, screened round by faintly rustling leaves, and guarded by sentinel birds of a peculiar species, that were fond of such trees, and who, sitting motionless among the boughs, emitted all day long a low, stream-like note, like an Aeolian harp played beneath the waves.

The interior of the palace was not less enchanting. Fountains played in the centre of the rooms, each of which opened into a conservatory devoted to the culture of a certain species of plant. Beautiful birds, tamed and highly trained, flew among the graceful leaves and blossoms, and every possible description of couch was scattered through the apartments.

It was evening. The sun was setting above the dark crests of a grove of chestnuts, and pouring his blood-red beams through the lofty window of stained glass which decorated one end of a room in the palace called "the Chamber of Poppies." Through this room a heavy narcotic odor diffused itself from an adjoining conservatory, which was filled with every species of soporific plant—an odor that merely soothed the nerves, or produced complete slumber, according as certain glass valves which formed a means of atmospheric communication were either closed or open. A fountain of delicate pink water played in the centre of the chamber, and its spray, lit by the crimson light of the sunbeams, assumed an aspect of prismatic splendor. Here, reclining on cushions of green velvet whose pile was so high that it resembled moss more than any artificial fabric, reposed Lord Incubus. At his feet, with a species of ivory mandoline in her hand, reclined a young girl of the most exquisite beauty. Her features were regular, and her complexion pale; and with eyes of the most lustrous darkness she combined the rare beauty of tresses that seemed like a mass of spider-webs dyed in liquid sunlight.

She was looking very sad and melancholy. Her mandoline lay in a listless hand, and she gazed at the sun that was sinking below the tree-tops as if she wished that she could die with it.

"Lereena!" said Incubus, gazing at her with a hideous leer of affection, "you look sad and melancholy. This must not be, or I shall cease to love you!" and the misshapen wretch laughed as if that would be one of the greatest of misfortunes.

The girl cast a glance of ineffable loathing at him, and sighed deeply.

"Ah! you sigh, Lereena!" the dwarf continued. "What is this secret grief? Are you lamenting the absent Pina? or, perhaps, it is the handsome Zoy for whom you are pining?"

Lereena started.

"Pina—Zoy!" she exclaimed earnestly; "where did you learn those names? Do you know aught about them? Oh, tell me, for pity's sake, tell me about my husband!"

"What charming conjugal affection!" cried Incubus, with affected enthusiasm. "What a pity that so faithful a pair should have been ever separated!"

"And my dear faithful Pina! Oh, if she were here, none would dare confine or insult me. She would avenge every dastardly glance;" and as she uttered these words she dashed her mandoline passionately on the marble pavement, where it shivered into a thousand fragments.

"How beautiful she looks in a passion!" murmured the dwarf to himself, in a tone of sneering admiration. "I like her beauty even better than when it is in repose."

"What do you know about my Zoy?" cried Lereena, turning round suddenly and casting a fierce glance at her companion. "You have by this mention of these names roused all that was brooding in my heart; take care that it does not overflow and sweep you into the nothing from which you should never have emerged."

If Lereena imagined that by this violence she was going to overawe Incubus, she was sadly mistaken. The dwarf was far too cool and self-possessed ever to feel absolute fear. He was brave on philosophical principles, because he knew that fear incapacitated one from taking proper care of one's self. So when Lereena stood before him, with flashing eye and advanced foot, and one hand grasping a small dagger that hung at her girdle, he only laughed and emitted the species of sound that one would use to an irritated cat.

"Be quiet, Lereena, will you?" he said contemptuously. "Sit down there; I have something to say to you."

Lereena bit her lip, but obeyed him.

"Now," continued Incubus, settling himself amid his pillows, "as you have imagined, I do know something about your handsome Zoy, and your dear faithful Pina. In fact, I may say, I know a good deal about them."

Lereena's eyes flashed, and she looked for an instant as if she was about to spring on him. She restrained herself, however, and contented herself with tearing the red and blue beads off of her slippers.

"I know," went on the dwarf, "that Zoy is in prison, and will perhaps remain there for life."

"Zoy in prison! oh, what has he done?"

"Simply this. He came on a wild-goose chase in search of you. He was found slumbering in the royal forest without a sleep certificate, and you know that the punishment for that, in a Cock-Crow, is imprisonment for life."

This was a pure invention of the dwarf's, for Zoy was at that moment working in the farm-yard, and there was no such punishment attached to sleeping without a certificate—a fine was all that the law exacted in such cases. But the falsehood had its full effect on poor Lereena, and she covered her face with her hands and wept bitterly.

"Now," continued Incubus, his eyes twinkling with pleasure at the sight of such grief, "I will restore Zoy to liberty, and also take dear, faithful Pina out of the nasty, filthy menagerie where she is confined in company with a wolf and three owls."

"You will!" cried Lereena, overcome with joy.

"Oh, I will bless you on one condition," said the dwarf in a solemn tone. "You know that I have long tried to win your love."

"Wretch!" cried Lereena, starting from him as one does from a snake when one's feet are bare.

"The time is now come. You are my slave; I bought you. Well, I want you to be something dearer to me. Love me, Lereena, and Zoy shall be free to-night, and Pina shall again gambol at your side and be at once your plaything and protector."

"And forget my husband, my beautiful Zoy? No, no, my Lord Incubus. You have it in your power to make me draw water and hew wood, but to make me love you is beyond your will!"

"You will not consent, then?"

"Never! never! never!"

"You will think better of it. If you do not, fair Lereena, you will feel my vengeance. I leave you here to think over my offer. I will return in half an hour, and if you still refuse, why, we shall see."

And with a horrid laugh the dwarf skipped up from his cushions, and locking the door behind him, was gone before Lereena could gather breath to reply.

The moment the monster was out of sight, all the pride that had supported her gave way. She buried her head among the cushions and wept bitterly. Almost unwillingly, her fancy went back to the times when she lived a pure, happy life with her Zoy, among the mountains. She thought of the anxious watches she spent when he was out hunting the deer with Pina, and wild infantine joy when he returned laden with spoil. Her pleasures were few, but each one was so fresh and unpalling that they were worth a whole year of city joys; and all this pure delicious freedom had been in a single day violently exchanged for the basest slavery. It was no wonder that poor Lereena should twist her fingers in her beautiful silken hair, and writhe among the cushions like one in the agonies of death. She lay in a sort of stupor, the consequence of intense excitement. A low murmur rang through the room, and shaped itself into a melody. Lereena scarce listened at first, but presently it seemed to fall more definitely on her ear. She raised herself from amid the soft pillows, and the following words were heard in a sort of whisper-song, with an accompaniment so aërial and spiritual that one might imagine it some angel playing upon a lyre whose strings were sunbeams:

> "Lereena, Lereena, the finger of dawn
> Has opened the lids of the night,
> And I must be gone to the hills where the fawn
> Flies along like some vapory sprite.
> But e'er I depart
> There's a voice at my heart,
> Which whispers to me soft and low—
> Lereena, Lereena,
> Like scent of verbena,
> Will your kiss be to me ere I go?
> Lereena!
> My queen, ah!
> You'll give me a kiss ere I go!

> "Lereena, Lereena, the flame dripping Sun
> Is kissing the lips of the sky;
> The white mists fling down, to each mountain-
> ous crown,
> Moist kisses; why not you and I?
> I'm off to the hill
> Where the vapors are chill;
> I'll want something warm 'midst the snow.
> Then Lereena, Lereena,
> My sweet little queen, ah!
> You'll give me a kiss ere I go—
> Lereena,
> Sweet queen, ah!
> Give one little kiss ere I go!"

"Zoy! Zoy! my own Zoy!" cried Lereena passionately, as the low notes of the last phrase died away. "Oh! come to me! speak to me!"

The doors that separated the conservatory from the room in which she was, opened gently, and amid a stream of narcotic perfume, which flowed from the plants with which it was filled, young Zoy glided into the arms of his bride. After the first passionate caresses had exhausted themselves, and they found words to speak, Lereena asked the youth how he had escaped from prison.

"Prison!" echoed Zoy. "I was in no prison, save for the first three days after my apprehension in the forest. I have been working in the farm-yard for the last month."

"What a dreadful liar that wretch Incubus is!" cried Lereena; "he told me that you were in prison, and would be condemned to confinement for life in consequence of being found asleep in the forest without a certificate; and he offered to have you released, if—if—I would love him."

"The monster!" said Zoy, grinding his teeth; "he will rue this. I have something to tell you about Incubus. You know a man of the name of Ivned."

"The Lord Chamberlain?"

"The same. Well, Ivned has received intelligence that Incubus intends to disgrace him with the King and deprive him of his office. Now he intends to be beforehand with the dwarf. A vast conspiracy is on foot, of which he is the head, to remodel the constitution, appoint new ministers, do away with the oppressive taxation, and liberate our countrymen, the unhappy Cock-Crows. The first step will be taken this evening. The dwarf must die."

"I would plead for his life, Zoy; but while he lives, we can never hope for happiness. Let him die. But we must be cautious. He will return here in a few minutes, to learn my answer to his infamous proposal. He must not find you here, or you are lost. By the way, how did you find me?"

"Ivned led me here. The dwarf is about to return, you say. So much the better. You must keep him in conversation, Lereena."

"Zoy! you surely would not—here, in my presence? Besides, if you fail, you will be executed."

"I will run no risk, Lereena; the execution of the plan is confided to one who is irresponsible to human law."

A low whistle sounded outside in the conservatory, and with a farewell embrace, Zoy glided hastily through the door leading to his retreat, almost at the same moment that Incubus entered by another.

"Ha! my fair Lereena," exclaimed Incubus, advancing joyously, rubbing his hands; "you look as bright as a May morning—a fair augury for my hopes. Come; you have reflected, and will listen to reason." So saying, he endeavored to pass his hand round her waist.

"Unhand me, monster!" she exclaimed, struggling to escape from his grasp; "unhand me, or you will rue it."

"Come, this is childishness," said Incubus, gnashing his teeth with fury. "I will not be baffled—by Heaven, I will not;" and he wound his long nervous arms around her like a cord.

"Help, help!" cried Lereena, rendered utterly powerless by the sinewy grasp of her assailant.

"Hush!" cried the dwarf; "you will be heard."

At this moment a strange sound rang through the room; the glass in the conservatory was heard to break, and a swift rushing, like that of an embodied storm, succeeded. Lereena turned her eyes for an instant in the direction of the sound, and to her she saw speeding with great bounds through the twilight, a huge animal, with glaring eyes, and tail that swept around like a pine branch tossed in the tempest. Two leaps more, and the ferocious animal had fastened its claws firmly between the shoulders of the dwarf.

"My God! what is this?" cried Incubus, as he found this unexpected burden on his shoulders; and loosing his grasp of Lereena, he staggered back, making furious efforts to free himself from his new assailant. Lereena, in the confusion of the moment, fancying that her last hour was come, veiled her face, and sank upon her knees. Meanwhile, the struggle between the dwarf and the leopard continued. Incubus, though deformed, was muscular, sinewy, and wonderfully active, and now fought more like a wild beast than a human being. The leopard still retained its original position between his shoulders, striving to drive its powerful white fangs into his vertebrae, while Incubus rolled on the floor, and twisted his body round and round in the attempt to strangle his indomitable antagonist. They rolled about inextricably mingled, and every now and then the dwarf's long legs or thin arms would be tossed aloft in the air, in the frantic attempt to grasp some vital part of the animal. Then the leopard would lash its tail, and taking a deeper hold with its talons, bury its fangs into the dwarf's sinewy neck. All this took place in perfect silence, broken now and then by a hoarse, guttural cry of despair and agony from Incubus, which the leopard would answer with a short impatient growl, as if he was enraged that the struggle should be so protracted. At length the dwarf's strength seemed to be exhausted; his wild contortions ceased, and he lay motionless on the floor with the leopard crouched upon his body. He was not yet dead: for a second or two all sound of combat ceased, and in the silence might be heard his heavy, stertorous breathing. The leopard then suddenly raised his head, and seemed for an instant about to forsake his prey, but the next instant his wide jaws opened; an agonized shriek burst from the dwarf—a dull sound, like the cracking of rotten wood, was heard. Incubus's body was suddenly contracted into a lump, by some powerful action of the muscles—then it quivered, straightened out again, and all was still.

The leopard lingered for a moment, raised his head, and looked steadfastly at the body, then leaped with a graceful swinging bound on to the floor, and coming to where Lereena knelt, crouched itself at her feet.

The door of the conservatory opened cautiously, and two men entered with a stealthy step. One was Zoy, the other Ivned.

"It is all over," said Ivned, pointing to the dwarf's body, which lay in a heap on the floor. "The monster will offend society no longer."

"We must lose no time," answered Zoy; "where is Lereena?"

"There she is," replied Ivned, "kneeling at the base of that pillar, with the leopard crouched at her feet."

"Lereena!" cried Zoy, "rejoice with us; our enemy is dead. See! our dear Pina has avenged us both."

But Lereena did not reply, and when Zoy hastened up to her and unfastened the folds of her veil, he discovered that she had fainted. A few drops of the icy water in the fountain, sprinkled upon her forehead, soon brought her to, and all her fears vanished when she recognized in the fierce animal, that she saw bounding through the gloom, her faithful and affectionate Pina.

Ivned now explained that there was no time to lose. In the death of the dwarf, the first step had been taken, and it was necessary to follow it up immediately. The conspirators were assembled in a large body outside Incubus's palace, and only awaited the signal from Ivned to march on the King's residence and demand the restitution of their rights and the abolishment of the sleep-tax. So without any more delay, Lereena, Zoy, and the demagogue hastened from the palace, followed by Pina, whose jaws were still smeared with the blood of the dwarf, and joined the multitude outside. Here Ivned made one of his violent speeches against the tyranny of the government; pledged himself to head the people when they went to demand their privileges from the King, and in the conclusion threw out an indefinite, but sufficiently tangible hint, that now as the dwarf-premier was dead, owing to an *accidental* encounter with a wild animal that had escaped from the King's menagerie, the best thing the King could do would be to place him, Ivned, in his place, and the best thing that the people could do was to insist upon its being done. As there were a great many allusions in this speech to the greatness of Nodland and Nodlanders in general, the people applauded; but when Ivned alluded to the enfranchisement of the Cock-Crows, a deadly silence fell over the multitude. Man looked at man, as if each feared the other. They cast their eyes upon the ground, put their hands in their pockets, and pursed up their lips into little funnels, but not a word was spoken. As King Slumberous truly said, "the Cock-Crow question was never discussed in Nodland."

Ivned, when he saw this, turned to Zoy and Lereena, who stood near him, and shrugging his shoulders, whispered something in their ears; whatever it was, it had the effect of producing their immediate departure.

"Come!" said Zoy to his young bride, "let us fly from this accursed country while there is yet time; we should never be any thing but slaves here, while if we go far in among the hills of our own dear land, we will live poor, unmolested and free. Leave Ivned to mingle in the stormy whirlpool of politics; the day will perhaps come, when he will be glad to exchange his tedious honors for our peaceful obscurity."

So saying, the Cock-Crow, followed by his bride and Pina, stole unobserved through the crowd while it was palpitating under the influence of some fiery sentence of Ivned's, and taking immediately to the fields, struck out for the borders of the Cock-Crow country.

Chapter V
The End of the Demagogue

It was a bright morning in spring, the wind blew freshly down the deep ravines, and the eagles that hung in the light-blue atmosphere, swung to and fro upon its currents. A little cottage stood nestled on the side of the hill, into a piece of green pasture, which was shaded gently off into inclosures, filled with springing corn. A waterfall on one side flashed through the foliage of some live oaks that backed the house, while on the other a small patch, evidently sacred to Vertumnus, blushed with all the flowers that spring could call up from the half-awakened earth. Outside the door of the cottage, and basking in the morning sunbeams, lay a beautiful leopard stretched at full length, while a ruddy bronze-skinned youth was standing close by, leaning on a spear. Presently a young girl issued from the cottage, with a leathern belt in her hand, to which were attached hooks to which the huntsman attached the slaughtered game; this she fastened around the waist of the youth, and then twining her arms around his neck, leaned against him, and turned her eyes lovingly upon his youthful face. It was a charming picture of young, unsatisfied love—she nestling in close to him as if she would work her way into his heart, and he enjoying the luxurious pleasure of such gentle demonstrations, without at the same time forfeiting the peculiar dignity of his sex.

"At what hour will you return, dear Zoy?" asked the girl in a low tone, that expressed something more than the question.

"Oh! I shall not be long, Lereena. If Pina there is not too lazy, we shall have a fat deer in less than an hour."

Pina gave a slight switch of her tail, as if to show that there was yet a portion of animal energy in her that had not evaporated in the hot sunshine.

"Who is that ascending the hill, dear Zoy?" asked Lereena, pointing to the distant figure of a man, who was slowly coming up the ravine. "I never see a stranger, that fear does not riot in my heart, lest it may be those horrid Nodlanders who have come to bear us into slavery."

"Fear not!" said Zoy, grasping his spear with a savage glance. "You will die by my hand, Lereena, before another manacle binds your arm."

"There is something familiar in the appearance of this stranger!" said Lereena, scanning the approaching individual rather anxiously; "but he appears very faint and weary, and his clothes are in tatters. Go to him, Zoy, and help him with your arm; he is weak."

"Why," cried Zoy, rushing down to meet the stranger, "it is Ivned! what can have brought him here?"

Pina opened one eye on the strength of all this hubbub, but seeing only her master and an old tattered beggar, she wisely concluded that any active measures on her part would be out of place, and closing it again resumed her slumbers.

It was Ivned. But how changed from the brisk favorite of fortune, whom Zoy had left leading a whole nation! He was thin and gray. His eye, once so bold and unquellable, was now sunken and unsteady. His gait was feeble and tottering; his clothes were in tatters, and it would have been indeed impossible to recognize in him the daring, reckless demagogue, for whom no task was too difficult and no assertion too impudent.

"Ah!" said he, when in the evening he was seated at the fire in Zoy's cottage, "I forswear politics for ever. When you fled from Nodland I was in a fair way to greatness. I made the King submit to my terms. The sleep-tax was abolished, and every burgher and mechanic in the nation was my friend. Trade improved, because every body was more attentive than when they had to pay for their sleep. That commodity being taxed, people thought that they were extravagant if they did not take the value of their money; the consequence was, they slept the full legal allowance, which was several hours more than they used to sleep before. But under my administration all this was reformed, and the commerce of Nodland recovered from its lethargy. I found the King a feeble man, and I ruled him judiciously. I made him do exactly what I liked, but those measures were always for the good of the people. I consequently became a popular favorite, and when the King and I drove out together, twice as many people cried, 'Long life to Ivned,' as to King Slumberous."

"Hum!" said Zoy, in rather a disapproving tone.

"Well, one day I made a covert sneer at the King, which I never intended he should see, and which he never would have seen if it had not been for the Prince of Fungi, who explained the satire to him after his usual manner. The joke was a severe one, and his Majesty never forgave me. But a short time afterwards I was accused of high treason, and of entering into a plot to dethrone the King, and place myself in his stead. I was innocent, but I was imprisoned. However, by the aid of some gold, I effected my escape, and here I am in this delightful rural retreat of yours, among a new people where all is innocence, and who only want a scientific constitution to be perfect. I shall be very happy here, I know."

"I think not," said Zoy gravely, "if your happiness lies, as it did once, in political turmoil and endless quarrel. Listen to me, Ivned: We are an innocent people, we Cock-Crows; we have retired up into these hills which are beyond the reach of the Nodlanders, and we intend to retain our purity. We want no brawling demagogues here; we have no politics, therefore we want no politicians. If you cannot live in peace, and must have excitement and dissension, return to Nodland or to your native island. Your speeches here will not be listened to, and your appeals against tyranny will go for nothing, for every one is free. But if you are content to settle down as one of us; to hunt the deer, instead of pursuing popular opinion; to cultivate muscle instead of cunning, and to change your political baton into a huntsman's spear, then we will give you the welcome of a man, and you shall be honored among us."

"You are very kind," said Ivned bitterly, "but I will not trespass upon the hospitality of a country that prescribes rules to its guest. I will return to Nodland, where a scaffold or a throne awaits me: either is preferable to your pastoral obscurity."

So saying, Ivned arose, and shaking the dust from off his feet, passed out of the house. Zoy made no effort to detain him, but turning to Lereena, he kissed her, and said, "I am sorry, but perhaps it is as well. He could not live in peace, and our country is better without him. He is a dangerous man."

And the husband and wife again embraced; and Pina waved her tail gently, until she found that she was waving it into the fire and burning it, when she got up and went growling to the other end of the room; and the deer hung from the rafters; and the noise of the waterfall at the back stole soothingly in through the half-opened window; and all was still and peaceful; and amid this peace, with the hope that it never was disturbed, we leave Zoy and Lereena.

The Dragon-Fang Possessed by
the Conjuror Piou-Lu

Chapter of the Miraculous Dragon-Fang

"Come, men and women, and little people of Tching-tou, come and listen. The small and ignoble person who annoys you by his presence is the miserable conjuror known as Piou-Lu. Every thing that can possibly be desired he can give you. Charms to heal dissensions in your noble and illustrious families. Spells by which beautiful little people without style may become learned Bachelors, and reign high in the palaces of literary composition. Supernatural red pills, with which you can cure your elegant and renowned diseases. Wonderful incantations, by which the assassins of any members of your shining and virtuous families can be discovered and made to yield compensation, or be brought under the just eye of the Brother of the Sun. What is it that you want? This mean little conjuror, who now addresses you, can supply all your charming and refreshing desires; for he is known every where as Piou-Lu, the possessor of the ever-renowned and miraculous Dragon-Fang!"

There was a little dry laugh, and a murmur among the crowd of idlers that surrounded the stage erected by Piou-Lu in front of the Hotel of the Thirty-two Virtues. Fifth-class Mandarins looked at fourth-class Mandarins and smiled, as much as to say, "we who are educated men know what to think of this fellow." But the fourth-class Mandarins looked haughtily at the fifth class, as if they had no business to smile at their superiors. The crowd, however, composed as it was principally of small traders, barbers, porcelain-tinkers, and country people, gazed with open mouths upon the conjuror, who, clad in a radiant garment of many colors, strutted proudly up and down upon his temporary stage.

"What is a Dragon-Fang, ingenious and well-educated conjuror?" at last inquired Wei-chang-tze, a solemn-looking Mandarin of the third class, who was adorned with a sapphire button, and a one-eyed peacock's feather. "What is a Dragon-Fang?"

"Is it possible," asked Piou-Lu, "that the wise and illustrious son of virtue, the Mandarin Wei-chang-tze, does not know what a Dragon-Fang is?" and the conjuror pricked up his ears at the Mandarin, as a hare at a barking dog.

"Of course, of course," said the Mandarin Wei-chang-tze, looking rather ashamed of his having betrayed such ignorance, "one does not pass his examinations for nothing. I merely wished that you should explain to those ignorant people here what a Dragon-Fang was; that was why I asked."

"I thought that the Soul of Wisdom must have known," said Piou-Lu, triumphantly, looking as if he believed firmly in the knowledge of Wei-chang-tze. "The noble commands of Wei-chang-tze shall be obeyed. You all know," said he, looking round upon the people, "that there are three great and powerful Dragons inhabiting the universe. Lung, or the Dragon of the Sky; Li, or the Dragon of the Sea; and Kiau, or the Dragon of the Marshes. All these Dragons are wise, strong, and terrible. They are wondrously formed, and can take any shape that pleases them. Well, good people, a great many moons ago, in the season of spiked grain, I was following the profession of a barber in the mean and unmentionable town of Siho, when one morning as I was sitting in my shop waiting for customers, I heard a great noise of tamtams, and a princely palanquin stopped before my door. I hastened, of course, to observe the honorable Rites toward this new-comer, but before I could reach the street, a Mandarin, splendidly attired, descended from the palanquin. The ball on his cap was of a stone and color that I had never seen before, and three feathers of some unknown bird hung down behind his head-dress. He held his hand to his jaw, and walked into my house with a lordly step. I was greatly confused, for I knew not what rank he was of, and felt puzzled how to address him. He put an end to my embarrassment.

" 'I am in the house of Piou-Lu, the barber,' he said, in a haughty voice that sounded like the roll of a copper drum amidst the hills.

" 'That disgraceful and ill-conditioned person stands before you,' I replied, bowing as low as I could.

" 'It is well,' said he, seating himself in my operating-chair, while two of his attendants fanned him. 'Piou-Lu, I have the toothache!'

" 'Does your lordship,' said I, 'wish that I should remove your noble and illustrious pain?'

" 'You must draw my tooth,' said he. 'Woe to you if you draw the wrong one!'

" 'It is too much honor,' I replied, 'but I will make my abominable and ill-conducted instruments entice your lordship's beautiful tooth out of your high-born jaw with much rapidity.'

"So I got my big pincers, and my opium-bottle, and opened the strange Mandarin's mouth. Ah! it was then that my low-born and despicable heart descended into my bowels. I should have dropped my pincers from sheer fright if they had not caught by their hooked ends in my wide sleeve. The Mandarin's mouth was all on fire inside. As he breathed, the flames rolled up and down his throat, like the flames that gather on the Yellow Grass Plains in the season of Much Heat. His palate glowed like red-hot copper, and his tongue was like a brass stew-pan that had been on the salt-fire for thirty days. But it was his teeth that affrighted me most. They were a serpent's teeth. They were long and curved inward, and seemed to be made of transparent crystal, in the centre of which small tongues of or-ange-colored fire leaped up and down out of some cavity in the gums.

" 'Well, dilatory barber,' said the Mandarin, in a horrible tone, while I stood pale and trembling before him, 'why don't you draw my tooth? Hasten, or I will have you sliced lengthwise and fried in the sun.'

" 'Oh! my lord,' said I, terrified at this threat, 'I fear that my vicious and unendurable pincers are not sufficiently strong.'

" 'Slave!' answered he, in a voice of thunder, 'if you do not fulfill my desires, you will not see another moonrise.'

"I saw that I would be killed any way, so I might as well make the attempt. I made a dart with my pincers at the first tooth that came, closed them firmly on the crystal fang, and began to pull with all my strength. The Mandarin bellowed like an ox of Thibet. The flames rolled from his throat in such volumes that I thought they would singe my eyebrows. His two attendants, and his four palanquin-bearers came in and put their arms round my waist to help me to pull, and there we tugged for three or four minutes, until at last I heard a report as loud as nine thousand nine hundred and ninety-nine fire-crackers. The attendants, the palanquin-bearers, and myself all fell flat on the floor, and the crystal fang glittered between the jaws of the pincers.

"The Mandarin was smiling pleasantly as I got up from the floor. 'Piou-Lu,' said he, 'you had a narrow escape. You have removed my toothache, but had you failed, you would have perished miserably; for I am the Dragon Lung, who rules the sky and the heavenly bodies, and I am as powerful as I am wise. Take as a reward the Dragon-Fang which you drew from my jaw. You will find it a magical charm with which you can work miracles. Honor your parents, observe the Rites, and live in peace.'

"So saying, he breathed a whole cloud of fire and smoke from his throat that filled my poor and despicable mansion. The light dazzled and the smoke suffocated me, and when I recovered my sight and breath the Dragon Lung, the attendants, the palanquin, and the four bearers had all departed, how and whither I knew not. Thus was it, elegant and refined people of Tching-tou, that this small and evil-minded person who stands before you became possessed of the wonderful Dragon-Fang with which he can work miracles."

This story, delivered as it was with much graceful and dramatic gesticulation, and a volubility that seemed almost supernatural, had its effect upon the crowd, and a poor little tailor, named Hang-pou, who was known to be always in debt, was heard to say that he wished he had the Dragon-Fang, wherewith to work miracles with his creditors. But the Mandarins, blue, crystal, and gilt, smiled contemptuously, and said to themselves, "We who are learned men know how to esteem these things."

The Mandarin Wei-chang-tze, however, seemed to be of an inquiring disposition, and evinced a desire to continue his investigations.

"Supremely visited conjuror," said he to Piou-Lu, "your story is, indeed, wonderful. To have been visited by the Dragon Lung must have been truly refreshing and enchanting. Though not in the least doubting your marvelous relation, I am sure this virtuous assemblage would like to see some proof of the miraculous power of your Dragon-Fang."

The crowd gave an immediate assent to this sentiment by pressing closer to the platform on which Piou-Lu strutted, and exclaiming with one voice, "The lofty Mandarin says wisely. We would like to behold."

Piou-Lu did not seem in the slightest degree disconcerted. His narrow black eyes glistened like the dark edges of the seeds of the water-melon, and he looked haughtily around him.

"Is there any one of you who would like to have a miracle performed, and of what nature?" he asked, with a triumphant wave of his arms.

"I would like to see my debts paid," murmured the little tailor, Hang-pou.

"Oh, Hang-pou!" replied the conjuror, "this unworthy personage is not going to pay your debts. Go home and sit in your shop, and drink no more rice-wine, and your debts will be paid; for Labor is the Dragon-Fang that works miracles for idle tailors!"

There was a laugh through the crowd at this sally, because Hang-pou was well known to be fond of intoxicating drinks, and spent more of his time in the street than on his shop-board.

"Would any of you like to be changed into a camel?" continued Piou-Lu—"say the word, and there shall not be a finer beast in all Thibet!"

No one, however, seemed to be particularly anxious to experience this transformation. Perhaps it was because it was warm weather, and camels bear heavy burdens.

"I will change the whole honorable assemblage into turkey-buzzards if it only agrees," continued the conjuror; "or I will make the Lake Tung come up into the town in the shape of a water-melon, and then burst and overflow every thing."

"But we would all be drowned!" exclaimed Hang-pou, who was cowardly as well as intemperate.

"That's true," said Piou-Lu, "but then you need not fear your creditors," and he gave such a dart of his long arm at the poor little tailor, that the wretched man thought he was going to claw him up and change him into some frightful animal.

"Well, since this illustrious assembly will not have turkey-buzzards or camels, this weak-minded, ill-shapen personage must work a miracle on himself," said Piou-Lu, descending off of his platform into the street, and bringing with him a little three-legged stool made of bamboo-rods.

The crowd retreated as he approached, and even the solemn Wei-chang-tze seemed rather afraid of this miraculous conjuror. Piou-Lu placed the bamboo-stool firmly on the ground, and then mounted upon it.

"Elegant and symmetrical bamboo-stool," he said, lifting his arms, and exhibiting something in his hand that seemed like a piece of polished jade-stone—"elegant and symmetrical bamboo-stool, the justly-despised conjuror, named Piou-Lu, entreats that you will immediately grow tall, in the name of the Dragon Lung!"

Truly the stool began to grow in the presence of the astonished crowd. The three legs of bamboo lengthened and lengthened with great rapidity, bearing Piou-Lu high up into the air. As he ascended he bowed gracefully to the open-mouthed assembly.

"It is delightful!" he cried; "the air up here is so fresh! I smell the tea-winds from Fuh-kien. I can see the spot where the heavens and the earth cease to run parallel. I hear the gongs of Pekin, and listen to the lowing of the herds in Thibet. Who would not have an elegant bamboo-stool that knew how to grow?"

By this time Piou-Lu had risen to an enormous height. The legs of the slender tripod on which he was mounted seemed like silk-worms' threads, so thin were they compared with their length. The crowd began to tremble for Piou-Lu.

"Will he never stop?" said a Mandarin with a gilt ball, named Lin.

"Oh, yes!" shouted Piou-Lu from the dizzy height of his bamboo-stool. "Oh, yes! this ugly little person will immediately stop. Elegant stool, the poor conjuror entreats you to stop growing; but he also begs that you will afford some satisfaction to this beautifying assemblage down below who have honored you with their inspection."

The bamboo-stool, with the utmost complaisance, ceased to lengthen out its attenuated limbs, but on the moment experienced another change as terrifying to the crowd. The three legs began to approach each other rapidly, and before the eye could very well follow their motions, had blended mysteriously and inexplicably into one, the stool still retaining a miraculous equilibrium. Immediately this single stem began to thicken most marvelously, and instead of the dark shining skin of a bamboo-stick, it seemed gradually to be incased in overlapping rings of a rough bark. Meanwhile a faint rustling noise continued overhead, and when the crowd, attracted by the sound, looked up, instead of the flat disk of cane-work on which Piou-Lu had so wondrously ascended, they beheld a cabbage-shaped mass of green, which shot forth every moment long pointed satiny leaves of the tenderest green, and the most graceful shape imaginable. But where was Piou-Lu? Some fancied that in the yellow crown that topped the cabbage-shaped bud of this strange tree they could see the tip of his cap, and distinguish his black roguish eyes, but that may have been all fancy; and they were quickly diverted from their search for the conjuror by a shower of red, pulpy fruits, that commenced to fall with great rapidity from the miraculous tree. Of course there was a scramble, in which the Mandarins themselves did not disdain to join; and the crimson fruits—the like of which no one in Tching-tou had ever seen before—proved delightfully sweet and palatable to the taste.

"That's right! that's right! perfectly bred and very polite people," cried a shrill voice while they were all scrambling for the crimson fruits; "pick fruit while it is fresh, and tea while it is tender. For the sun wilts, and the chills toughen, and the bluest plum blooms only for a day."

Every body looked up, and lo! there was Piou-Lu as large as life strutting upon the stage, waving a large green fan in his hand. While the crowd was yet considering this wonderful reappearance of the conjuror, there was heard a very great outcry at the end of the street, and a tall thin man in a coarse blue gown came running up at full speed.

"Where are my plums, sons of thieves?" he cried, almost breathless with haste. "Alas! alas! I am completely ruined. My wife will perish miserably for want of food, and my sons will inherit nothing but empty baskets at my death! Where are my plums?"

"Who is it that dares to address the virtuous and well-disposed people of Tching-tou after this fashion?" demanded the Mandarin Lin, in a haughty voice, as he confronted the new-comer. The poor man seeing the gilt ball, became immediately very humble, and bowed several times to the Mandarin.

"Oh, my lord!" said he, "I am an incapable and undeserving plum-seller, named Liho. I was just now sitting at my stall in a neighboring street selling five cash worth of plums to a customer, when suddenly all the plums rose out of my baskets as if they had the wings of hawks, and flew through the air over the tops of the houses in this direction. Thinking myself the sport of demons, I ran after them, hoping to catch them, and— Ah! there are my plums," he cried, suddenly interrupting himself, and making a dart at some of the crimson fruits that the tailor Hang held in his hand intending to carry them home to his wife.

"These your plums!" screamed Hang, defending his treasure vigorously. "Mole that you are, did you ever see scarlet plums?"

"This man is stricken by Heaven," said Piou-Lu gravely. "He is a fool who hides his plums and then thinks that they fly away. Let some one shake his gown."

A porcelain-cobbler who stood near the fruiterer, immediately seized the long blue robe and gave it a lusty pull, when, to the wonder of every body, thousands of the most beautiful plums fell out, as from a tree shaken by the winds of autumn. At this moment a great gust of wind arose in the street, and a pillar of dust mounted up to the very top of the strange tree, that still stood waving its long satiny leaves languidly above the housetops. For an instant every one was blinded, and when the dust had subsided so as to permit the people to use their eyes again, the wonderful tree had completely vanished, and all that could be seen was a little bamboo-stool flying along the road, where it was blown by the storm. The poor fruiterer, Liho, stood aghast looking at the plums, in which he stood knee deep.

The Mandarin, addressing him, said sternly,

"Let us hear no more such folly from Liho, otherwise he will get twenty strokes of the stick."

"Gather your plums, Liho," said Piou-Lu kindly, "and think this one of your fortunate days; for he who runs after his loses with open mouth does not always overtake them."

And as the conjuror descended from his platform it did not escape the sharp eyes of the little tailor Hang, that Piou-Lu exchanged a mysterious signal with the Mandarin Wei-chang-tze.

The Chapter of the Shadow of the Duck

It was close on nightfall when Piou-Lu stopped before Wei-chang-tze's house. The lanterns were already lit, and the porter dozed in a bamboo-chair so soundly, that Piou-Lu entered the porch and passed the screen without awaking him. The inner room was dimly lighted by some horn lanterns elegantly painted with hunting-scenes; but despite the obscurity, the conjuror could discover Wei-chang-tze seated at the farther end of the apartment on an inclined couch covered with blue and yellow satin. Along the corridor that led to the women's apartments the shadows lay thick; but Piou-Lu fancied he could hear the pattering of little feet upon the matted floor, and the twinkling of curious eyes illuminating the solemn darkness. Yet, after all, he may have been mistaken, for the corridor opened on a garden wealthy in the rarest flowers, and he may have conceived the silver dripping of the fountain to be the pattering of dainty feet, and have mistaken the moonlight shining on the moist leaves of the lotus for the sparkles of women's eyes.

"Has Piou-Lu arrived in my dwelling?" asked Wei-chang-tze from the dim corner in which he lay.

"That ignoble and wrath-deserving personage bows his head before you," answered Piou-Lu, advancing and saluting the Mandarin in accordance with the laws of the Book of Rites.

"I hope that you performed your journey hither in great safety and peace of mind," said Wei-chang-tze, gracefully motioning to the conjuror to seat himself on a small blue sofa that stood at a little distance.

"When so mean an individual as Piou-Lu is honored by the request of the noble Wei-chang-tze, good fortune must attend him. How could it be otherwise?" replied Piou-Lu, seating himself, not on the small blue sofa, but on the satin one which was partly occupied by the Mandarin himself.

"Piou-Lu did not send in his card, as the Rites direct," said Wei-chang-tze, looking rather disgusted by this impertinent freedom on the part of the conjuror.

"The elegant porter that adorns the noble porch of Wei-chang-tze was fast asleep," answered Piou-Lu, "and Piou-Lu knew that the great Mandarin expected him with impatience."

"Yes," said Wei-chang-tze; "I am oppressed by a thousand demons. Devils sleep in my hair, and my ears are overflowing with evil spirit. I can not rest at night, and feel no pleasure in the day; therefore was it that I wished to see you, in hopes that you would, by amusing the demon that inhabits my stomach, induce him to depart."

"I will endeavor to delight the respectable demon who lodges in your stomach with my unworthy conjurations," replied Piou-Lu. "But first I must go into the garden to gather flowers."

"Go," said Wei-chang-tze. "The moon shines, and you will see there very many rare and beautiful plants that are beloved by my daughter Wu."

"The moonlight itself can not shine brighter on the lilies than the glances of your lordship's daughter," said the conjuror, bowing and proceeding to the garden.

Ah! what a garden it was that Piou-Lu now entered! The walls that surrounded it were lofty, and built of a rosy stone brought from the mountains of Mantchouria. This wall, on whose inner face flowery designs and triumphal processions were sculptured at regular intervals, sustained the long and richly laden shoots of the white magnolia, which spread its large snowy chalices in myriads over the surface. Tamarisks and palms sprang up in various parts of the grounds like dark columns supporting the silvery sky; while the tender and mournful willow drooped its delicate limbs over numberless fish-ponds, whose waters seemed to repose peacefully in the bosom of the emerald turf. The air was distracted with innumerable perfumes, each more beautiful than the other. The blue convolvulus; the crimson ipomea; the prodigal azaleas; the spotted tiger-lilies; the timid and half-hidden jasmine, all poured forth, during the day and night, streams of perfume from the inexhaustible fountains of their chalices. The heavy odors of the tube-rose floated languidly through the leaves, as a richly-plumaged bird would float through summer-air, borne down by his own splendor. The blue lotus slept on the smooth waves of the fish-ponds in sublime repose. There seemed an odor of enchantment through the entire place. The flowers whispered their secrets in the perfumed silence; the inmost heart of every blossom was unclosed at that mystic hour; all the magic and mystery of plants floated abroad, and the garden seemed filled with the breath of a thousand spells. But amidst the lilies and lotuses, amidst the scented roses and the drooping convolvuli, there moved a flower fairer than all.

"I am here," whispered a low voice, and a dusky figure came gliding toward Piou-Lu, as he stood by the fountain.

"Ah!" said the conjuror, in a tender voice, far different from the shrill tones in which he addressed the crowd opposite the Hotel of the Thirty-two Virtues. "The garden is now complete. Wu, the Rose of Completed Beauty, has blossomed on the night."

"Let Piou-Lu shelter her under his mantle from the cold winds of evening, and bear her company for a little while, for she has grown up under a lonely wall," said Wu, laying her little hand gently on the conjuror's arm, and nestling up to his side as a bird nestles into the fallen leaves warmed by the sun.

"She can lie there but a little while," answered Piou-Lu, folding the Mandarin's daughter in a passionate embrace, "for Wei-chang-tze awaits the coming of Piou-Lu impatiently, in order to have a conjuration with a devil that inhabits his stomach."

"Alas!" said Wu, sadly, "why do you not seek some other and more distinguished employment than that of a conjuror? Why do you not seek distinction in the Palace of Literary Composition and obtain a style. Then we need not meet in secret, and you might without fear demand my hand from my father."

Piou-Lu smiled almost scornfully. He seemed to gain an inch in stature, and looked around him with an air of command.

"The marble from which the statue is to be carved must lie in the quarry until the workman finds it," he answered, "and the hour of my destiny has not yet arrived."

"Well, we must wait, I suppose," said Wu, with a sigh; "meantime, Piou-Lu, I love you."

"The hour will come sooner than you think," said Piou-Lu, returning her caress; "and now go, for the Mandarin waits."

Wu glided away through the gloom to her own apartment, while the conjuror passed rapidly through the garden and gathered the blossoms of certain flowers as he went. He seemed to linger with a strange delight over the buds bathed in the moonlight and the dew; their perfume ascended into his nostrils like incense, and he breathed it with a voluptuous pleasure.

"Now let the demon tremble in the noble stomach of Wei-chang-tze," said Piou-Lu, as he re-entered the hall of reception laden with flowers. "This ill-favored personage will make such conjurations as shall delight the soul of the elegant and well-born Mandarin, and cause his illustrious persecutor to fly terrified."

Piou-Lu then stripped off the petals from many of the flowers, and gathered them in a heap on the floor. The mass of leaves was indeed variegated. The red of the quamoclit, the blue of the convolvulus, the tender pink of the camelia, the waxen white of the magnolia, were all mingled together like the thousand hues in the Scarfs of Felicity. Having built this confused mass of petals in the shape of a pyramid, Piou-Lu unwound a scarf from his waist and flung it over the heap. He then drew the piece of jade-stone from his pocket, and said:

"This personage of outrageous presence desires that what will be, may be shown to the lofty Mandarin, Wei-chang-tze."

As he pronounced these words, he twitched the scarf away with a rapid jerk, and lo! the flower-leaves were gone, and in their place stood a beautiful mandarin duck, in whose gorgeous plumage one might trace the brilliant hues of the flowers. Piou-Lu now approached the duck, caught it up with one hand, while with the other he drew a sharp knife from his girdle and severed the bird's head from its body at a single stroke. To the great astonishment of Wei-chang-tze the body and dismembered head of the bird vanished the moment the knife had passed through the neck; but at the same instant a duck, resembling it in every respect, escaped from the conjuror's hands and flew across the room. When I say that this duck resembled the other in every respect, I mean only in shape, size, and colors. For the rest, it was no bodily duck. It was impalpable and transparent, and even when it flew, it made no noise with its wings.

"This is indeed wonderful!" said Wei-chang-tze—"let the marvelous conjuror explain."

"The duck formed out of flowers was a duck pure in body and in spirit, most lofty Mandarin," said Piou-Lu, "and when it died under the knife, I ordered its soul to pass into its shadow, which can never be killed. Hence the shadow of the duck has all the colors, as well as the intelligence of the real duck that gave it birth."

"And to what end has the very wise Piou-Lu created this beautiful duck-shadow?" asked the Mandarin.

"The cultivated Wei-chang-tze shall immediately behold," answered the conjuror, drawing from his wide sleeve a piece of rock-salt, and flinging it to the farther end of the room. He had hardly done this when a terrific sound, between a bark and a howl, issued from the dim corner into which he had cast the rock-salt, and immediately a large gray wolf issued wonderfully from out of the twilight, and rushed with savage fangs upon the shadow of the beautiful duck.

"Why, it is a wolf from the forests of Mantchouria!" exclaimed Wei-chang-tze, rather alarmed at this frightful apparition. "This is no shadow, but a living and blood-thirsty beast."

"Let my lord observe and have no fear," said Piou-Lu, tranquilly.

The wolf seemed rather confounded when, on making a snap at the beautiful duck, his sharp fangs met no resistance, while the bird flew with wonderful venom straight at his fiery eyes. He growled, and snapped, and tore with his claws at the agile shadow that fluttered around and over him, but all to no purpose. As well might the hound leap at the reflection of the deer in the pool where he drinks. The shadow of the beautiful duck seemed all the while to possess some strange, deadly influence over the savage wolf. His growls grew fainter and fainter, and his red and flaming eyes seemed to drop blood. His limbs quivered all over, and the rough hairs of his coat stood on end with terror and pain—the shadow of the beautiful duck never ceasing all the time to fly straight at his eyes.

"The wolf is dying!" exclaimed Wei-chang-tze.

"He will die—die like a dog," said Piou-Lu, in a tone of savage triumph.

And presently, as he predicted, the wolf gave two or three faint howls, turned himself round in a circle as if making a bed to sleep on, and then lay down and died. The shadow of the beautiful duck seemed now to be radiant with glory. It shook its bright wings, that were lovely and transparent as a rainbow, and mounting on the dead body of the wolf, sat in majesty upon this grim and shaggy throne.

"And what means this strange exhibition, learned and wise conjuror," asked Wei-chang-tze with a sorely troubled air.

"I will tell you," said Piou-Lu, suddenly dropping his respectful and ceremonious language, and lifting his hand with an air of supreme power. "The mandarin duck, elegant, faithful, and courageous, is an emblem of the dynasty of Ming, that true Chinese race that ruled so splendidly in this land before the invaders usurped the throne. The cowardly and savage wolf is a symbol of the Mantchou Tartar robbers who slew our liberties, shaved our heads, and enchained our people. The time has now arrived when the duck has recovered its splendor and its courage, and is going to kill the wolf; for the wolf can not bite it, as it works like a shadow in the twilight and mystery of secret association. This you know, Wei-chang-tze, as well as I."

"I have indeed heard of a rebel Chinese named Tién-té, who has raised a flame in our peaceful land, and who, proclaiming himself a lineal descendant of the dynasty of Ming, seeks to dethrone our wise and Heavenly Sovereign Hién-foung."

"Lie not to me, Wei-chang-tze, for I know your inmost thoughts. Chinese as you are, I know that you hate the Tartar in your heart, but you are afraid to say so for fear of losing your head."

The Mandarin was so stupified at this audacious address that he could not reply, while the conjuror continued:

"I come to make you an offer. Join the forces of the Heaven-descended Emperor Tién-té. Join with him in expelling this tyrannical Tartar race from the Central Kingdom, and driving them back again to their cold hills and barren deserts. Fly with me to the Imperial Camp, and bring with you your daughter Wu, the Golden Heart of the Lily, and I promise you the command of one-third of the Imperial Forces, and the Presidency of the College of Ceremonies."

"And who are you, who dare to ask of Wei-chang-tze to bestow on you his nobly-born daughter?" said Wei-chang-tze, starting in a rage from his couch.

"I!" replied Piou-Lu, shaking his conjuror's gown from his shoulders and displaying a splendid garment of yellow satin, on the breast of which was emblazoned the Imperial Dragon, "I am your Emperor, Tién-té!"

"Ha!" screamed a shrill voice behind him at this moment, "here he is. The elegant and noble rebel, for whose head our worthy Emperor has offered a reward of ten thousand silver tales. Here he is. Catch! beautiful and noble Mandarins, catch him! and I will pay my creditors with the head-money."

Piou-Lu turned, and beheld the little tailor Hang-pou, at whose back were a whole file of soldiers, and a number of Mandarins. Wei-chang-tze shuddered, for in this compromise of his character he knew that his death was written if he fell into the Imperial hands.

The Chapter of "All Is Over."

"Stately and temperate tailor," said Piou-Lu calmly, "why do you wish to arrest me?"

"Ho! because I will get a reward, and I want to pay my debts," said Hang-pou, grinning spitefully.

"A reward for me! the miserable and marrowless conjuror, Piou-Lu. Oh! elegant cutter of summer-gowns, your well-educated brains are not at home!"

"Oh! we know you well enough, mighty conjuror. You are none other than the contumacious rebel Tién-té, who dares to claim the throne held by the wise and merciful Hién-Foung, and we will bear you to the court of Pekin in chains, so that you may wither in the light of his terrible eyes."

"You think you will get a reward of ten thousand silver tales for my head," said Piou-Lu.

"Certainly," replied the little tailor, rubbing his hands with glee—"certainly. His Unmatched and Isolated Majesty has promised it, and the Brother of the Sun never lies."

"Listen, inventive closer of symmetrical seams! listen, and I will tell you what will become of your ten thousand silver tales. There is a long avenue leading to the Imperial treasury, and at every second step is an open hand. When the ten thousand tales are poured out, the first hand grasps a half, the second hand an eighth of the remaining half, the third hand grasps a fourth of the rest, and when the money-bags get down a little lower, all the hands grasp together; so that when the bags reach the little tailor Hang-pou, who stands stamping his feet very far down indeed, they are entirely empty; for Tartar robbers surround the throne, and a Tartar usurper sits upon it, and the great Chinese nation toils in its rice-fields to gild their palaces, and fill their seraglios, and for all they give get neither justice nor mercy. But I, Tién-té, the Heavenly Emperor of this Central Land will ordain it otherwise, and hurl the false Dragon from his throne; for it is written in the Book of Prognostics, a copy of which was brought to me on the wings of a yellow serpent, that the dynasty of Han shall rule once more, and the Tartar wolves perish miserably out of the Land of Flowers."

"This is treason against the Light of the Universe, our most gracious Emperor," said the Mandarin Lin. "You shall have seventy times seven pounds of cold iron put upon your neck for these blasphemies, and I will promise you that many bamboo splinters shall be driven up under your rebellious nails."

"Let our ears be no longer filled with these atrocious utterances!" cried Hang-pou. "Oh, brave and splendid Mandarins! order your terrifying tigers to arrest this depraved rebel, in order that we may hasten with him to Pekin."

"Before you throw the chains of sorrow around my neck, O tailor of celestial inspirations!" said Piou-Lu, with calm mockery—"before the terrible weight of your just hand falls upon me, I pray you, if you would oblige me, to look at that duck." So saying, Piou-Lu pointed to where the shadow of the duck was sitting on the body of the wolf.

"Oh, what a beautiful duck!" cried Hang-pou, with glistening eyes, and clapping his hands; "let us try and catch him!"

"It is indeed a majestic duck," said Mandarin Lin, gravely stroking his mustache. "I am favorable to his capture."

"You will wait until we catch the duck, illustrious rebel!" said Hang-pou to Piou-Lu, very innocently, never taking his eyes off of the duck, to which they seemed to be glued by some singular spell of attraction.

"I will talk with the Mandarin Wei-chang-tze while you put your noble manoeuvres into motion," answered Piou-Lu.

"Now let us steal upon the duck," said Hang-pou. "Handsomely-formed duck, we entreat of you to remain as quiet as possible, in order that we may grasp you in our hands."

Then, as if actuated by a single impulse, the entire crowd, with the exception of Wei-chang-tze and Piou-Lu, moved toward the duck. The Mandarins stepped on tip-toe, with bent bodies, and little black eyes glistening with eagerness; Hang-pou crawled on his belly like a serpent; and the soldiers, casting aside their bows and shields, crept, with their hands upon their sides, toward the beautiful bird. The duck remained perfectly quiet, its variegated wings shining like painted talc, and its neck lustrous as the court robe of a first-class Mandarin. The crowd scarcely breathed, so intense was their eagerness to capture the duck; and they moved slowly forward, gradually surrounding it.

Hang-pou was the first to make a clutch at the bird, but he was very much astonished to find his hand closing on empty air, while the duck remained seated on the wolf, as still as a picture.

"Miserable tailor!" cried Mandarin Lin, "your hand is a sieve, with meshes wide enough to strain elephants. How can you catch the beautiful duck? Behold me!" and Mandarin Lin made a rapid and well-calculated dive at the duck. To the wonderment of every one except Piou-Lu and Wei-chang-tze, the duck seemed to ooze through his fingers, and escaping, flew away to the other end of the room.

"If my hand is a sieve," said Hang-pou, "it is evident that the noble Mandarin's hand is not a wall of beaten copper, for it lets ducks fly through with wonderful ease."

"It is a depraved and abominable duck, of criminal parentage," said Mandarin Lin, in a terrible rage; "and I vow, by the whiskers of the Dragon, that I will catch it and burn it on a spit."

"Oh, yes!" cried the entire crowd—Mandarins, soldiers, and the little tailor—all now attracted to the chase of the duck by a power that they could no longer resist. "Oh, yes! we will most assuredly capture this little duck, and, depriving him of his feathers, punish him on a spit that is exceedingly hot."

So the chase commenced. Here and there, from one corner to the other, up the walls, on the altar of the household gods—in short, in every possible portion of the large room, did the Mandarins, the little tailor, and the soldiers pursue the shadow of the beautiful duck. Never was seen such a duck. It seemed to be in twenty places at a time. One moment Mandarin Lin would throw himself bodily on the bird, in hopes of crushing it, and would call out triumphantly that now indeed he had the duck; but the words would be hardly out of his mouth when a loud shout from the rest of the party would disabuse his mind, and turning, he would behold the duck marching proudly down the centre of the floor. Another time a soldier would declare that he had the duck in his breeches pocket, but while his neighbors were carefully probing that recess, the duck would be seen calmly emerging from his right-hand sleeve. One time Hang-pou sat down suddenly on the mouth of a large china jar, and resolutely refused to stir, declaring that he had seen the duck enter the jar, and that he was determined to sit upon the mouth until the demon of a duck was starved to death. But even while uttering his heroic determination, his mouth was seen to open very wide, and, to the astonishment of all, the duck flew out. In an instant the whole crowd was after him again; Mandarin Hy-le tumbled over Mandarin Ching-tze, and Mandarin Lin nearly drove his head through Hang-pou's stomach. The unhappy wretches began now to perspire and grow faint with fatigue, but the longer the chase went on the hotter it grew. There was no rest for any of them. From corner to corner, from side to side—now in one direction, now in another—no matter whither the duck flew, they were compelled to follow. Their faces streamed, and their legs seemed ready to sink under them. Their eyeballs were ready to start out of their heads, and they had the air of government couriers who had traveled five hundred *li* in eleven days. They were nearly dead.

"Those men will surely perish, illustrious claimant of the throne," said Wei-chang-tze, gazing with astonishment at this mad chase.

"Let them perish!" said the conjuror; "so will perish all the enemies of the Celestial sovereign Tién-té. Wei-chang-tze, once more, do you accept my offer? If you remain here, you will be sent to Pekin in chains; if you come with me, I will gird your waist with the scarf of Perpetual Delight. We want wise men like you to guide our armies, and—"

"And the illustrious Tién-té loves the Mandarin's daughter," said Wei-chang-tze, roguishly finishing the sentence. "Light of the Universe and Son of Heaven, Wei-chang-tze is your slave!"

Piou-Lu—for I still call him by his conjuror's name—gave a low whistle, and, obedient to the summons, Wu's delicate shape came gliding from the corridor toward her lover, with the dainty step of a young fawn going to the fountain.

"Wu," said Piou-Lu, "the marble is carved, and the hour is come."

"My father, then, has consented?" said Wu, looking timidly at her father.

"When the Emperor of the Central Land condescends to woo, what father dare refuse?" said Wei-chang-tze.

"Emperor!" said Wu, opening her black eyes with wonder. "My Piou-Lu an Emperor!"

"I am indeed the Son of the Dragon," said Piou-Lu, folding her to his breast, "and you shall sit upon a throne of ivory and gold."

"And I thought you were only a conjuror!" murmured Wu, hiding her head in his yellow gown.

"But how are we to leave this place?" asked Wei-chang-tze, looking alarmed. "The guard will seize us if they get knowledge of your presence."

"We shall be at my castle in the mountains of Tse-Hing, near the Kouëï-Lin, in less than a minute," answered Piou-Lu; "for to the possessor of the Dragon-Fang all things are possible."

Even as he spoke the ground began to slide from under their feet with wonderful rapidity, leaving them motionless and upright. Houses, walls, gardens, fields, all passed by them with the swiftness of a dream, until, in a few seconds, they found themselves in the mountain-castle of Tién-té, where they were welcomed with a splendid hospitality. Wu became the favorite wife of the adventurous Emperor, and Wei-chang-tze one of his most famous generals.

The day after these events some Tartar soldiers entered Wei-chang-tze's house to search for the Mandarin, when, in the reception-hall, they were confounded at finding a number of men lying dead upon the floor, while in the midst sat a beautiful duck, that immediately on their entrance flew out through a window, and was seen no more. The dead men were soon recognized, and it was the opinion of the people of Tching-tou that Wei-chang-tze had poisoned all the soldiers and Mandarins, and then fled. The tailor, Hang-pou, being among the corpses, was found to have given his creditors the slip forever.

Victory still sits on the banner of Tién-té, and he will, without doubt, by the time that the tea is again fit to gather, sit upon the ancient throne of his ancestors.

Everything is now gracefully concluded.

Notes

"A Voyage in My Bed"

"A Voyage in My Bed" is a charming, imaginative fantasy that would make a stunning *Little Nemo* script, or *Little Nemo Grown Up*. Moments of drama and horror make it a serious work as well, though rendered safe by the dream framework. The reference to *Arabian Nights* in this and in "From Hand to Mouth" gives evidence to the inspiration for his first known story, "An Arabian Nightmare."

The story appeared anonymously in *The American Whig Review* for September 1852 and has never been reprinted.

"A Terrible Night"

The horror tale "A Terrible Night" was anthologized by Julian Hawthorne in 1907 and was included in a rare selection of Fitz's stories cumberously titled *The Golden Ingot, The Diamond Lens, A Terrible Night, What Was It? A Mystery* (1923) as well as *Famous Authors' Handy Library* that same year, the tale's only reprintings after its appearance in *Harper's New Monthly Magazine* for October 1856, the source of the present text.

Wolle called it "a ghostly tale of lonesomeness and fear in the woods of northern New York, done with tremendous effect." Though of minor theme, it is excellently developed.

"A Day Dream"

"A Day Dream" is a small whimsy published in Fitz's column "A Man About Town" in *Harper's Weekly*, February 21, 1857, and never reprinted. It's a comic retelling of the earlier, horrific "A Terrible Night" and typifies Fitz's cavalier interest in violence and his fascination with dreams.

"The Other Night"

Originally untitled, "The Other Night" was an introductory vignette for "The King of Nodland and His Dwarf," itself part of a cobbled series of poems, tales, and commentaries that appeared anonymously in *The American Whig Review* for August, September, November, and December of 1852.

The overall title of this fascinating patchwork of writings (including also "A Voyage in My Bed" and some fine macabre poems) was "Fragments from an Unpublished Magazine." It is, in its entirety, a remarkable tour de force, presuming to be the work of sundry hands compiled by a would-be editor whose magazine never materialized.

The text is from the December 1852 *American Whig Review*.

"The Crystal Bell"

"The Crystal Bell" is taken from *Harper's New Monthly Magazine* for December 1856, never before reprinted. A minor tale, it is yet thoroughly imaginative, original, and moody. It and "A Dead Secret" show similarities of structure and reveal as well the influence Fitz had on his close chum Thomas Bailey Aldrich, whose minor classic "The Chevalier de Resseguier," originally in *Century Magazine*, May 1893, bears a startling resemblance to Fitz's dream tales.

"How I Overcame My Gravity"

The punningly titled "How I Overcame My Gravity" betrays Fitz's interest in scientific discoveries and invention, although in this case he is ultimately more whimsical than in his other science fantasies, of which "The Diamond Lens" is most noted. The central theme of "How I Overcame My Gravity" anticipates Jules Verne and modern science fiction.

This was his last story, published posthumously in *Harper's New Monthly Magazine* for May 1864, never before reprinted.

"Three of a Trade; Or, Red Little Kriss Kringle"

"Three of a Trade; Or, Red Little Kriss Kringle" appeared in the *Saturday Press* for December 25, 1858. The journal was the brain-child of Henry Clapp, Jr., and served as a de facto house organ for the Bohemians who met in Pfaff's Cellar. The comic magazine created a stir and many notable authors were eager to contribute, from Whitman to Twain and even that stuffy conservative William Dean Howells. But Clapp, an abolitionist, advocate of women in the arts, and a cynical wit *par excellence* (comparable only to the biting, sparkling witticisms of Oscar Wilde), was never able to obtain a popular following. When funds were running out, he and his staff of writers would block off the entrance to the office and hold creditors at bay. When a new "angel" was discovered to keep the project afloat a while longer, the monies were quickly divided among his chums and they went to work for as long as it took the new angel to realize there would be no return on the investment.

It was a noble effort but ultimately only another of many failed dreams organized around the table at Pfaff's. Many years later, dissolute and virtually alone, Clapp was to drink himself to death in conscious imitation of Poe. The famed "King of Bohemia" chose a proper Bohemian demise.

By 1858 Dickens had already long established the fantastic tale as a necessary adjunct to Christmas, hence the inclusion of Fitz's yarn in the December 25 issue of the weekly. As "The Wondersmith" was in homage to Hoffman and "The Child That Loved a Grave" shows the influence of Dickens and many of Fitz's tales owe much to Edgar Allan Poe, "Three of a Trade; Or, Red Little Kriss Kringle" bows to the honor of Hans Christian Andersen (with echoes of Dickens as well). Fitz listed it as one of the stories he wished collected, but William Winter for some reason excluded it from the 1881 volume. It was reprinted in *Good Stories*, Part III (1868), and *Famous Stories* (1880). The present text is from the 1868 anthology.

"From Hand to Mouth"

Francis Wolle called "From Hand to Mouth" unconvincing and offers a backhanded compliment regarding its ingenuity and "fantastic queerness which stimulated the curiosity and wonder of the reader as to what even passably plausible conclusion the author can invent for such outlandish premises." Sam Moskowitz, on the other extreme, introducing the tale in *Horrors Unknown* (Walker, 1971), its only appearance in an anthology of our century, declares it to be "one of O'Brien's most extraordinary novelettes" and "the single most striking example of surrealistic fiction to predate *Alice and Wonderland.*" The real merits of the tale lie somewhere between Wolle's disappointment in his favorite author and Moskowitz's simple hyperbole.

What no critic seems to have noted is that the story is snide, cynical, and remarkably funny. The going rates for rooms in the hotel consists of three columns a day, and the tenants eat brains and the creativity of others. Fitz is writing about magazine and newspaper publishing that paid, in the 1850s, as little as one dollar the printed page, if you could collect it—the real cannibals of the literati. Today the wooden carrots are somewhat larger, but publishers are still the foes more often than they are the compatriots of authors, so the satirical points of "From Hand to Mouth" remain topical.

The story appeared as a serial, written for the money and without much respect for the people who paid him so little. The chapter heading "A Stupid Chapter and I Know It" is very telling. He wrote his "three columns a day" or, more precisely, one episode a week, biting the thoroughly bitable hands that fed him; and he did it so cleverly the editors and publishers never knew they'd lost some fingers. Fitz's intellect and wit delivers punch after punch, the crowning touch being that he even refused to complete his meandering fantasy, that never had any overall scheme beyond the immediate jest. The closing chapter is generally credited to his editor Frank H. Bellew (who had wanted Fitz's contribution mainly to cash in on the sudden fame engendered by "The Diamond Lens") but could as easily have been done by Bellew's sub-editor William Pool (who was later murdered). The hasty close is *somewhat* in the manner of Fitz's dream stories, so he probably couldn't complain.

None of this is to suggest Fitz set out willfully to write something inferior; indeed, his devil-may-care attitude, by which he lived his life, is seen in its purest form here, as he cared not one whit who was chided in the serial. He let his imagination run full steam without the strictures of artificial logic or the illusory, false structure most fiction imposes on reality. The story is by all means delightful and a fine window into Fitz's complex, creative, jaded, aware, comic, critical, bemused, and devious mind. "From Hand to Mouth" can be considered a minor classic of absurdist fantasy.

The story appeared in Bellew's weekly *The New York Picayune* from

March 27, 1858, to May 15, 1858. It achieved a posthumous success in being one of only three of Fitz's stories reprinted in the 1860s ("The Diamond Lens" and "Three of a Trade; Or, Red Little Kriss Kringle" being the others). After its serialization in *The Picayune*, it languished until 1868 when it was included in *Good Stories*, Part IV, reprinted again in 1880 in *Famous Stories*, with cheap editions in decades thereafter. The present text is from the 1868 anthology.

"The Wonderful Adventures of Mr. Papplewick"

The only story similar to "From Hand to Mouth" was Fitz's earlier comedy "The Wonderful Adventures of Mr. Papplewick." It lacks the cynicism and as such is of lesser importance, but is more purely comical than "From Hand to Mouth" and charming throughout. Francis Wolle pointed out, "Even this ridiculous yarn contains examples of the technique upon which O'Brien's fame as a writer of weird tales was to rest— the localization of fantastically unbelievable events in well-known, even prosaic surroundings," such as Barnum's museum or a New York hotel.

Because "Mr. Papplewick" reflects some of the real interests of the time, it is an interesting look at popular culture of the day. Mr. Papplewick becoming magnetized shows Fitz's, as well as the general public's, interest in science. In "What Was It? A Mystery," "The Diamond Lens," and "A Pot of Tulips," the supernatural is approached with a scientific attitude, whereas in "How I Overcame My Gravity" and in the portrait of the inventor in "The Phantom Light," we see that science is also a source of whimsy in Fitz's thinking.

The polar escapades are also derived from public interests. On a far more serious note, one of Fitz's most popular poems, less interesting for today's reader, was "Kane" (1857), written on the death of a well-loved Arctic explorer. (As a curious aside, Elisha Kent Kane was also a believer in spiritualism and married one of New York's most successful mediums— one of a triad of sisters for whom the word "medium" was first used in such a context. Though Fitz's fiction is riddled with an interest in dramatic and/or comic supernaturalism, his circle of Bohemians was not superstitious, and made great fun of a gullible society.)

As with "From Hand to Mouth," Fitz never finished his serial, as he had begun writing for the better (and better-paying) magazines. But one gets the feeling that Mr. Papplewick's adventures could have ended almost anywhere, and the abrupt end is of slight importance. The six chapters (the last two each called "Chapter V" in the original) appeared intermittently from March 13 to May 8, 1852, in John Brougham's sometimes sophomoric weekly *The Lantern*, with illustrations by Frank Bellew, who was a close friend of Fitz's. The text is from *The Lantern* and has never before seen republication.

"The Comet and I"

"The Comet and I" is a successful, whimsical fantasy included in Fitz's nonfiction column "The Man About Town" in *Harper's Weekly* for May 23, 1857. The column was generally a grand reflection of weekly events in the city. The second chapter of "The Comet and I" was run June 27 with the subtitle "Many a Slip 'Twixt Cup and Lip." Part two reveals precisely Fitz's attitude toward his own finances, for which his friend the Comet provides as good an excuse as any. The text is from the weekly paper from which it was never previously republished.

"The Man Without a Shadow: A New Version"

"The Man Without a Shadow: A New Version" is the shortest and least of Fitz's fantasies. The title and opening reference is to the classic German Romantic fantasy "Peter Schlemihl, the Man Without a Shadow" by Adalbert von Chamisso, first published in 1813 and often reprinted in English translation. But Fitz's story is in reality a parody of Poe's prose poem "Shadow."

This vignette appeared only in *The Lantern* for September 4, 1852, from which the present text was taken. Fitz wrote much for *The Lantern*, chiefly poems, but was really too good for it. It was the first paper to welcome him wholeheartedly but he very quickly graduated to *The American Whig Review* and *Harper's New Monthly Magazine* and was never again seen in obscure publications unless as a favor to close friends, such as for Frank Bellew's *Picayune* or Henry Clapp's excellent failure *The Saturday Press*.

"An Arabian Nightmare"

Never before reprinted, "An Arabian Nightmare" is from Charles Dickens's *Household Words* for November 8, 1851. Francis Wolle somewhat tentatively identified this as Fitz's story after inspecting the magazine's pay records. In New York, Fitz claimed an association with Dickens's magazine, and "An Arabian Nightmare" is really the only plausible prose candidate, along with tentatively identified poems.

The story does seem pure Fitz in his dream story mode, and it is definitely the case that *The Thousand and One Nights,* along with other Orientalia, influenced him. I am inclined to second Wolle's opinion. This would be Fitz's first known short story, discounting a legend incorporated into the novella "The Phantom Light" and reprinted separately in Volume One: Macabre Tales of *The Supernatural Tales of Fitz-James O'Brien.* Many of Fitz's later themes can be detected in this early work.

"The King of Nodland and His Dwarf"

When William Winter compiled the 1881 edition of Fitz's stories and poems, he excluded many stories that were Fitz's choice to be collected. In some cases this seems to have been due to difficulty in clearing copyright permissions, which was certainly the case of poems and stories from *The American Whig Review.*

"The King of Nodland and His Dwarf" was one of Fitz's favorites, but has never been republished from the December 1852 *The American Whig Review.* It's his most important work from the early period, his most remarkable both in humor and incident. He makes his most innovative use of dreams that were so central to much of his writing. Nodland is given as an isle in the Pacific, but at the same time it is clear that it is a world within a dream—a very sophisticated ambiguity.

This is also Fitz's most Swiftian satire with jibes at slavery which was still practiced in the southern United States, and at the political structure of England. The story can also be read partly as a precursor to modern heroic fantasy as derived from fairy tales, this one set in an entirely fabricated world, in a manner often said to have been innovated by William Morris more than forty years later.

"The Dragon-Fang Possessed by the Conjuror Piou-Lu"

Intentionally naïve and richly textured in the ornamentalist style, "The Dragon-Fang Possessed by the Conjuror Piou-Lu" begs comparison to the French Romanticist Théophile Gautier and the later Judith Gautier and other Parnassians. The "Kai Lung" stories of Ernest Bramah were the last pure inheritors of the form, but, as the earliest and one of the finest examples of nineteenth-century high fantasy, "The Dragon-Fang Possessed by the Conjuror Piou-Lu" may well be considered the starting point of much high and heroic fantasies right up to the present day.

Théophile Gautier was a contemporary of Fitz and, as Fitz kept abreast of French literature, he would have been well aware of the Frenchman's *nouvelles*. Henry Siedel Canby's 1909 suggestion that the story is derived in part from Lamb and De Quincy strikes me as farfetched. It is certainly unique in Fitz's canon, resembling nothing so much as "An Arabian Nightmare" and "The King of Nodland and His Dwarf"—and not even these very closely.

Wolle praises the story exceedingly, "exquisite in finish, a gem of its type." It was included in the Winter editions and thereafter in most selections of Fitz's stories, hence it is one of his best-known pieces and deservedly so. The present text is from the original appearance in the March 1856 issue of *Harper's New Monthly Magazine*.

Fitz-James O'Brien was an Irish-born American writer. From his arrival in New York in 1852 until he died of an infected wound in the Civil War, O'Brien contributed numerous poems and minor stories to the magazines. His importance rests on a handful of brilliantly original science fiction tales, which were influential not only on subsequent science fiction but also on the development of the short-story genre.

Jessica Amanda Salmonson has published five novels, of which *Ou Lu Khen and the Beautiful Madwoman* is the most recent. She is also a poet *(Innocent of Evil)* and World Fantasy Award-winning anthologist *(Amazons!)*. Her most recent books include a collection *A Silver Thread of Madness;* an anthology, *Heroic Visions II;* and a contemporary horror novel, *Anthony Shriek.*